The Rake's Bride

Reformed Rakes, Book 1

Kelsey Swanson

DRAGONBLADE PUBLISHING, INC.

ARE YOU SIGNED UP FOR DRAGONBLADE'S BLOG?

You'll get the latest news and information on exclusive giveaways, exclusive excerpts, coming releases, sales, free books, cover reveals and more.

Check out our complete list of authors, too!

No spam, no junk. That's a promise!

Sign Up Here

www.dragonbladepublishing.com

Dearest Reader;

Thank you for your support of a small press. At Dragonblade Publishing, we strive to bring you the highest quality Historical Romance from some of the best authors in the business. Without your support, there is no 'us', so we sincerely hope you adore these stories and find some new favorite authors along the way.

Happy Reading!

CEO, Dragonblade Publishing

Additional Dragonblade books by
Author Kelsey Swanson

Reformed Rakes Series
The Rake's Bride (Book 1)

Spy Society Series
Courting the Duchess (Book 1)
Seducing the Spy (Book 2)
Bedding the Marquess (Book 3)

For Omi.
Beloved sister, wife, mother, grandmother,
and great-grandmother.

IF ONE RESEARCHED the word "rake", one would likely discover an etching of the sinfully handsome visage of Rafael Hart, Viscount Blackwood, provided as its sole definition.

The man changed his paramours more often than the world did its seasons. Many a lady had bemoaned the fact that she had failed to be the one to convince him to settle down and give up his wild ways.

He was, according to more than one tabloid, "absurdly handsome," thanks to his dark coloring, lean height, and pleasantly athletic physique.

He possessed a caustic wit and ready smile, as well as a reputation that made debutantes salivate and their mamas steer them as quickly as possible in the other direction.

He'd been but a young buck when he'd inherited his title his last year at University, born as the second of only two children from parents more advanced in age than was customary. His impending birth had been touted as a pleasant surprise—a miracle—until his mother died of a fever without ever leaving the birthing bed.

The old viscount had been torn between joy at finally having a son and heir, and irrationally blaming an innocent babe for the death of his wife of nearly two decades. As a result, young Rafe had been left with his elder sister as his only advocate and replacement mother figure. Ten years his senior, Alice had shown her tiny brother love and unfailingly reassured him that he was never a burden, nor had his birth been a mistake. Despite her best efforts, this had not always canceled out their father's hard words of criticism or his grief-fueled rage whenever he looked upon the son who so looked like the mother who'd given her life for his first breath. To Rafe, Alice had been one of the only truly good things in his existence, and he'd have done absolutely anything for her.

This was why the news of her sudden death alongside her husband in a carriage accident had crippled Rafe.

When he'd have rather crawled into a hole and allowed death to claim him as well, he hadn't even been afforded that courtesy. His brother-in-law's solicitors had arrived on his doorstep and asked him what they should do with his sister's children: a boy of ten, a girl of three, and an infant girl not yet weaned. Apparently (and for some unknown and ill-advised reason), their will had stipulated that Rafe, of all people, receive guardianship of the children in the unlikely event that they both perished.

Rafe, feeling particularly bewildered and lost, had been un-characteristically frustrated that Alice hadn't had the forethought to remember that Rafe's life never went according to plan, and putting his name on that document had all but ensured he'd be the one to wind up caring for these children when he didn't know the first thing about how to do so.

"There is also an Aunt Agatha Hart mentioned as an alterna-tive," hedged one of the solicitors who, upon taking one glance around the house, saw not one bit of warmth and comforts one would expect in a home where children would be raised. If anything, the home was little more than a façade in the literal sense—mismanagement of the Blackwood holdings prior to Rafe's inheritance meant he'd received little more than the shabbily furnished home in which they stood, and a paltry annual income from the dregs that remained of the estate's holdings that was barely enough to keep him clothed in the appearances befitting his station. It certainly was not enough to house, clothe, and educate three children as befitting their noble blood. He did not know the first thing about children above their universal love of sweets and presents, but even he knew they were not inexpensive.

Though the solicitor had indicated there was another option…

Rafe barely suppressed a shudder at that woman's name. Agatha was their father's spinster sister, whom Alice had always feared as a girl—there was a reason Agatha had never married, and it wasn't purely her bulbous nose and permanent scowl. Unfortunately, she was also the last living relative either of them had. Alice's husband, while he'd been a good and kind man whom Rafe had genuinely liked, had brought with him a tragic dearth of relations. These poor children certainly were not spoiled for choice. As Rafe saw it, they'd either become wildlings beneath his unworthy hand, or they'd whither beneath Aunt Agatha's strict cane and unkind, rheumy eyes. Joy would be a thing of the past if their great-aunt had her way.

And this was how Rafe, one of London's most notorious hell-raising rakes, inherited three small children.

It was also how, after a few months of living with said children—being thrust from the free life of a titled bachelor to that of a pseudo-father figure—he concluded that he needed to commit the ultimate sin: He needed a wife. As abhorrent as he found the situation of marriage, it was clear that a woman's hand was required to manage the situation…not to mention he was in dire need of the influx of capital a hefty dowry would provide.

It made him nauseous, but Rafe would have to trade his title for a mother to his nephew and nieces, and money in his coffers.

Following his acceptance of the responsibility, the solicitors had immediately launched into an explanation of all the intricacies involved in taking on three small charges. Rafe lost his grip on his final shred of hope and watched it flutter away upon a brittle breeze. Though his nephew had inherited a title and some funds upon his parents' demise, payment of the death tax and safeguards put in place by solicitors who were clearly skeptical of Rafe's ability to be responsible (likely even more so now that they'd seen the depressingly inadequate interior of his home), the boy's income was tied up too tightly to make any difference until he reached his majority.

All that said, Rafe required a *rich* wife...and he needed her fast.

Chapter One

London Society has been invaded by America's version of royalty! Shipping king, Benjamin Rockford, has arrived on English shores for what some say is a scouting mission for possible expansion of his empire to the London dockyards. Rockford Shipping has, in the last several decades, become a goliath in the trading world. Mr. Rockford earned his fortune utilizing his in-depth knowledge of the seas and a keen sense of supply and demand to build a formidable fleet. His holdings include warehouses along America's Eastern coast and vessels numbering in the dozens; bringing his business across the Atlantic could mean proper competition for local companies. Touting fairer wages and more desirable working hours, Rockford Shipping has the potential to become a real contender in the ring as the fight for shipping supremacy expands in our ever-growing world.

"You're muttering to yourself."

Victoria chose not to acknowledge her brother's comment and merely pressed her lips together. The line they formed grew tighter and thinner the more she read the sheet that had been printed and delivered just that morning.

But business does not seem to be Mr. Rockford's only aim. He has brought his son and heir, Mister Luke Rockford, to continue his education at his father's side so he might one day take over the lucrative venture. This author feels it is notable that he has also brought his beloved—and admittedly entirely lovely—daughter, Miss Victoria Rockford. The sophistication of London is a world away from the streets of New York City, but it appears Miss Rockford has already taken quite well to this broadening of her horizons. The Rockford trio has already been sighted enjoying a performance at The Mask & Lyre, attending a ball hosted by the Duke and Duchess of M., as well as numerous other dinner parties, and gatherings fairly overflowing with names of impeccable quality (the Duke and Duchess of R., the Earl and Countess of A., Viscount and Viscountess S., Viscount B., Mr. and Mrs. S., to hint at but a few of the illustrious individuals). One wouldn't have considered these up-and-coming Americans to garner so much attention in such a short time, but, in addition to their intelligence and charm, the Rockford offspring are remarkably well-groomed, polite, and attractive. Mr. Rockford the Younger appears at each event cloaked in impeccable tailoring with nary a hair out of place, while his sister is always in the height of fashion. With looks (and a fortune!) such as theirs, this author feels it will be a miracle if neither of them is snapped up by the voracious (and notorious) London Marriage Mart! One thing is certain: Mr. Rockford could certainly do worse than allowing his children to form attachments here in London; his business acumen could only be strengthened by the introduction of hardy English blood, after all.

"Well that's rather insulting," Victoria groused and balled up the gossip rag in her hands before tossing it across the table.

"You'd do better to ignore whatever they say," her brother, Luke, commented somewhat distractedly. He had yet to glance up from the pile of correspondence that had been delivered that morning. His breakfast plate remained untouched.

"And you'd do better to remember to eat your food. Wouldn't want you to start wasting away lest your 'impeccable tailoring' no longer fit."

"Is that what's upset you?" A quizzical smile tugged at the corners of his mouth. Oh, to be a man with a steady future ahead and not a doubt in his mind—to have the luxury of being able to ignore the drivel in such tabloids.

"I don't think I shall ever become used to this backhanded way they have of speaking here. A single sentence can feel like a compliment and an insult at the same time. How is that even possible?" She held up her hands like the precariously balancing trays of a scale and adopted an exaggerated English accent. "The Rockfords are such a handsome family; they'd do well to marry Brits because their American bloodlines are sorely lacking. We're all so impressed with how well they use a fork and knife, though!"

The last earned a chuckle from her brother. "Don't take it to heart."

"That is easy for you to say. Everyone is marveling at your intelligence and status as the crown prince of Rockford Shipping; meanwhile, I am whittled down to 'entirely lovely' and 'fashiona-ble.'"

"Only because they do not know you." Luke set aside the letter, and his light hazel eyes met hers. "You and I shared the same education—if anything, you excelled in several areas where I struggled."

"I do believe that was the first time I've heard you admit I am the smarter sibling," she chirped with a grin.

Luke leveled a finger at her. "Not what I said, but I will let you have that small victory since you're perturbed by that meaningless English tabloid." Victoria giggled and motioned for him to continue. "They're jealous. Our family scraped and fought for every dollar, every ounce of success, and we, from our 'upstart' country, have attained an unfathomable level of success in only two generations. And now we've crossed the Atlantic and threaten their shipping industry."

"We are simultaneously objects of curiosity and derision."

"They want to be us, and they resent that fact." He shook his head at Victoria's bark of laughter. He explained, "We don't have the constraints of a title, the loyalty to a monarchy, and we are not guilted into adhering to antiquated customs. We are foreign to them in more ways than one. If they take interest in us for these things, then it is because we are fascinating, not because we are something to be looked down upon; do not ever allow anyone to make you feel less than because our family has worked for its good fortunes. You are and will always be a Rockford."

Though she tried to take comfort in her brother's words, Victoria knew the last was not necessarily true. Luke may be unerringly proud of how far their family had come—she was, too—but she did not have the benefit of being intentionally deaf to all criticisms that came from carrying working-class blood in her veins. She often wondered if his purposefully flippant nature was a trait all men shared, or if she simply noticed it more because he was her brother. She'd had a lifetime of comparing and contrasting their personalities, after all.

They had yet to be in London a full two weeks, and they'd already been inundated with invitations and events they "simply must attend" if they desired to be "seen in the right circles." Victoria didn't know why it mattered so much; she'd only been informed that that was the case by a pushy, if well-intentioned, wife of one of her father's associates who'd been tasked with chaperoning and showing Victoria around London. This meant Victoria had seen a great deal of Mayfair drawing rooms and the inside of carriages, but little else. She'd been forbidden to accompany her father and brother to the dockyards, so she'd taken her guide's words to heart and busied herself selecting the most interesting from the steadily increasing stack of invitations.

The Rockford family had attended the opening night of a new show at one of the city's premier theaters, which she'd thorough-ly enjoyed and passed along her appreciation to the lead performers. News traveled remarkably quickly for a city as large as London, and that appearance had resulted in a veritable waterfall of calling cards and finely engraved letters on the front table of their rented home overlooking Grosvenor Square in Mayfair.

They'd met the Duke and Duchess of Morton at the Mask & Lyre. Her father's associate had facilitated the introduction to the strikingly beautiful duchess and her handsome, imposing husband, but Victoria's quick wit and easy sense of humor had earned her and her family an invitation to share the private Morton box at the theater. The nerves she'd felt at conversing with the glittering aristocrats quickly dissipated when she realized the duchess was perhaps the least duchess-like person she might have imagined. Of course, the woman was regal in bearing and dress, but she had a wide smile and a casual way of speaking that instantly put Victoria at ease. And when they began speaking about books, well, Victoria's heart was all but lost.

"The shop is called Thorpe & Son?" Victoria had asked as the duchess detailed all manner of reading materials she was able to acquire through her longstanding relationship with the London retailer.

"It is more than a shop!" Lady Morton had replied. "It is the very best in Town and a veritable haven for lovers of the written word. Mr. Thorpe built the foundations upon making publications more accessible; his son has expounded upon it and takes great pride in the company's charitable efforts. Thorpe & Son books fill the shelves at Mrs. Worthy's Home for Girls." The duchess fairly beamed when she spoke of the asylum to which she and her husband devoted much of their efforts, in one fashion or another. "Thorpe can obtain any manuscript or publication I request—sometimes doing so before even I know it is something I wish to read."

"You must be one of the most well-read women in existence with Thorpe & Son at your disposal," Victoria had commented with a grin. "May I ask what your favorite novel has been? Perhaps I will venture to the bookstore and obtain a copy."

The corner of the duchess's lush lips twitched, and she cast Victoria's family a thoughtful glance before leaning in. "How long will you be in England?"

"Likely through the summer," she'd replied, but failed to understand the significance of the question.

The duchess replied with a decisive nod. "Then I will loan

you a copy of *Lady Chaste*—you can ask at Thorpe & Son, but they won't have copies readily available…too scandalous, you see." Victoria's eyes had widened, and she felt her cheeks warm with delight at the possibilities. Was the duchess—a woman who was supposed to be a paragon of English propriety—loaning her a copy of a scandalous book too incendiary for the average patron? How wonderful could one woman be? "And," the duchess continued, "if you enjoy it and are not too put off by the material, you may attend a meeting of my Reading Society."

"You host a reading society as well?" She was in awe of this woman.

"I do, indeed." Lady Morton actually winked at her. Winked! "And it is far from tame. The invitations are quite coveted."

"Well, I am greatly honored."

"Are you recruiting another minion to your Reading Society, my dear?" The duke had left Victoria's father and brother to a conversation at the box's entrance and joined the ladies in the velvet-upholstered chairs. Victoria might have thought the duke was mocking them were it not for the hint of mischievous glitter in his striking, hawklike eyes.

"Always, darling," Lady Morton replied airily, displaying all the confidence of a woman who was secure in the knowledge that her husband loved her enough that he would deny her little—if anything. That was it. Victoria adored the woman. In fact, she hoped she might one day be just like the duchess: confident, graceful, unapologetically herself, warm, and welcoming.

Victoria had been so taken with the congenial and outspoken duchess that she'd accepted her written invitation to dinner the following day without bothering to consult her father or brother. Fortunately, the Rockford men were used to following in Victoria's wake, so—unless business was scheduled—they went where and when they were told to do so, both happy to indulge her. Balls and musicales, masquerades and more dinner parties were all planned for the coming weeks, but it was impossible to accept all the invitations...nor would Victoria have desired to do so.

"Would that I could so easily brush off all the labels being applied to me," Victoria grumbled. Why couldn't she be left in peace to enjoy her blossoming friendships and explore what this new country had to offer? Her time in England was so limited, and she'd much rather her memories of it were filled with pleasant experiences rather than all the times she'd been mentioned in the tabloids with varying degrees of criticism.

Luke chuffed. "It's quite simple. Ignore it."

She emitted a rather unladylike snort in response. "You distill my experience down to the written word. It is easy to simply not purchase a tabloid or gossip rag; it is another thing entirely to witness the stares and hear the whispers as if I were a creature in a zoo. Eat your food, Luke."

Used to her abrupt changes in topics, her brother merely shook his head and popped a single blueberry into his mouth, all the while never removing his eyes from the papers in his hands.

Victoria had learned quite quickly that the *ton* was morbidly fascinated with the "wealthy Americans", as if they were some objects in one of the museums Victoria had yet to visit. Some turned their noses up at their "new money", though that wasn't all that dissimilar from back in New York. There, the line between Old and New Money was a fortress from which the Old imagined they could look down upon those grasping newcomers. In London, the difference was how the Rockfords were viewed as interesting purely for their Americanness.

They were ogled for the diversity of their tastes, their accents and inflection, their views of the world, and it seemed that every well-off household in Town desired the novelty of being able to say they'd hosted "The Americans." Victoria was used to being in the spotlight of Society, but she was unused to the reasons the English aristocracy found her fascinating.

As if sensing the sinking direction of her thoughts, Luke said, "I will eat my food if you stop your ruminating. I fear your brain will begin to make unpleasant sounds if you continue to seethe so violently."

Victoria huffed and sat back in her chair, wriggling until her stays no longer bit into her ribs. "If only everyone could be as relaxed as you."

He cocked a dark, wry brow at her. "I thought you enjoyed telling me how high-strung I am."

"Single-minded."

"See? There is your answer." Luke popped another berry into his mouth and chewed. "Become single-minded and nothing else will bother you."

Victoria rolled her eyes toward the ceiling, but a smile tugged at her lips.

Chapter Two

OVER THE NEXT two weeks, Victoria was swept up into the world of social calls, soirees, and other events deemed vital by Society's elite. Women asked her what the fashions were in New York—What did they eat at dinner parties? Which dances were popular? Would she teach them the steps sometime?—but, as keenly intelligent as she was, she very quickly learned these people were more interested in America, her family's wealth, and what she could provide them rather than actually becoming her true friend. This made the Duchess of Morton's friendship all the warmer and more welcoming.

As promised, Lady Morton had delivered to her a copy of *Lady Chaste*. It was a slim book bound simply and cleanly in brown leather. She held it in her hands and wondered what made it so special to be the duchess's chosen book.

Two chapters in, however, and Victoria no longer wondered.

She hadn't known what to expect, but it certainly hadn't been the liberal tale of a woman exploring what it meant to live unashamedly and unapologetically. Lady Chaste smoked cheroots, drank whiskey, rode astride in breeches, and—good heavens—she even took lovers.

Face burning, Victoria had set the book aside to press cooling hands to her cheeks, contemplating just how inappropriate even her indulgent father and brother would find the literature to be. Then she promptly picked it back up and read well into the night.

At its heart, the story was a commentary on societal restrictions placed upon females. It begged the question of what would happen if a woman simply acted as a man would. It was brilliant.

The next morning, she was so engrossed in reading the final chapter that she didn't realize Luke had entered the library until he was practically standing beside her.

"What has you so enraptured?"

His voice came as such a shock that she jumped in her seat and actually tossed her book into the air. "Good God, Luke!"

Being the unfairly agile man he was, he managed to snatch the book out of the air. "*Lady Chaste*, hm?" he commented, reading the title. "No author?"

"The author wished to remain anonymous," Victoria huffed and reached to snatch back her reading material before he could thumb through the pages. *Dear Lord*, what if he stumbled upon the scene in the carriage? She felt the skin of her throat burn at the thought.

"Interesting title."

"It was sent by Lady Morton," she said truthfully, clutching it to her breast.

"Oh? You two seem to be getting along well."

Victoria made a thoughtful sound in reply, fully intending to write a letter to the duchess as soon as she finished the final few pages of the book, eagerly inquiring as to when the next Reading Society meeting would be held. Victoria wished to be a part of any group that read such fascinating (and titillating) material.

She tilted her head and truly looked at Luke's face for the first time since he'd entered the room. Though he smiled at her, there was a weariness to his jaw, deepening the lines around his mouth; it lessened the intelligent gleam in his eyes.

As rough a go as Victoria had been having with the invasive tabloids and the snobbish *ton*, she suspected Luke might have been experiencing his own difficulties assimilating into this English world. She knew him well enough to recognize the fissures beginning to form in his normally unflappable façade. The poor man was practically mobbed by desperate marriage-minded mamas and their daughters—or at least the ones who didn't turn their noses up at the "unrefined" American. Luke was caught in an awkward place of having access to more wealth than a great many peers, but no title or breeding to lend it the necessary credence. Victoria could practically see the gold glinting in women's eyes as they appraised her brother. She always made sure to steer him far, far away from them. He deserved much better—as did she.

Unfortunately, there was a darker side to the discrimination against him, and he would have been greatly displeased if he knew Victoria was aware of it. Whereas many Englishmen of Luke's age were going to their clubs or raising hell, he was left out, not granted admittance to the same clubs. She'd even witnessed him being treated with thinly-veiled contempt by some men. She suspected his method of coping with the loneliness was to throw himself into his work for their company even more than usual. If he wasn't careful, Rockford Shipping would become his entire personality.

The plan had always been a three-month visit to England before returning to New York, but if it was determined that Rockford Shipping could benefit from expansion, then Luke would stay behind alone to oversee the venture. He'd always been one of the most driven men of Victoria's acquaintance, but the treacherous waters of this new life in London, coupled with the desire to prove to their father that he could manage an English branch of the company, drove him to new heights. That made Victoria worry for her brother. Without her nearby to arrange outings, distractions, and social obligations, it was entirely possible he would never speak to another being not directly involved in the shipping business.

When it became apparent that Luke was viewed as either a target or a rival in most of London's social situations, he began sitting more and more of them out, leaving Victoria to bear the brunt of the curiosity-seekers and parties inquiring after her handsome, eligible elder brother. At nine-and-twenty, possessive of an imposing build, dark chocolate hair and light hazel eyes, objectively, Victoria couldn't blame them. He'd have been a catch even if he had only half the brains and wealth he did.

"How are you, Luke?" she finally asked, tucking *Lady Chaste* beneath the folds of fuchsia pink fabric at her hip.

His eyes softened further; he didn't even attempt to redirect her because he knew she could read him too well and wouldn't stop until she received a satisfactory answer. "I won't be accompanying you to the ball tomorrow evening."

Victoria deflated. "Why not?"

"I have a meeting with some accountants for—"

"I thought Papa already met with the accountants," she interrupted him, not caring if she was beginning to sound like a petulant child.

"He did," Luke replied patiently. "But there are some new documents and figures to go over. A supper has been scheduled, and I will be attending instead of going to another ball."

"Won't Papa wish to be there for the meeting?"

"He has agreed to let me handle this on my own and will trust my reports on the matter." She did not miss how Luke stood a little straighter. Nothing made him prouder than earning their father's trust and having an opportunity to prove it was not misplaced—especially when it came to the company their grandfather had built. Still, she would have much preferred her brother attend the ball as well, because he had perfected the art of acting as a buffer to the eyes of the *ton*, and because he was so easy to converse with, making it easier to pass the time. However, she understood his decision.

"Admit it," Victoria groused theatrically. "You far prefer those stuffy, number-loving Englishmen to escorting your little sister around London."

Luke chuckled warmly. "You've found me out. I would have a thousand meetings with them to discuss an infinite number of dreadfully boring numbers if it meant I never had to set foot in another English dress shop with you."

AND SO, THE next evening, Victoria stood in a grand, gilded ballroom owned by a lord and lady whose name she could not recall, with her father by her side. Most young women her age might have felt put out at being left to spend the evening with their fathers, but, as much as she'd complained to Luke, it did not bother Victoria in the slightest. She adored Papa, and he, in turn, doted upon her. With his booming laugh and deceptively soft exterior, he'd always had a way of charming people and had never cared what anyone had to say to him or about him. He was fortunate enough to know and be secure in his place in the world, and he was damned proud of his success—and rightly so, if Victoria had anything to say about it. Her father's unflappable joviality and confidence in any situation were enviable. Lord knew Victoria would have benefited from inheriting some of her father's disposition on more than one occasion; alas, she was cursed with having the most readable face in Creation (or so one New York tabloid had once commented). As such, it was sometimes difficult for her to interact with a particularly acerbic matron without pulling at least once face.

This was, rather unfortunately, her current predicament.

A baroness with the jowls of a hound had taken it upon herself to educate Victoria on all the ways the English were superior to Americans. At first, she'd believed it all to be in jest, but she'd quickly learned that that was not the case. What the woman hoped to accomplish, Victoria couldn't quite comprehend, but she was all but cornered between a wall and her father, who was too engrossed in a conversation with another guest to hear what was being said to his daughter. Time and time again, Victoria had to snap herself to attention and remember to smile rather than grimace, to nod when she would have rather rolled her eyes.

"*Furthermore...*" the woman droned on indignantly, and it was everything Victoria could do not to give the woman the satisfaction of proving just how "savage" Americans could be. A well-placed flick of her fan to the woman's throat might stun her enough for Victoria to make her escape…

But no.

That would not do.

She'd always prided herself on her openness and honesty. As she'd come of age and experienced Society first in New York and now England, she'd learned some unpleasant lessons. What she interpreted as a manifestation of her soul's honesty, however, was not always well-received in English ballrooms. She'd discovered early on that the smiling faces and polite inquiries of the ladies at these events quite often acted as disguises for the most vicious venom. It was galling to do so, but she'd promised her father that she would do her best not to insult anyone of any import. The last thing Rockford Shipping needed was opposition from those who held actual sway in government (as opposed to those who simply held inflated opinions of themselves). She liked to play a game with herself as she tried to distinguish between the two, pasting a smile upon her face as she remained resolutely confident.

She did her best not to sag in relief when the baroness finally ran out of wind and moved onto a more receptive target. Her relief was short-lived when she looked out at the expansive room and realized she was being watched by no less than a dozen pairs of eyes.

To Victoria, the men at these events were more welcoming than the vipers' nests to be found in the clutches of women whispering behind their fluttering fans. Unfortunately for her, these men seemed to find her so interesting that she barely had time to breathe. Her dance card filled at an alarming pace, and to say that she was swarmed by admirers of the male persuasion would not have been an understatement.

Though she hid it well behind a practiced mask, Victoria found herself often overwhelmed by these Englishmen attempt-ing to snag her attention and garner her favor. Unfortunately, this only further villainized her in the eyes of the jealous women of the aristocracy who, more and more, saw her as their competition in what she'd quickly realized was the cutthroat field of the London Marriage Mart. Victoria wasn't deaf or blind—she heard the whispers calling her self-preservative ways sheer vanity. She was viewed as taking away rightful attention from women and daughters who'd had centuries of breeding on her.

Unlike those women, though, Victoria realized the male attention she received had little to do with her charm, beauty, or wit, and much more to do with her fortune. She'd have been quite happy if the attention ceased altogether, but that was hardly the case. In fact, it seemed to worsen as word of the Americans spread throughout England.

She longed to share a genuine laugh with someone outside of her family, to find someone who might be a friend and companion these months abroad. London, however, conspired against her, and most of the overtures of friendship she made were summarily shut down. She was grateful for the friendship of the Duchess of Morton and would attend the next meeting of her Reading Society held at Morton House the coming week, but, being a duchess, she was also quite busy with her various responsibilities and organizations. There was also the matter of the blossoming pregnancy Victoria imagined she could see beneath Lady Morton's fashionable skirts. To comment upon it would have been unseemly, but she believed it was the reason behind the duchess's aberration of morning calls. Even though she'd never been pregnant, she had enough acquaintances back home who'd experienced the state for Victoria to appreciate just how difficult it might be for a woman to adhere to social schedules when she felt unwell.

Though she was coming close with Lady Morton, this meant for the time being that Victoria was woefully without a true and consistent companion thus far in England, and she'd begun to despair of that ever changing.

Chapter Three

FROM ACROSS THE stifling ballroom, Rafe watched the dark-haired woman dressed in ivory, from the ribbons and brilliants woven into her complicated coiffeur to the elegant lace and beadwork of her outrageously expensive gown, right down to the dainty slippers that peeked out from beneath her skirts when she danced with partner after partner after partner. He jabbed an elbow into the tall blond man beside him and lifted his chin in the woman's direction.

"That is her—the American heiress."

Simon Stratford, Rafe's oldest and closest friend, despite their wildly different personalities, followed his gaze. "And?"

Rafe stifled a sigh. He cherished Simon like a brother, but sometimes he was a bit difficult to converse with. They'd formed a bond all the way back at Eton when Rafe had been naught more than a scrappy lad with a chip on his shoulder who couldn't stand by as Simon was tortured for no reason other than he was a bit different. The second son of the Earl of Aldborough had always been a bit too in love with his books, spoke too often about mathematics, and took little interest in the things other boys their age deemed most important. In the decades since Rafe had saved him from a cruel beating, their friendship had stuck. Though he didn't always understand Simon's idiosyncrasies and Simon couldn't comprehend Rafe's free, rakish lifestyle, they'd made it work.

Simon's wife, on the other hand, had made things a bit diffi-cult as of late. Odette (along with most of London) believed Rafe to be a poor influence. To be honest, it was probably truer than not. He hadn't garnered his reputation as an irreverent rakehell by chance. However, Rafe *was* the reason Simon had been at the theater the night he'd met Odette! They had him to thank for their wedded bliss—did that count for nothing? Couldn't her gratitude over that help her overlook the fact that he'd called off his affair with one of her old friends from the theater business? That had been a few months and at least five paramours ago, and *still* Odette was chilly around him. The fact that Odette was friends with the brokenhearted girl was regrettable, but Rafe had been nothing if not upfront about what he wanted from their liaison. It had never been malicious. Any of his interactions with the fairer sex were intended to be temporary and nothing more. If a woman built it up in her head that she'd be the one to make him turn over a new leaf, then, as far as Rafe was concerned, that was on her.

Simon's wife ended her conversation with another guest and saw where the men were looking. "The American?" she asked, easily interpreting the situation after a few years of practice. Rafe felt her eyes narrow on him. "Don't tell me you're planning on trying to make her your latest conquest?"

Rafe turned to Odette. Shorter than her husband by more than a head and elegantly curvaceous, she presented a lovely juxtaposition to all of Simon's harsh angles and inelegant manners. "What? You don't think I'll be able to?" He waggled his eyebrows suggestively, intentionally trying to earn a reaction from Odette.

She scoffed. "Of course not. I spent quite a bit of time speak-ing to her at Lady Morton's supper the other night—you were not invited to that dinner, were you?" Rafe missed the days when Odette had been much quieter and less confident in her barbs. "Miss Rockford seems quite self-sure and bright. If she can run the gauntlet of all these money-hungry men of the *ton*, then I don't think she'll find your brand of charm very moving. Besides, Lady Morton will be quite put out if you break Miss Rockford's heart; she likes her. She's even invited her to the Reading Society, and you know the duchess does not extend that privilege to just anyone."

Simon caught Rafe's eye over his wife's head. His oldest friend was the only one who had an inkling of Rafe's dire financial straits, and that was only because he'd known him for so long. Simon had witnessed the old viscount's neglect of his only son and watched Rafe's childhood home slowly deteriorate into shambles from apathy and neglect. He was aware of how difficult it had been for Rafe's sister, Alice, to make a decent marriage with a humiliatingly paltry dowry. It didn't take a person with Simon's brilliant intellect to deduce that an obscenely wealthy heiress was just the woman Rafe needed, and the one most likely to entice him to seek something more than a temporary arrangement.

"That sounds like an irresistible challenge to me."

With that, Rafe excused himself from their little group without waiting for Odette's retort and made direct progress toward the American heiress who had so consumed the tabloids as of late.

Rafe had spent the weeks since her arrival scouring the papers and gossip rags for any tidbits of substance about her—anything that might help ingratiate him with her. Unfortunately, those sources were predictably shallow. He may have learned that she was fashionable and looked quite lovely in the indigo blue frock she wore on a shopping excursion, and that she'd been in the company of quite a few notable members of the *ton*. However, it seemed she hadn't yet been connected with any man in particular, which left Rafe just the opening he needed.

A group of men currently surrounded Miss Rockford—each offering to bring her a drink, begging another dance, complimenting her on her otherworldly beauty with flourishing odes—none of them a threat to Rafe. It was no task for him to insert himself into the group, but it was another for him to set himself apart from the rest of the money-hungry men surrounding her.

And he knew precisely how to accomplish it: He would be nothing like them.

These men made their interest known. They all but threw themselves at her feet and begged her to look their way. They did nothing to mask their intent or interest; they desired only the opportunity to lay claim to her for the novelty of it, or for the undeniable draw of her fortune. Thinking of his wards asleep at home, Rafe knew no other man in London was more motivated than he.

He performed a quick scan of the men's familiar faces and knew instantly that none of them possessed his confidence or skill. He might have had some competition if the Marquesses of Kempton or Swanleigh were in the group; however, the former was escorting his current mistress to another function, and the latter was still in the deliriously happy early months of his marriage to their mutual friend, Caroline. While they may have had titles, the men encircling Miss Rockford were sorely lacking in the proper panache, gusto, and creativity. Rafe suspected not one of them possessed more of any of those things than Rafe did in his smallest finger. No. Compared to them, a little boldness would go a long way, and, judging from the slight pinch between Miss Rockford's dark, elegant brows, she wouldn't mind a reprieve from the gulls pecking at her from all sides.

"Miss Rockford," Rafe interjected, smoothly slipping between two of her admirers during a brief lull in conversation and holding his gloved hand out to her. "If you'll excuse the interruption, your presence is requested by the refreshment table."

Her rich hazel eyes assessed his outstretched hand, running up his arm to land on his face. He was startled to realize that she was more than passably pretty at this distance. Her irises were a unique blending of shades of green and brown, framed by long, kohl-black lashes. The bridge of her nose and the apples of her cheeks were splashed with faint constellations of freckles, and he found he admired the fact that she hadn't attempted to mask them with powder as so many women of his acquaintance would have. He'd objectively admired her figure from afar, but now he could fully appreciate the contrast of her hair—so dark a brown as to be nearly black—to the healthy blush of her skin. She was willowy, but not frail in the least; in fact, he suspected she'd outpace half the men in their circle in a footrace. Her breasts were small and high—nothing extraordinary, but, while Rafe appreciated a good set of tits, he far preferred the curves hidden beneath a woman's skirts. He would delight in exploring her.

In all, the woman wasn't a great beauty of ballads and epics, but, taken as a whole, her features made her stand out as uniquely attractive. Pleasing to the eye.

"And you are?" she said, her wide lips parting skeptically to reveal a very slight—unexpectedly charming—overlap of her white front teeth.

"Rafael Hart, Viscount Blackwood, at your service," he replied, a tilt to his head. The amused gleam in her eyes told him she was well aware of the unconventional way he'd approached her, rather than wait for a mutual acquaintance to perform the introduction. But would she have the guts to take his hand and the escape he offered her? Would she rather alight with him, the newcomer, or remain in the cloying safety of the group of admirers? "Our hostess is a friend of the family, and I was asked to retrieve you."

Another heartbeat passed before she placed her hand in his. Rafe ignored the zing he felt when pulling her hand into the crook of his arm as he extricated her from the frustrated glares of men left in their wake.

"I am no fool," Miss Rockford murmured to him as she politely returned another guest's smile.

"I do not believe you are," Rafe replied lightly, and she shot him a sidelong glance.

"Then why?" She didn't need to elaborate.

"Can a man not be allowed to play knight when he sees a woman overwhelmed?"

"So you are a knight? I thought you said you were a viscount; would that be a demotion?" She cocked an impressively saucy brow at him. "I fear I am still learning the hierarchy of the English nobility."

She was playing with him… "A demotion in title, but not in soul," Rafe answered smoothly. "I do not believe there is anything more noble than rescuing a fair maiden."

"So you believe I required rescuing?"

He nodded gravely. "They might have smothered you had they stood much closer."

"And you don't believe I could handle myself? That you were the only man capable of saving me from such a fate?"

"I was, wasn't I?" His tone might have been flippant, but the words were intended to draw attention to the differences between him and the other men vying for her attention.

"That was rather bold of you."

"I've never before been accused of being subtle."

"Or modest?"

Rafe's head whipped to the side just quickly enough to catch the wry tilt to her lips before it disappeared. Intriguing.

"Nor that," he replied.

"Am I expected to believe your absconding with me had a purely altruistic aim?"

"I have never pretended to be that selfless."

Miss Rockford emitted a brief breath of laughter before she could stifle it. "Then you are no better than the men I've just left."

"You wound me, Miss Rockford," Rafe said, pressing a hand to his chest. "Am I not allowed to enjoy the jealous stares of other men as I make off with the loveliest lady here tonight?"

Rather than blush as any English chit might have, Miss Rockford erupted into a gale of laughter far louder than what was appropriate in a public setting. He found himself entranced by the way she didn't care one whit.

"Hardly," she finally said. "Only one of the wealthiest."

That was, by far, the last response Rafe had expected. The American bluntness was something the tabloids had mentioned, but to be confronted with it in the face of his charm was jarring. An Englishman didn't discuss money, and a lady didn't call fortune-hunters out to their faces; one simply knew who and what they were and went about their business.

"Come now," Miss Rockford added with a motherly pat to his hand. "Given your earlier actions, I thought you'd have appreciated a bit of candor. Everyone here knows who I am and what I am worth; any interest in my person is solely for the size of my purse and my ties to an American shipping company. I am not so delusional as to believe I am a great beauty when compared to your English roses. I intrigue them, but they will not be so blunt as to admit to themselves or to me the reasons why. No one here speaks directly of the taboo topic of wealth, even when they wallow in it, covet it, and use it to fund the lavish facades everyone here is so fond of."

The dart struck remarkably close to home for Rafe, and he was beginning to realize he hadn't given this woman enough credit. "You are quite observant."

"Do not patronize me, Lord Blackwood," she said with a scoff. "I am not observant, merely more straightforward than most of the people I've met since setting foot on his island." The words could have been bitter and biting, but the glitter in her eyes told him she enjoyed the banter. She was weighing him—seeing if he'd be put off by her speech and her mien. Little did she know, he enjoyed a bit of spice…and he was desperate enough that he'd have pursued her, were she twice his age and missing half her limbs. Seeing this spark in her, the flat sense of humor, the willingness to test him, was like a chisel in stone, lending permanence to his determination. It made him smile.

"Would you care to dance?" Rafe asked suddenly, just as the last notes of another song wrapped up.

"I believe this next song has already been claimed." She stammered slightly, caught off guard by his abrupt change of subject.

"By whom?"

She skimmed the dance card affixed to her wrist by a bright pink ribbon. "Baron Trote."

Rafe chuffed. "That dullard isn't worth your time." Without giving Miss Rockford a moment to reconsider, Rafe swept her into his arms and onto the floor. He wished he'd paid better attention to the type of dance—a novice mistake brought on by the pressing need to make headway with her before the night was through—because the reel had them parting ways and spinning so often that they had no time at all to converse. He did, however, have plenty of opportunity to watch her wide red mouth grin unabashedly at everyone she passed.

The candlelight did wondrous things to her skin and her hair, making her glow as if she'd been born from the sunset—the perfect combination of gold and shadows. Her ivory gown, splashed in beads and gems, glittered, making her the center of attention whether she cared for it or not. Lord knew Rafe couldn't tear his eyes away.

She wound up in his arms once more as the dance concluded. He held her a moment too long before they parted to bow and curtsey to the other couples around them, and then he took her arm once more and led her from the floor.

"Regardless of your intentions, I must thank you for your rescue," Miss Rockford said slightly breathlessly from the vigorous steps. "The escape was quite refreshing, but I fear my respite has now passed." She tilted her chin to gesture to the fresh wave of men approaching them, their eyes fixed on her like hounds on a vixen.

"Is it always like this for you?" Rafe asked, slightly surprised by how much he did not care for those predatory gazes upon her. "These men eyeing you like dogs with a bone to be fought over?"

She nodded but raised a brow at his description. "I will choose not to take offense at being likened to a bone; but yes, this is what most events are for me. I never have a moment of peace. Sometimes my feet are so sore from dancing and being trodden upon that I cannot walk the following day."

Coming to an instantaneous decision, Rafe snatched a pair of crystal champagne flutes from a passing servant and murmured beneath his breath for Miss Rockford to duck behind the potted plant near the veranda doors. She did precisely what he'd asked, shooting him a mischievous smile.

"Gentlemen!" Rafe grinned at the approaching flock of disgruntled peers.

"Blackwood," said one of them in greeting, though his eyes remained occupied as they tried to discern where Miss Rockford had gotten off to.

"If you are searching for Miss Rockford, I believe she's ducked off to the ladies' retiring room. She should return momentarily." He leaned in conspiratorially. "Might I suggest camping out near the far entrance to the ballroom? You should be able to catch her just as she returns."

Several of the men clapped him on the shoulder, others muttered their thanks, and a few dashed off without bothering to acknowledge what he said just so they might scout the best position before the others got there.

Rafe scoffed. She hadn't been lying; she was as near to being hunted as a woman might be.

Good thing he was an excellent shot.

"Surely, you cannot expect me to believe you and your friends have *jousted*?" Victoria laughed incredulously. "I might have believed you were this the sixteenth century, but even I, in my ignorance, am quite certain that such events have not taken place in England for some time." She took another sip of the chilled champagne Lord Blackwell had handed her, quite enjoying the way the icy bubbles tickled her nose and the way the drink struck the perfect note between sweet and dry.

"I assure you, I am quite serious about this," the viscount said, leaning in closer as the golden candlelight danced in his eyes, illuminating his mirth and charm. He couldn't have been much older than his mid-twenties, but the corners of his eyes crinkled when he grinned, telling her of a man who laughed well and often. "Really!" he insisted. The infectiousness of his laughter had increased as the minutes passed in the back garden of the party they'd abandoned. She shook her head and tried to wave off his absurd claim, but his fingers gently closed around her wrist, and she felt the lightning of it travel all the way up her arm. Every muscle from her face to her smallest toes froze; her eyes locked onto that point of contact. They both wore gloves, but the heat of him—his gentle power—was nearly as intoxicating as the drink she held in her other hand.

What—what was this?

"The Marquess of Swanleigh and I were schoolmates, and we've remained close through the years. He claimed he could sit a horse better than I; I countered that, not only could I sit a horse better, but I could do so doing *any* activity."

Why did the last thing he said make her stomach flutter? What did that even mean? Clearly, logic was not in play any longer when it came to her senses.

"Lord Brinley was the one who mentioned jousting," he added.

"And you interpreted that as a brilliant idea?"

"Naturally!" Blackwell tilted his chin and puffed out his chest in an exaggerated posture of pride so absurd that Victoria was forced to bite her lips to prevent a bark of laughter.

"Did it end as poorly as my imagination suspects?"

Blackwell still hadn't released her wrist, and his thumb now caressed the underside of her palm, sending tendrils of warmth spreading through her. He leaned in close, until his warm breath tickled the shell of her ear. "Worse," he murmured.

"Oh my…"

Taking her words as shock and dismay over the situation in which he'd landed himself, the viscount sought to reassure her. "Do not fear. There were no lasting ill effects from the lark."

"I am glad to hear it," she replied a little less steadily than she'd hoped before tipping the last of her champagne between her lips. Blackwell immediately relieved her of the glass and set it down beside his on the unoccupied half of the bench they'd claimed upon their escape from the ballroom.

She knew she never should have ducked away with him—should never have allowed herself to be alone with this man—but it felt so good to laugh freely outside of her home, and without a dozen eyes upon her weighing her every movement. And Lord Blackwell…he was far from a chore to look at and interact with. He was witty, sarcastic, and unbearably handsome. She had enough sense to recognize that he was a man who would cut a swath through London Society without trying, and she should keep her wits about her, but his candor was so refreshing as to be irresistible.

His lightly sun-bronzed skin and dark hair, the sharp angle of his jaw and elegant nose, the sultriness of his fathomless chocolate eyes, all served to draw her in; however, his deep chuckle, winning smile, and effervescent sense of humor kept her there. He made it nearly impossible for Victoria to regret her poor judgment when she snuck away with him. And, when his eyes met hers, as soulful as a loyal hound's, her lungs stuttered.

"I sense you are in need of a friend here in London, Miss Rockford." He spoke low and soft, just like his touch upon her wrist. "I should like very much to be that friend for you, if you would allow me to."

How had this man read her so well when he'd known her for so short a time? She'd spent weeks in London without anyone making her feel so comfortable, so much herself, and it was tempting to allow it. She'd come close with Lady Morton, but she couldn't very well cling to the duchess like a barnacle—she had her own life to attend to, and Victoria had more dignity than that. She also missed New York. She missed her friends. And he was offering her a way to feel a little less alone.

She'd have been a fool to turn it down, wouldn't she?

As long as she kept her head about her and maintained realistic expectations, why couldn't she enjoy the possibility of friendship with this viscount? Besides, even if he turned out to be a bore, looking at him wasn't a chore in the slightest.

The corner of his lips tilted in a hint of a self-deprecating smile. "I would understand if your hesitation were due to what is said about me in the gossip columns."

"No!" she cut him off. She couldn't deny that she had read about "Viscount B" in the gossip rags. Many of the tabloids utilized nicknames and abbreviations to help prevent libel suits; he, Marquess K and Lord B, were mentioned often as charmers, flirts, and toeing the edge of what was proper behavior. His account of the jousting incident was confirmation that those tabloids were, indeed, describing the man before her. But, if she were honest, she hadn't read anything that made her think she should run far away from him. And wasn't she the last person who should be hesitant to form a friendship with someone over what was written about them? Besides, the viscount had been nothing but solicitous and charming, and who was she to turn down an offer of friendship? Another friend for the duration of her stay in England was an enticing prospect. She'd made the acquaintance of several women whom, given enough time, she might see herself forming a friendship with, but none of them had been quite so forthcoming as to outright request this sort of attachment from her.

"I would like very much for us to be friends," she finally said. Perhaps, when she looked back on that night, Victoria might think herself foolish or overeager, but she'd been so unexpectedly annoyed by what the tabloids were saying and how she was treated in certain Society circles that she couldn't help but grasp this straw that had been offered to her. She would not leap blindly, but she would take it for what it was. Viscount Blackwell made her laugh, and she desired at least the opportunity to see if their companionability might last beyond this evening in the shadows.

Besides, the dimpled, surprisingly boyish grin he gave her in return did odd things to her heart...and she quite liked that as well.

Chapter Four

THANKS TO HIS numerous connections, it was no difficulty for Rafe to discover which event the Rockfords would be attending next and wrangle an invitation for himself. Now that he'd caught Miss Rockford's attention, he knew the trick lay in keeping it. He had to set himself apart from the other men pursuing her...by *not* directly pursuing her.

Oh, of course, he'd set his sights upon her, but to attempt to perform an open seduction would make him no better than those bloodhounds from whom she'd fled at the ball. No. He had to offer her what the other did not. He'd witnessed the gleam in her eyes when he'd extended the possibility of friendship; he knew it was the way past the defenses she'd built to guard herself against the other fortune-hunting Englishmen, and into her good graces. Luckily for him, she was far less aloof than reports had led him to believe. Her laughter came more easily, her smile was broader, and even her shoulders relaxed somewhat when she was not beneath the assessing eyes of London's unforgiving *ton*. Having spent his entire life beneath their scrutiny, he knew it could wear down even the hardiest of souls—to throw a young woman unused to the customs and culture into the fray was surely overwhelming. Rafe knew he had to become the sanctuary for Victoria in London's shark-infested waters.

As Rafe scanned the crowd at the Atkinson dinner soiree, he felt that description was quite apt, indeed. Men circled desirable women like predators. Girls and their chaperones huddled together like schools of brightly colored, well-coordinated fish. The matrons watched him warily as they guarded their broods; the chits eyed him desirously like a shiny lure cast into their midst, irresistibly tempting despite the obvious danger. For his part, Rafe had eyes for only one creature of the American variety.

Eventually, he spotted Miss Rockford on the far end of the long, narrow parlor. She was dressed in diaphanous blue of the richest hue he'd ever seen. She dripped with matching sapphires and diamonds—not a single paste gem to be found on her person. Elegance and refinement were the words best used to describe her that evening...until Rafe caught sight of the cut of her gown. It was daringly low-cut and revealed a great swath of her flawless decolletage. While the skirts floated around her legs like the froth of an agitated sea, the bodice was so form-fitting that there was no way the garment wasn't a bespoke piece from the finest modiste. It cradled her bosom to perfection, hiking the pale globes up for his attention, barely covering enough of her to conceal her nipples. And that sent his mind down a dangerous path.

Delicious.

That was the adjective his stuttering mind latched onto and decided to apply—quite appropriately—to the American heiress.

Not since he'd been a lad had he gone so long without a bed partner. He'd broken off his latest arrangement the minute he decided to pursue a wealthy heiress to fill his depleted coffers. Lesser men might not have taken that step, but that was the only point where Rafe drew a line. If he were finally going to seriously court a woman, he might as well do it properly. Now, faced with Miss Rockford's deliciously enticing wares, his pulse began to throb in a most concerning manner.

Rafe knew he had to keep his wits about him if he was going to be successful in his venture. He couldn't allow his lust to drive his actions, no matter how tempting the prospect was.

"Miss Rockford," he drawled as he approached her from just

behind her left shoulder. Was it his imagination, or did her eyes glitter at the sight of him?

"Lord Blackwood," she greeted him and tilted her head up and to the side, as if both amused and perplexed by his appearance.

Rafe bowed over her hand with all the charm and grace he possessed. "A true pleasure to see you again so soon."

"You have been introduced?" inquired a man's deep voice.

Rafe straightened to find a tall, dark-haired man watching their exchange with narrowed eyes. From the looks of it, he'd recently returned from retrieving a refreshment for Miss Rockford. Though the men were of similar height, Rafe stood a little straighter when he realized the newcomer likely outweighed him by nearly a stone. He was as broad as one of the ships his family owned.

"We have," Miss Rockford answered. It did not miss Rafe's notice that she did not remove her hand from his...not even when her brother's hazel eyes snagged on their point of contact. "At the ball earlier in the week—the one you were unable to attend."

A muscle in the other man's jaw twitched.

"Viscount Blackwood," Rafe interjected by way of introduction. "We have not formally met, but you must be Mr. Luke Rockford, unless I am mistaken?"

The American grunted and handed his sister the glass he'd been carrying; it had looked absurdly small in his enormous fist. "Is my Americanness so obvious?" he asked, a sardonic lilt to his clipped words.

Rafe made a thoughtful sound and looked between the siblings. "I would say it's more in the eyes. You share the unique color of that feature." Miss Rockford nearly choked on the sip of her drink she'd rather unfortunately attempted. That muscle in her brother's jaw ticked again. Rafe always enjoyed unnerving overprotective male family members.

This was going to be even more fun than he'd thought.

BY THE END of the evening, Victoria's sides ached from all the laughter she'd had to stifle. Though they hadn't been seated very closely together at supper, Blackwood had still found ways to draw her attention and dramatically increase her enjoyment of the evening. She was quickly learning that he was a man who could embody an evening's entertainment all on his own.

He could send her into a fit of giggles with only a sidelong glance. When the wealthy businessman to her left droned on about his collection of carved ivory tobacco pipes, she'd have dozed off right into the soup course had she not caught a well-timed eye roll from the viscount's direction. How he managed to pull faces at a table full of people without being caught was beyond her, but surely it was an acquired skill he'd honed into an art form. It certainly made the meal a great deal more enjoyable for her.

She hadn't expected the viscount to be in attendance that evening—his name had not been brought up as one of the attendees in any prior discussion of the event—but she was pleased to discover that she was far from disappointed. In fact, her pulse had tripped when he'd appeared at her side before the meal like a guardian angel sent to save her evening from the uncomfortable one it was shaping up to be.

Prior to Blackwood's arrival, she'd been snubbed by several of the female guests. It was shocking to her that women who were old enough to be her mother could treat another woman with such blatant disregard and issue a cut direct. Were she ever in such a position, Victoria vowed that she would be like Lady Morton and open her arms to one and all, no matter the rumors or what was written in the gossip rags. There was far more to a person than the whispers that were translated onto a page.

Following the meal, the women retired to the parlor, and the men were left to their drinks and cigars. Victoria's cheeks ached from so many hours spent with a false smile upon her face, from grinning and bearing every little barb thrown her way. She could only take it so long before she needed a respite from it all. Not caring whether it was rude, she excused herself from the room under the guise of visiting the privy. As soon as she was in the hallway, however, she closed her eyes and sighed heavily, savoring the way she felt instantly lighter without so many eyes upon her.

Her eyes fluttered open, and there, appearing once more like an angel summoned from the mists of the shadows, was Viscount Blackwood.

"Just the lady I was hoping to encounter," he drawled, his white teeth flashing in the dim lighting.

"You were hoping I would wander into the hallway?" she asked, proud that her slight breathlessness sounded more coy than in awe of him. How did he always know where to find her? And how did he have any right to be so handsome? He was, once more, impeccably dressed in expertly tailored evening wear, his dark hair was artfully mussed, and the knife-sharp cut of his jawline was smooth from a recent shave.

"Is it so wrong to hope?" He stepped closer and she tried not to read too much into his words. He had offered her friendship, and she reminded herself that she desired nothing above that. Looking at the carved angles of his handsome, angelic face made that voice in her head fall softer and softer, so she averted her eyes and noted the honey glow of brandy in the snifter cupped nonchalantly in his left hand.

"So, you abandoned the rest of the men on a hope?"

He chuffed gently. "Men have committed far worse sins for far less." He held the glass out to her. "Would you like to try some?"

Victoria's cheeks burned when she realized he'd caught the aim of her gaze even in the dim lighting. She hoped his keen eyes would not pick up on her increasing flush. "Do you not think it is unfair that Society women are told to refrain from imbibing spirits, yet men are expected to partake?" she asked as she accepted the drink. The glass was warm from his touch as she cradled it in her gloved palm and examined the rich hue of the liquid. "In my experience, very little business is done without at least a dram of whiskey or a snifter of brandy present. Men's studies and offices possess well-stocked sideboards." She held the glass to her nose and tested the bouquet—sweet, like caramelized sugar, and slightly smoky. "And women...we are expected to weather the lion's den of your *ton* events without so much as a stiff drink to calm our nerves." She sipped from the glass with practiced grace, her eyes sliding closed as she savored the rich explosion of flavors, the pleasant burn of the spirits as they trickled down her throat and curled languidly in her stomach. An appreciative murmur escaped her throat. The brandy could only be French—terribly expensive, hard to come by, and likely smuggled onto English soil—and it was all the more delightful for it.

When she opened her eyes, she found Blackwood's dark gaze focused intently upon her. While she had not known him long, she'd never seen him look thusly...as if his eyes burned like banked coals and the firm line of his lips was the only thing holding his words in check. She found she very much desired to know what he had to say.

"Don't you agree?"

That seemed to snap the viscount out of whatever had held him rapt. He blinked rapidly and cleared his throat. "Quite." He brushed an imaginary wrinkle from his sleeve. "You may finish that if you'd like. I've had quite enough for one evening."

"Thank you; I do believe I will." Victoria smiled and enjoyed another sip of the brandy. She did not miss the way he followed her every small movement, and she suspected he watched her just as closely as she did him. For a man offering friendship, he seemed rather interested in her lips when she spoke.

Blackwood cleared his throat once more and said, "You escaped the rest of the ladies for a reason. Why?"

Victoria nibbled her lower lip. "Nothing new."

"The room was stifling in its stuffiness?" he guessed.

"And certain areas were rather chilly," she grumbled.

Blackwood made a thoughtful sound. "They are not worth a moment of your time."

Victoria's eyes flew to his face; his expression was impressively passive. "Society might say otherwise."

"Then they need to sod off," he said with a nonchalant lift of his shoulder. Victoria covered her mouth but couldn't stave off a small giggle of surprise. "I am quite serious," he added gravely, though mirth crinkled the corners of his eyes.

"I believe you are," she said with a smile. "Are you always this irreverent?"

"I am afraid so. It is quite the deadly affliction."

"Oh, is it?"

"I fear the prognosis is grim."

Victoria swatted lightly at his shoulder and was impressed by the solidness of it. There was no padding beneath that coat.

Blackwood finally unleashed his grin, and it was glorious. Already unbearably handsome, the expression made him shine with all the blinding light of the summer sun. It also made her knees go slightly weak. Much like the ball the other evening, she found herself wishing she did not have to return to the rest of the guests—that she and the viscount might continue to chat and laugh uninterrupted and unobserved.

THREE WEEKS, TWO balls, three dinner parties, and four fortuitous meetings while strolling in Hyde Park, and Rafe was confident he had ingratiated himself quite sufficiently with Miss Rockford. She was more comfortable with him each time they met; she laughed more readily around him, and it did not go unnoticed by her doting father.

Despite his amiable smile and ready generosity, Rafe had heard the American shipping tycoon was considered unpolished amongst most of the *ton*—likely more to do with the fact that it was bad form that a man who had come from nothing possessed a fortune that dwarfed much of English Society. For his part, Rafe enjoyed the man's loud laughter, so juxtaposed to the father-figure with which he'd been raised. In fact, he didn't think he'd ever heard the old viscount laugh, and he was quite certain the man's face would have shattered had he so much as attempted a smile.

"Blackwood!"

Mr. Rockford, the elder, clapped Rafe on the shoulder hard enough to make him choke on air, but he recovered quickly and offered Miss Rockford's father a welcoming smile.

"Mr. Rockford. A pleasure." Both men watched as Miss Rockford executed the complex steps of the current dance with her partner, an overeager young buck too much like a spaniel to present any threat to Rafe's position. "How are you enjoying the evening?"

"Too hot. Too crowded. Too starched."

A chuckle escaped Rafe's throat at the unexpected candor. Leave it to an American to distill a high society event down to such simplicity...apt as it was.

He leaned in and spoke from the side of his mouth. "Lord and Lady West have never been known for their exemplary hosting."

Mr. Rockford grunted. "That information would have been much more useful before we accepted the invitation. Though Victoria seems to be enjoying herself a great deal." He lifted his chin toward his daughter, and Rafe realized the man was right. Her cheeks were crested with delighted color, and her movements were free and graceful. Her eyes glittered each time she turned and caught Rafe's gaze, making his skin warm. None of it was lost on the American, whose keen assessment Rafe felt as tangibly as Miss Rockford's. "In fact, her enjoyment seems to be directly correlated to your presence, my lord," he added thoughtfully.

Rafe tore his eyes away from the dance floor and met the other man's intelligent, piercing blue eyes. He'd have been a fool to underestimate him; he was, first and foremost, a shrewd businessman. A man did not reach his station in life without a ruthless business acumen and a decent judgment of character.

This was the moment Rafe had been waiting for—the one that would present him the opportunity to shift his budding relationship with Miss Rockford from friendship to one of courtship and (hopefully) a quick marriage.

"I am pleased to hear that," Rafe said evenly, allowing Mr. Rockford to set the tone and show him how to proceed. Would the man be open to allowing a relationship between them, or would Rafe need to redouble his efforts with Miss Rockford to earn her father's blessing?

"Do you ride, Blackwood?"

The abrupt change in topics nearly caused Rafe's head to spin, but his mind was quick, and his tongue was quicker. "As often as my schedule permits." He didn't need to admit that he no longer owned any horses of his own and, instead, borrowed those of his closest friends when the need arose. Everyone benefited from the arrangement; the horses received their exercise, and Rafe needn't truly go without.

"Tomorrow morning, then. Dawn. I ride in the park, and you will join me—that is, if you don't find yourself in too bad a way after tonight's festivities."

Rafe eyed the glasses of watered-down punch with barely masked disdain. "I don't believe that will be a problem at all." His pulse thrummed with anticipation. This was his opportunity. He'd already worked his way into Miss Rockford's life; to earn the trust of her father could only help him to cement his place as primary suitor—whether Miss Rockford realized it or not.

Given the narrowed eyes and obvious distaste he displayed, Rafe doubted that he'd ever fully win over the younger Mr. Rockford, but that did not concern him overmuch.

The father controlled the wealth.

The father signed the marriage contracts.

The father paid the dowry.

The corners of Rafe's mouth tilted in a smile. The end was in sight.

THE NEXT MORNING, Rafe reined in the gelding he'd borrowed from Swanleigh's mews. The beloved chestnut with a white spattering of markings on its nose was the marquess's favorite mount, but he trusted Rafe to care for the animal and immediately gave his blessing when approached with the request. The horse and its tack were finer than anything Rafe could have hoped to afford, so the image presented was precisely the one Rafe hoped to convey to the elder Mr. Rockford. Swanleigh was not expressly aware of Rafe's dire financial straits, but, even if he suspected the reason behind the request when Rafe admitted he was riding with the American, he was a good friend and made no comment.

Rafe patted the horse's thick neck. "Good lad, Posy." The name was undignified for a horse so large, but Caroline had named him, and Swanleigh had never been able to say no to the woman who was now his wife and mother to his son and heir.

Straightening in the saddle, Rafe scanned the rolling green with its paths and trees as his mind struggled to comprehend the depth of the attachment that had formed between his two friends. They were deliriously in love now and had been for some time before admitting it to the world. He'd watched it develop over the years, but no matter how he turned it this way and that, his mind couldn't seem to decipher it. Swanleigh and his wife were one of only two examples of true romantic love he'd witnessed in his life; the other was Alice and Richard. His sister's love had been tragically brief and burned with blinding brightness, manifesting in her three beloved children. Rafe didn't ever expect to experience or even to understand such an all-consuming emotion, but he could do the next best thing. He could allow his sister's love to live on in her children by giving them the best life he could.

Miss Victoria Rockford was the key to that.

"Blackwood!" The shouted greeting was accompanied by the reverberation of heavy hooves on soft earth, the jangle and squeak of tack.

Rafe pivoted his mount with a small press of his heel and an adjustment to the reins to see Mr. Rockford approaching from the east. The horse he rode was a stunning dappled mare so large, she was similar in size to Posy. The American wore tailored riding clothes in navy blue and buff, with polished gold buttons. His seat was smooth and comfortable, rolling with the horse's motions much like Rafe suspected he did atop a ship's deck.

Rafe raised a hand in greeting. "Pleasant morning." The mist had not yet burned off, and the grey of dawn hung low around them. The pinks and golds of morning were just beginning to make their presence known. Soon enough, the day would change and London would come to life.

Mr. Rockford filled his barrel-like chest with the fresh air. "Indeed." His grin was amiable enough, but there was something calculating in his eyes.

Should Rafe have brought a weapon? He nearly chuckled at the absurd thought, then wondered if being so flippant was the absurdity in that situation. Hardly anyone visited Hyde Park at this time of day. Rafe hadn't spotted any other riders as he'd stretched and warmed Posy's muscles. What did the American have in store for him? Posy side-stepped, sensing Rafe's unease. He gave him another pat.

"Shall we?"

"How about we follow the path, hm? Then we can have a chat."

There it was.

Rafe wasn't sure if he should feel triumphant or terrified. He'd spent his entire adult life avoiding conversing with a woman's father, and now it felt as if his entire future hinged upon it.

He forced a pleasant tilt to his lips and inclined his head to have Mr. Rockford lead the way.

The men settled into a fast walk; slow enough that they might converse, but quick enough that the horses didn't grow too bored. The birdsong above their heads was increasing as the morning drew on. Mr. Rockford was the first to speak.

"My son has reservations about you," the American said with

unapologetic bluntness.

"Oh?" Rafe replied flatly. He wouldn't pretend to be surprised by the admission, and, judging from Mr. Rockford's amused grin, this had been the right play.

"You see, Luke is an excellent judge of character...but he is also very protective of his sister."

"As is his right," Rafe said, thoughts of Alice making his heart clench before he could stop it.

Mr. Rockford nodded once. "Then you also understand why, as soon as he made your introduction, he immediately brought to me the tabloids recounting the exploits of one, 'Viscount B'. It does not take a brilliant mind to deduce who those articles were discussing, so I've no idea why these English papers even bother with the false names."

Rafe's heart began to pound, but he reminded himself that he'd made very sure that the papers caught wind of no bad behavior on his part for just this reason.

"They call you and your friends the 'Rank of Rakes', do they not?"

"Rather unfortunate, isn't it? They have always given us more credit than was due."

"Are you denying the title?"

"The Marquess of Swanleigh is happily wedded to Miss Caroline Wells now. I will not speak for the other members of our group of friends, but I can tell you that no behavior committed by any of us has been cruel or malicious," he began with sincerity. "Have outrageous feats been performed? Certainly. Were any of them above what one might expect from the wildness of youth? Not necessarily. Young men toe the line of propriety; it is expected here in England, as I am sure it is in America. These tabloids are notorious for their exaggeration and the liberties they take with the truth, as I am sure you and your family are familiar with."

Rafe knew the last was precisely the right thing to say, because Mr. Rockford's lips thinned and he nodded in agreement.

Of course, Rafe avoided detailing just how he'd fallen into the habit of exhibiting outrageous and attention-garnering behavior. He'd cut off his right arm before he admitted to the father of the woman he intended to marry that the old Viscount Blackwood had possessed deplorable paternal instincts, only showing an interest in his heir when the lad acted out. What began as disrespecting his instructors and schoolyard tussles morphed into irreverent pranks, the seduction of women, and generally cavorting with all the "wrong" sorts of people. Rafe could not find it in himself to regret any of it, however, because his friends—the Rank of Rakes—were more family to him than his own father had ever been.

Mr. Rockford adjusted his seat before he said, "Be that as it may, I did also make inquiries of my own after it became apparent that you and my daughter were enjoying one another's company."

It was suddenly difficult for Rafe to swallow. He was impressed that his voice was as even as it was when he said, "I would expect nothing less."

"I discovered some interesting information."

"I find my life to be fairly uninteresting." Rafe chuckled unevenly. "I look forward to learning what you found 'interesting' about me." Mr. Rockford's keen eyes met Rafe's, and he refused to look away. He waited patiently for the older man to speak.

"You are in need of funds."

"As are most peers. Most every arrangement, engagement, agreement, and contract is built upon this foundation."

"True, but your need stems back quite a way, doesn't it?"

Rafe went silent, his mind working with impressive speed as he fought to determine which angle would be preferable. He should have known that someone who was as shrewd a businessman as the elder Mr. Rockford would investigate anyone who had the potential to become close with his daughter. The real question was how deeply he had looked. Was he aware of his wards? The children's presence in his home and his life was not something he shared openly; never having guests in his home made keeping the secret far easier. However, if the right questions were asked of the right people, then the information would not be too difficult to uncover.

"Your title is centuries old, yet you are the last of your family. Over the years, the Blackwood lands have been whittled away from significant holdings to almost nothing. I might have blamed your youth for poor investments or financial planning, but most of this seems to have taken place before you inherited. Am I correct?"

Rafe gritted his teeth. It had been years since he'd had to answer to anyone about money. To say it was uncomfortable was an understatement, but he also knew it was something he needed to endure if he was going to prove to Mr. Rockford that he was worthy. He couldn't risk offending the man.

Not trusting his words, Rafe could only nod.

"And I suspect your interest in my Victoria to be motivated by this fact?"

"To a one, the men pursuing your daughter are unashamed fortune-hunters," Rafe said firmly.

"And you do not count yourself among their numbers?"

"I do not." The lie was bitter, but he had to sell it. He had to be convincing.

Mr. Rockford raised a questioning brow.

"Miss Rockford is more than a purse. She is more than an heiress."

"Is she?" Her father sounded skeptical. "I did not bring her here to find a husband. My aim was not to buy a title for her. I know wealthy Americans are doing this now—I have friends who have done it for their daughters, for God's sake!—but I am not that man. I couldn't care less about the color of her future husband's blood, so long as she is happy." Their eyes met squarely, unflinchingly. "Of all the men who've danced attendance upon her, who've escorted her around the many ballrooms, who've called at our house, *you* are the one she seems most comfortable with. Happiest."

Rafe's heart stuttered in a most unexpected way.

After a pause, Mr. Rockford said, "I would like to hear why you believe there is more to my daughter than the money she might bring to a marriage."

"She is witty and charming," Rafe began with full honesty, surprised that he did not have to craft an appropriate response. Miss Rockford was, indeed, both of those things, and more. "She is outspoken, but not brash. She is unafraid of laughter. I have yet to witness a hint of cruelty from her; only the most refreshing honesty. Miss Rockford is different from any other woman of my acquaintance."

Mr. Rockford's eyes danced across Rafe's face, examining every one of his features and even his posture for the truth. Rafe did not squirm. Nothing he'd said had been a falsehood, and that bolstered his confidence.

He narrowed his gaze at Rafe and asked, "Nothing about her looks? Is she not attractive?"

Rafe nearly swallowed his tongue. He hadn't thought to describe Miss Rockford's loveliness to her own father. "Of course—That is—She is—" He stammered uncharacteristically until he was finally saved by a great, booming laugh from the American.

"Don't have a fit, Blackwood!" Mr. Rockford slapped his own thigh in amusement, and his mount snorted in response.

Rafe exhaled his anxiety and tried again. "Miss Rockford is a lovely young woman."

"That she is. And it will take the right man to partner her." He looked Rafe up and down again. "She comes from solid, hardy stock. Generations of her family have worked the docks and ships. Her grandfather was captain of a vessel. I spent my life on or near the water; she and my son have done the same."

"Are you saying this to warn me off?" Rafe cocked a brow.

"I am telling you the bald truth of it," he replied frankly. "Not a drop of noble blood can be found in our lineage. We are a new breed of aristocrat, Viscount Blackwood. My family earned their place in the world through blood and sweat, ingenuity and sheer determination. Thus far, England has not always treated my daughter with the respect she is due. I suspect your intentions and, if I am reading them accurately, then I must know that you are a man who is willing to stand for her when your peers will not; I must know that you see her as more than a woman who might refill your coffers to overflowing."

"Do you have this conversation with every man who speaks to your daughter?"

"No. No, I do not."

Rafe met his eyes.

"I invited you to join me today because you've struck me as a man who enjoys my daughter's company in more than just the superficial capacity. I also believe she feels the same about you." Why did that make Rafe's pulse trip? "Frankly, I liked your answers earlier." He seemed to pause for effect. "There is more to my daughter than her family's fortune, and what you said showed me that you've seen that. You could have spouted pretty words or flattered me as her father, but you did not.

"The fact remains that you require funds. While Victoria certainly has them, I suspect that the two of you have the potential for so much more than a transactional arrangement."

A large part of Rafe chafed at that assessment. Everything about the conversation was making him uncomfortable, as if every part of his clothing had been doused in powdered starch, causing his skin to itch and burn. Not only was he discomfited by Mr. Rockford's interpretation of Rafe's relationship with his daughter, but also by the other man's belief that Rafe was even capable of forming an attachment above the superficial. A great deal of faith bled from those words, and Rafe didn't know if he'd ever had someone say such a thing to him—especially not when the stakes were so high.

It took Rafe several tries to swallow past the thick knot in his throat. Finally, he said, "And you are saying—"

"That you are earning my permission to court my daughter officially," the American spoke over him. To Rafe, his tone was too light for the import of the decision he'd just announced; it did not match the weight of the impact it was about to have on Rafe's world. "I wish to have the opportunity to know you better first, but I will give you my blessing if I find it appropriate. I say we meet again tomorrow for another ride, partake another of these chats, and, if all goes well, then I am hopeful my daughter will be amenable to your suit." He paused again before warning, "This is a privilege I've never allowed. Do not make me regret it."

"I do not intend to." The pounding of Rafe's blood was like the roar of a furious ocean in his ears.

"DID YOU TRULY go riding with Papa yesterday morning?" Victoria had caught Viscount Blackwood's sleeve and quite literally yanked him out the door and onto the back terrace of the Mayfair home where she and her family had been invited to attend a poetry reading. It wasn't something that had ever been of any particular interest to her before, but she'd come to expect Blackwood's appearance at any event she attended, and it was the only socially acceptable way she could all but guarantee seeing him.

"Lord, but don't you have a powerful grip?" the man groused dramatically, brushing at his coat and affecting a dandified carriage he knew would make it difficult for her to maintain a straight face.

"Do not try to distract me," she said, jabbing a finger into his chest and noticing for the first time just how firm it was. Now *that* was distracting.

"Yes, I went riding with your father. Three times this past week, as a matter of fact." His eyes met hers, and he cocked an imperious brow. "Should I have asked your permission? Am I allowed to be friendly with only one Rockford at a time? I fear your brother may have a long while to wait—"

"Three times?" Victoria had taken a few moments to process

his words, but the shock of them set in rather quickly after that.

"Why, yes. Did he not tell you?"

She shook her head. No, he certainly had not. Of course, she didn't expect her father to run his entire social calendar by her for approval, but he hadn't allowed anyone to accompany him on his rides since they'd arrived in England. Those early morning outings were normally his most contemplative, and he didn't care to be interrupted. The fact that he'd invited Lord Blackwood—and on several occasions, no less!—was astonishing to her.

"I rose early yesterday and heard him return from his ride. I now know it was you I saw riding away from the mews."

The soft, warm smile Blackwood offered her melted her insides, and he took her hand in his. It was warm even through the layers of their gloves. "Does it displease you that I was riding with your father?" he inquired gently.

"No—that is, I do not suppose I have feelings about it one way or the other. My father is a grown man."

"Then are you jealous that I have not accompanied you on a ride yet? I am more than happy to remedy that."

Victoria's bark of laughter was unladylike, but she couldn't help it with how off-guard his comment had caught her. "That is not it at all!"

"Then are you curious about what he and I discussed on these long rides at ungodly hours?"

Victoria pulled her lips between her teeth rather than answer. That maddening brow of his rose a little higher before he leaned in as if imparting a delicious secret.

"I should like very much to call upon you formally at your home, Miss Rockford, if that is agreeable to you."

Her breath hitched. She did not know what she had expected, but it certainly hadn't been that. Was she that blinded by her desire for a sense of belonging in London that she hadn't noticed his less-than-platonic interest in her? Had it been there all along, or had it developed over time?

Blackwood continued, saying, "Your father has given his

blessing for us to begin meeting in such a capacity. All that is left is your approval." He straightened to his full height, and she was shocked to realize they'd moved together so now barely a breath of air separated them. She could feel the heat of his body; she could do nothing but breathe the air scented with pine and sweet tobacco.

"If you do…then you will become like every other man I've met in London," she replied, the tragedy of the fact leaking into her words. Is that what their friendship would be reduced to? Would he fade into the crowd of uninspired fortune-hunting suitors? Victoria thought with a sense of loss how she would miss the easy, amiable time spent in his company; how keenly she would feel the absence of his intoxicating laughter.

Rather than sober him, her statement seemed only to thrill him. The viscount's smile split into a full grin.

"Sweeting," he purred, "I am nothing like those men." And he closed the last little gap between them to cover her mouth with his, shaking Victoria's normally solid reserve to her core.

She had experienced a few chaste kisses in her life from the bolder of her suitors back home in America, but those had been nothing like the toe-curling, sensational onslaught unleashed upon her by Lord Blackwood. He pulled her in with a strong arm around her waist, pressing their bodies together in an unyielding embrace that left her breathless. This man, who'd spent the last several weeks making her laugh, earning her trust, and becoming her friend, wanted her…and she was helpless to resist the pull.

Blackwood's lips met hers with practiced expertise, drawing a sigh of rapture from her breast as he licked at the seam of her mouth. He tasted of something intoxicatingly sweet and smoky— whiskey and brown sugar, warm and inviting, drugging in its sensual leisure. Helpless in the face of his skill, she tilted her head with only the slightest provocation from his thumb at her jaw and granted him access to more of her. And take, he did. He devoured her. His tongue swept deeply, claiming her until she clung to his lapels lest her legs give out. She could feel the heavy thud of his heart against her knuckles, and she was certain it beat as the perfect counterpart to her own hammering pulse.

They took turns tasting one another, giving and taking in equal measure. The tightening of his arms around her emboldened Victoria. His slight groan when she gave his lower lip a teasing nip spurred her on, but he met her challenge and demonstrated just how little she truly knew of physical passion and pleasure. His hands danced down her back, sending ripples of gooseflesh across every inch of her skin. She arched into him and accepted everything he gave her until, quite suddenly, he released her.

She'd been kissed so soundly that her mind was still lost in the clouds, leaving her to teeter precariously. Lord Blackwood steadied her with a maddeningly pleased look on his handsome face, his eyes dark pools of carnal knowledge the likes of which she could not fathom. It didn't seem fair that a man could be so beautiful…surely, he'd always been forgiven anything in return for a smile and a wink.

"I will call upon you tomorrow," he said. Was it her imagination, or was his voice slightly huskier than usual? "I know your directions."

Victoria's cheeks flared with heat as if she'd stared into the hearth for too long—sought its warmth and been scorched so slowly that she hadn't realized it until it was too late.

Her sluggish mind had no opportunity to comment before she was ushered back into the buzzing parlor, the rest of the guests none the wiser for what had taken place in the dim hallway. She barely resisted the urge to press her gloved fingertips to her lips. Surely, they were pink and swollen from Blackwood's thorough kissing; would they not give away what had transpired?

But no.

Everyone was quite enthralled by the poetry reading that was still somehow taking place despite her recent transcendent experience. She supposed it was a good thing this was surely the world's longest poem, or else her absence might have been noticed.

Or Blackwood's.

Her eyes scanned the crowd and, sure enough, his dark, handsome frame had reentered through another doorway on the opposite side of the room with all the forethought of a man used to such scenarios.

And his coal-fire gaze was trained right at her.

The rest of the evening passed in a blur, and Victoria considered that she might truly have discovered a touch of excitement in London.

Chapter Five

Two Months Later

VICTORIA FINGERED THE ruby and garnet ring on her third finger, tracing the intricate network of gold prongs used to create the cluster of red and pink stones set into a ring that had once belonged to Blackwood's mother. Even though she'd known the proposal had been coming, she'd still been struck quite breathless when the words had been spoken—when the viscount had offered her the ring and asked for her hand. Much to Luke's chagrin, Blackwood had already obtained her father's blessing for the match, but Victoria appreciated that he still thought to allow her to ultimately accept or decline.

They had Papa's approval. She and Lord Blackwood got on extremely well. The marriage would be societally advantageous both in England and America, where the novelty of peerage would make her quite fashionable. She was quite attracted to the viscount. And, perhaps most of all, she could not stop thinking about their first stolen kiss in the darkened hallway. Not since that night had he attempted to repeat the interaction, but that did not stop Victoria from experiencing little frissons of excitement each time he touched her. No matter how innocent the gesture— whether helping her alight from a carriage or leading her to the floor for a dance—her heart reacted as if it were in mortal danger of being lost forever. The sensation was foreign and wretchedly inconvenient when one was attempting to maintain one's composure.

As soon as Luke discovered that their father had given his

permission to Blackwood to formally court Victoria, her brother had immediately set about doing his best to convince her to discourage the match. Each time "Viscount B" was mentioned in the tabloids, he handed it to her over breakfast; each time he garnered a new bit of gossip about Blackwood's history with women, he made sure to share it with her; each time they attended the same function, Luke would make no effort to mask his distaste over the possibility that his sister would marry an Englishman.

"What has he done?" Victoria finally demanded on the carriage ride home one evening after a night at the theater. They'd once more been invited to accompany the Duke and Duchess of Morton in their private box; Luke and Blackwood had been invited as well. Much to Victoria's mortification, Luke had done everything in his power to make the evening as uncomfortable as possible. Long silences, narrowed eyes, and suspicious glances were cast in Blackwood's direction the entire evening. Luke did such a poor job of hiding his disdain for the man that Victoria recognized hints of discomfort in their hosts' demeanors—and the Mortons were not easily unsettled people. "Why did you feel the need to behave in such a manner? You are not usually so careless or graceless, Luke!"

At least he'd had the good grace to cast his eyes downward in a minor show of regret before he leaned back against the squab, crossed his arms over his chest, and said, "He's nothing more than another fortune-hunter."

"Who? Blackwood?" Victoria asked with a frown.

Luke grunted. "Did you know the Blackwood title is all but impoverished?"

Victoria reared back at the comment. The viscount certainly did not dress or carry himself like a man without funds, but what she found more shocking was the fact that her brother had invested the time and energy into ferreting out the information. "So, you hired an investigator to look into him?" The more she'd pondered it, the more the idea had made her skin burn. Who was her brother to perform such an invasion?

"Of course I did! Someone had to; Papa has ridden out with Blackwood a handful of times and all but welcomed him into the family. Don't you wish to know why the man did not disclose this information to you himself?"

Victoria's stomach made an uneasy lurch. Of course, she would have preferred to know the viscount's financial circumstances, but she could understand why he might not have discussed it with her. What man wanted to admit that he had pockets to let...let alone an English lord? The English were all about appearances, she'd learned, and to tear down the façade of one's wealth would be a terrible sin. A mortification from which one would likely never recover. The fact that Blackwood had so carefully guarded his dire financial straits made her experience a wave of protectiveness for him, which was odd. Didn't this put Blackwood in the same category as every other fortune-hunter who'd pursued her in London? Didn't it? But, for some reason, it didn't. She wanted to feel the same righteous indignation Luke did; she didn't care for the unfamiliar position of disagreeing with Luke's opinion of the man. Never had they been so at odds, and perhaps the stakes had something to do with that.

Victoria's future hung in the balance.

"I believe it is actually quite easy to understand why a man might not wish to disclose this information in casual conversation."

"But he hid it—"

"Would you rather he dressed in rags? Wear a sign disclosing his worth?"

Luke narrowed his eyes at her, but he did not argue against her logic.

"You are not being entirely fair to him."

"Fair?" Luke scoffed. "Fair would be for a man not to be so duplicitous when it involves my sister. Blackwood approached you under the guise of friendship, did he not? He ingratiated himself with you, and then with Papa, and now he has his future all but secured with an heiress."

Victoria's face flushed. "And do you not think that I resigned myself long ago to the fact that money would always be a factor in whatever match I made?" Luke's mouth snapped shut as she continued. "Mightn't it also be feasible that a man could like me for who I am, recognize that I might make an admirable partner, and my inheritance would only be a boon?" Victoria knew this might have been an optimistic exaggeration of her relationship with Blackwood. Still, her pride had been wounded by Luke's insistence that the viscount was pursuing her only for her money. Not for the first time, she told herself that it wasn't unreasonable to believe that his offer of friendship had been sincere, and his desire to wed her had developed over the course of their acquaintance. She wanted to believe it with quiet desperation. "Is it so unbelievable that a man might also want *me*?" Victoria's voice cracked painfully.

"You know that is not what I am saying, Victoria," Luke huffed and then scrubbed at his face.

"Isn't it?"

"No! It is only one of many items that make him unsuitable for you," Luke said with all the confidence of a professor about to launch into a lengthy diatribe. He listed each of Blackwood's perceived sins, from what the tabloids said about his numerous mistresses, his torrid affairs, his debauched activities, and his rakehell antics with his group of close friends. "This does not seem to me like a man who wishes to take a wife and live as a married man should."

Each of Luke's marks against Blackwood only made Victoria's fists clench more tightly. He was being unfair. Of course, Blackwood was no saint—she firmly believed any man who claimed to be one was likely closer to devil than angel—but never had he ever made her feel unsafe, manipulated, or used. What was worse, Luke seemed to be placing so much weight upon what was being said in the tabloids, as if they were the preeminent authority on all things that summed up a man's worth. How often had he told her that she should ignore what those articles said? How often had Luke reassured her that those tabloids were worth less than the paper on which they were printed? And now, there he was, using them against Blackwood. The hypocrisy was almost more than she could handle.

They arrived at their rented home, and Luke followed her as she stormed up the stairs. Victoria hadn't realized she'd begun to shed angry, frustrated tears until her father, seeing how distraught she was as she attempted to storm past him and toward her own chamber, caught her arm.

"What has happened?" he asked, looking between his children. He must have returned from his appointment some time prior because he'd already removed his coat and unwound his cravat.

"Luke is determined to warn me off Viscount Blackwood as a suitor."

"And she is determined to paint him as a paragon when he's hidden his deplorable financial status from her—from us!"

Her father's head whipped toward Luke. "What?"

"Blackwood! He has hardly two shillings to rub together. He—"

"I heard you," their father suddenly snapped, startling both of them. "What I want to know is how you came upon that information."

Luke stood a little straighter, much like when he'd been a boy and was preparing himself for a lecture. "I made discreet inquiries of the right people," he explained.

"Because you did not trust my judgment when it came to Victoria's suitor?" Papa said icily. Luke's jaw tightened. "Do you think I would entrust her care with just anyone? That I would not do my due diligence?" This finally seemed to cow Luke and quell the strength of his fire. "I would not be where I am today if I were so negligent, and you would do well to remember that."

"Yes, sir," Luke replied steadily.

"I will not listen to another word about this. I have given my blessing, and that is final." Papa looked at her. "At least until Victoria decides to accept or decline the match." She squeezed her father's hand in gratitude and slipped off to her chamber.

Her maid helped her to change into her nightshift and wrapper before retiring for the evening, leaving Victoria to curl up in a chair before the hearth and stare pensively into the flames.

She had always known that no man was ever going to come along and be entirely immune to the size of all she stood to inherit—of all her family held and controlled. It was the least she could do to marry a man she liked.

And she had come to like Blackwood a great deal.

There was a tentative knock upon her door before Luke's dark head poked into the room.

"I thought you might still be awake," he said quietly.

"If you've come to berate me some more, you can turn around right now and take a long walk into the Thames."

He emitted a single low chuckle before entering the room and pressing the door closed behind him. He did not ask permission before taking up the chair across from her.

She wanted to be childish and ignore him until he left her alone, but his heavy sigh made her hesitate.

"You do know I am only trying to look out for you, don't you?" he finally asked, gently, plaintively. It was not a tone she was used to hearing from her brother.

"I do," she responded only slightly begrudgingly. "But I also do not feel that it is fair of you to villainize Lord Blackwood."

"And I do not believe it is fair to you to tie yourself to a man with a rakish reputation and a poor financial record."

"Oh, Luke..." she chided him gently and reached across the space to pat his hand. "We have been the subjects of gossip since we set foot on this island; we have laughed over the inaccuracies and exaggerations contained in the tabloids. Should we not be some of the first people to recognize that sensationalized accounts might be just that? A way to sell more papers? Besides, no man was ever going to be good enough for me in your eyes...no matter who he was." Her brother's countenance darkened, but he did not refute her statements. "Blackwood has been nothing but kind and solicitous to me, and I have no reason to believe we will not be content in our marriage."

"I do not care to think you are settling."

Victoria scoffed lightly. "If I were resigned to settling, then I would have accepted any of the other half-dozen offers over the past few years." She sighed and slumped back into her chair. "You cannot understand what it is like for a woman who comes from wealth. No matter how long I wait, I will never be able to tell who wants my attention for my money, and who wants me for *me*. Do not frown at me, Luke. Your priority has been Rockford Shipping, and marriage is quite possibly the furthest thing from your mind, though perhaps one day you may consider it." She ignored his dismissive snort. "Rockford Shipping is your destiny, but it cannot be mine. I came to terms long ago with the fact that my inheritance would play at least a small part in whatever match I accepted. While I appreciate how much you care, I can only do my best to reassure you that I am not making a grave mistake, and trust that Papa's safeguards for my inheritance will keep me secure in any circumstances.

"Blackwood may have a reputation, his title may not have limitless funds, but I believe in my heart that he is earnest. Or at least dedicated and determined enough to persist and stand out amongst the other men here in London and even convince Papa of his worthiness." She knew their father's effusive praise of Lord Blackwood had been grating on Luke, but she couldn't resist reminding him of it. As amiable as he could be, not many men could say they'd worked their way into the elder Mr. Rockford's private circle.

Except Blackwood.

Only Blackwood.

The viscount was charming, persistent, friendly, and he made her laugh. Besides, he had impressed her father, which was perhaps the most important and remarkable thing of all. If her father trusted him, then Victoria would as well. Papa had never led her astray before, and she had to believe there were reasons he felt Blackwood was a suitable match. Even if she was not privy to all her father's thoughts on the matter, the fact remained that her father had given his blessing and would support the match.

Despite Luke's best attempts to change her mind, she accepted Blackwood's formal proposal, and she would go through with the wedding. There would be no turning back after that.

Chapter Six

THE MORNING OF Victoria's wedding to the viscount dawned sunny and surprisingly warm for England. The ceremony would take place at St. George's, after which a wedding breakfast would be served. Papa had tried to convince her that they could host a more lavish affair, but Victoria had staunchly declined. She knew such a spectacle would be expected. St. George's was still considered highly fashionable amongst the Mayfair elite, and it would accommodate enough guests to make it an appropriately grand affair, but it would also allow Victoria to maintain some control. As much as she could, she invited only those people who had been kind to her and her family during their time in London. The wedding would be her first official event in England, and she was determined to set the proper tone. She would not accept deplorable treatment; she would not grin and suffer through snide comments. Once the vows were said, she would have a title to back up her wealth, and she would make a name for herself. She would follow Lady Morton's lead and use her status for good, and she would not allow anyone to make her feel less because her family had worked hard for everything they had. She would be proud of her origins. Besides, not once had Blackwood ever batted an eye at her Americanness, nor the way they'd earned their fortune. So long as that support continued, Victoria felt she could weather most anything the *ton* brought her way.

The door to Victoria's chamber swung open after a perfunctory knock. In stepped her father, looking rather refined in his bespoke formalwear with its crisp lines and coattails. His dear face split into a broad grin, the lines at the corners of his eyes deepening in his joy. Victoria smoothed the skirts of the ice-blue gown she'd had specially made for the day. The garment was impossibly heavy, but the intricate beadwork made it worth it. A pattern of Forget-Me-Nots and vines had been sewn into the dyed satin to create a custom design that was truly one of a kind. The beadwork clicked and dazzled when she moved, making every movement a spectacle. And she felt truly beautiful in the gossamer wrap of ivory lace, so fine it appeared almost cloud-like, which softened the daring cut of the pleated bust and empire waist.

"Stunning," her father murmured. "Absolutely stunning." His eyes were suspiciously bright.

Before her own tears spilled over, Victoria closed the gap between them and pressed a kiss to her father's slightly leathery cheek, weathered from too many hours spent outdoors. "Thank you, Papa."

He held her at arm's length and looked her up and down again. "And you look so like your mama."

Victoria's throat tightened painfully, her eyes burned, and her breath clogged her throat. Words failed her. She and Luke missed their mother each day, but she knew their father missed her even more. They'd all learned to cope after more than a decade without her, but events such as this made her absence felt even more keenly than usual.

"Imagine!" Papa said with an overabundance of cheer. "My Victoria, a true lady and a viscountess!" Her father beamed. "As long as you are happy, of course," he added sincerely. "I desire your happiness above all else."

Victoria patted his hand, kissed his cheek again, and reassured him that she was, indeed, happy that she'd accepted Blackwood's offer. "Yes, Papa; I am pleased with the decision." She huffed a cleansing breath, stood up straighter, and said, "Shall we?"

As HER FATHER escorted her up the narrow central aisle of the church, Victoria's heart raced in anticipation. It took everything in her to continue her measured, careful steps when faced with Blackwood's sinful half-smile and impeccable appearance. He was glorious. Tall and lean, broad of shoulder, artfully hewn features, eyes rich and striking. Before then, she'd done her best to temper her longing glances, her awe of his unnatural physical perfection and unfair amount of charm, but she would have the right to indulge in her gazing for the rest of her life from that moment forward. It was a sobering realization only underscored by the binding recitation of their vows.

With her gloved hand in his, the rest of the scene—the guests, her father and brother watching from the front pew, and Mr. Simon Stratford standing up beside her soon-to-be-husband—all seemed to melt away like spun sugar. Gone were the familiar faces of her father's business associates, the few ladies she'd met and befriended during her time in London, and even Blackwood's closest companions, who comprised a majority of the small assemblage on the groom's side of the church. They all became inconsequential in the presence of this man who would take her as his wife for all the rest of their days.

The unexpected tremble began in her toes and slowly danced up her calves. It made her stance unsteady as it traveled through her spine and made her fingers shake.

Until that point, she'd managed to stave off the unease that perhaps they were moving too quickly. Was she acting rashly in accepting this man's suit? Could Luke be correct with his words of caution? Did she truly wish to spend the rest of her life in England? Could she be away from the only family she'd ever known?

And then, Blackwood's fingers tightened around hers, and the corner of his mouth lifted reassuringly in a private smile just for her.

The trembling instantly stopped.

A calm, like the cool breeze after a storm, washed over her, and she squeezed his fingers back.

The kiss he pressed to her lips at the conclusion of the ceremony was nothing like the one they'd shared before. Still, she knew the softness and the skill in his touch hinted at the passion hiding just beneath the surface. Warmth spread through her limbs, and she barely resisted the urge to press her fingers to her tingling lips.

She barely remembered walking back up the aisle and making their way, along with the rest of the guests, to her family's rented home nearby. Lady Morton had stepped in as a guiding hand during the planning process when it became clear that Victoria was overwhelmed by everything that needed to be accomplished, as well as the incorporation of English traditions with which she was unfamiliar. For that, Victoria would be eternally grateful. The parlor and dining room had been swathed in netting and draped with ivy and summer blooms in shades of blue, pink, and purple. The air was scented with sunshine and sweet floral aromas dancing on the breeze that traipsed through the open windows and doors leading out to the back garden. The wedding breakfast had been coordinated to perfection; served on fine bone china from polished silver chaffing dishes, the meal would be remembered and emulated—or so Victoria was assured by Lady Morton.

"Everything came out to perfection, did it not?" the duchess asked after kissing the air beside Victoria's cheeks.

"I could not have done it without you," Victoria replied sincerely.

"Of course, you could have!" Lady Morton waved a dismissive hand.

"You give me too much credit."

"You do not give yourself enough." Victoria barely had time to process the compliment before two ladies approached them. One was shorter with pale blond hair, sapphire eyes, and pleasantly soft features; the other was taller, long of limb, with burnished rose-gold hair.

"Ah, Lady Blackwell. You have made the acquaintance of the Marchioness of Swanleigh and Mrs. Simon Stratford, have you not?"

It took Victoria several heartbeats to realize the duchess was addressing her by her new title. She'd been Miss Victoria Rockford her entire life; she would be Lady Blackwell for the rest of it. That she was now stepping into a new identity was more than a little sobering.

"Y—Yes," she stammered slightly. "Thank you so much for coming." She greeted the women properly—by order of precedence.

"Thank you for the invitation," said the taller of the two women with a broad smile. Victoria had previously met the marchioness at one of the meetings of Lady Morton's Reading Society, and she'd also learned that, before her marriage to the Marquess of Swanleigh, the woman had once been counted amongst Blackwood's Rank of Rakes. At first, Victoria hadn't been entirely sure what to think of the woman whose reputation had once been so tarnished that she'd thought nothing of being unchaperoned amongst a group of London's rakes, but she'd only needed to witness Lady Swanleigh and her husband once to have her mind put to rest. The two were clearly enamored with one another, and they spent so much time at home with their young son and heir that Victoria had only had one or two other occasions to speak with them in her entire time in London.

"Yes, thank you," said the other woman. "The decorations are glorious. I daresay this will be an event that is talked about for many months to come." Mrs. Stratford was more reserved than Lady Swanleigh, though she was also a member of the Reading Society, so Victoria needn't have worried that she was one of the stuffy ladies who would look down their noses at her. Victoria found her sweet and reserved, mindful and conscientious in the things she said. Blackwood had asked Mr. Stratford to stand up with him at the wedding, and Victoria was certain two more different men could not have existed in the world. Where

Blackwood could be loud and animated, Stratford was quiet and observant. For such a tall, objectively attractive man, he somehow managed to blend in with the paneling of the walls. He often seemed lost in his thoughts and relied upon his wife to carry out conversations on his behalf. Victoria might have felt sorry for Mrs. Stratford, except she'd also witnessed the small gestures of affection between the two of them. There was a distinct air of adoration in the marriage that made their relationship make sense.

"I appreciate the compliments, but I ask that you direct them to Lady Morton. She had a great deal more to do with this event than I."

"Oh, hush!" Lady Morton gently tapped Victoria's arm with her fan. "Your first lesson in being a part of English nobility: Accept compliments, especially when they relate to your abilities as a hostess, especially when any assistance you employed has *expressly* indicated that you are to take all the accolades for yourself."

"Very well," Victoria laughed lightly.

"I have a good feeling about you, Lady Blackwood," Lady Swanleigh said with another wide smile. "My husband had begun to despair that anyone could entice Blackwood to settle down; I was always insistent that it would simply take the right woman. Who knew the right woman had to sail all the way here from America? Though it makes sense…Blackwell never did like to do things the easy way if there was a more interesting way to be had."

"Why settle for an Englishwoman when there is a beautiful, bright American?" Lady Morton chimed in with an airy laugh as she claimed a drink from a passing servant. Coming from anyone else, the comments might have been underhanded or snarky, but these women had been nothing but supportive of Blackwood and their relationship. And Victoria hoped she might continue to count on them as she settled into her new role. She could only guess at the challenges a newly minted viscountess might encounter. She would need their support if she was going to make her way in this world.

"Indeed," intoned Mrs. Stratford. The marchioness and duchess were quickly pulled into another conversation, leaving Victoria alone with the wife of the man who had so recently stood up in her wedding. Mrs. Stratford had always been polite and kind, but Victoria could tell there was more behind the woman's smile than she let on.

Deciding to have it out, Victoria asked, "Won't you join me on the terrace for a moment? I require a bit of air." Indeed, the room had grown quite full of all the guests now having meandered over from the church.

Mrs. Stratford nodded amiably and followed Victoria's lead. The women filled their lungs with the heady summer air, and Victoria resolved to clear whatever it was that lay between them. "Our husbands are quite close, and have been for most of their lives, have they not?"

"That is correct," Mrs. Stratford replied with a nod. Intelligence flashed in her blue eyes, letting Victoria know there was more to the woman than a pretty face.

"Then I would like for you and me to have the same opportunity, since I suspect we will see one another often. I hope I have done nothing to offend you, and, if I have, please accept my apologies—"

"Oh, it is nothing like that at all!" she rushed to reassure Victoria. Her eyes averted as if she were weighing her next words.

"Then please tell me what you wish to say. Today is a day of new beginnings, and I do not want there to be any shadows lying in wait."

Mrs. Stratford nibbled her plump lower lip for another moment before she met Victoria's gaze once more. "I have always found you quite likable, Lady Blackwood," she admitted. "You are charming and intelligent—Lady Morton feels the same."

"I thank you for the compliment, but I cannot help but wonder how this is concerning?"

"The viscount, well…please forgive me for speaking plainly."

"I would not have it any other way between friends."

This seemed to reassure the other woman, because a fleeting smile of appreciation crossed her lips. "Then I will say that Lord Blackwell has not always presented the most favorable side of himself to me." Victoria's eyes widened, and she was suddenly unsure if she wished to hear more. "You are aware that he has a bit of a reputation that follows him around?" Victoria nodded once. "My, but you've gone quite ashen!" Mrs. Stratford reached out and took Victoria's hand. "I promise it is not as bad as whatever you have in your mind right now. He simply had a relationship with an old friend of mine, and it did not end on the best of terms. He wasn't cruel," she hurried to add when she saw the question begin to form in Victoria's eyes. "He merely bruised her heart. We women from the theater stick together to protect one another. I admit that I am holding onto the grudge a bit longer than is perhaps seemly, but…" She lifted her shoulder in a Gallic gesture.

"You are standing beside your friend," Victoria supplied.

"Yes." Mrs. Stratford deflated a little in relief. "I am glad you understand."

"I do." Victoria squeezed her fingers. "As long as you don't hold my husband's past against me, then all will be well."

"Certainly not! And I vow, in the name of this blossoming friendship, that I will do my best to forgive him his sins."

"Well, now…let us not be too generous."

The women giggled together and regained their composure before returning to the wedding breakfast.

Chapter Seven

"THANK YOU, FRAN," Victoria murmured as her maid bobbed a curtsey and quit the room.

The unfamiliar room.

The room in an opulent hotel where she would reside until she and her new husband boarded a ship for their honeymoon trip.

Her husband...

And she was now Lady Victoria Hart, Viscountess Blackwell. It wasn't the first time that day the realization had crossed her mind, but it was setting in a little bit more on each occasion. She wondered when it would stop being a novelty and simply become her reality. She nearly reprimanded herself for her silliness, then decided to give herself some grace. She'd been married less than twelve hours; she could hardly be expected to change her entire perception of herself in that amount of time!

And there were a great many things with which she now must come to terms...like how much she enjoyed looking at her new husband.

Just as she'd explained to Luke, Victoria had long ago accepted the fact that the man she married might not love her—and that was her current situation, since the viscount had never so much as hinted at the word—but what would happen to her if she were to give in to the way Blackwood made her feel? How could she handle herself for the rest of her life when faced with the persistent flutter in her chest whenever he smiled at her? Or her incessant desire to have him hold her and touch her?

It was damned difficult to maintain her composure when faced with his charm; it was even more difficult now that they'd spent the last couple of months getting to know one another. She'd learned the shape of his smile, the difference in his laughter when it was just the two of them as opposed to when there was more of a crowd, and that there was substance behind his lighthearted demeanor—there had to be if he'd won over her father.

Could she allow herself to explore her attraction to the man she'd married?

Would she?

None of Society's constraints applied any longer; they'd been freed from them as soon as the ink had dried on the register. But the idea of admitting to her growing attraction felt a bit like handing over too much control. She'd spent so long keeping her emotions in check and disguising her feelings from the vipers and harpies who would feast upon her weakness that it caused her no small discomfort to think of doing otherwise.

If she couldn't do this with Blackwood, then with whom could she? He was her husband, after all.

Victoria had still been contemplating that much when they arrived at their suite of rooms from the lavish wedding breakfast, as the maid had helped her slip from her elegant wedding gown and into the gauzy ivory nightdress trimmed in sapphire blue ribbon, and she waited in silence thick with anticipation.

HER EYES DANCED across the ornately carved marble of the mantle, the elegant crown molding, the walls papered in rich blue stripes; her bare toes wriggled in the thick pile of the rug. None of it truly distracted her from the hammering of her heart against her ribcage—especially not when she heard the handle of the door to the adjoining chamber turn.

Certainly, there was nothing in existence that could calm her pulse when her husband walked through the door, somehow even more devilishly handsome in his dishabille. The collar of his crisp white linen shirt was undone, affording her a view of the strong column of his throat; his sleeves were rolled to his elbows, revealing his corded forearms and their dark dusting of hair. It was absurdly, incredibly intimate, this glimpse of his arms.

It took a great deal of effort, but she was finally able to drag her eyes back to his face…and he smiled when their eyes met. It was broad and unguarded; his eyes crinkled at the corners and his sharply angular features softened.

Once again, her stomach performed that hopeless flip.

RAFE HAD DONE the unthinkable.

He, the Rake of London, one of the notorious Rank of Rakes, was well and truly wedded.

What was more impressive? He'd managed to snag one of the wealthiest heiresses on the Marriage Marts on both sides of the Atlantic.

In a matter of months, he'd singlehandedly managed to turn his fortunes around—quite literally.

Mr. Rockford had offered a most generous sum as settlement for the marriage agreement, along with an annual income that would keep them all quite comfortable. Of course, the younger Mr. Rockford hadn't been able to resist throwing his weight around, and he'd insisted upon stipulations for his sister's happiness.

"My son insisted upon a few terms as well," Mr. Rockford had said, tapping his thumb on the paperwork between them. "Though I was reluctant, I must admit that his stipulations were not unreasonable. The annual stipend will be paid out only after personal testimony to the solicitors by Victoria that she remains satisfied in the marriage. If she is at all unhappy or displeased, then the disbursement will be frozen. She will still be able to request funds for personal use, but nothing will be disbursed to the Blackwood estate. Not a cent. Not a pound. Not a farthing."

Anxiety had briefly tightened across Rafe's chest. He'd been arrogant to believe that all his troubles would be over after the vows were recited when he'd entered negotiations with such a shrewd businessman. His future—and that of his wards—would continue to hang in the balance and depend upon his ability to maintain a good rapport with the woman he would marry. He'd bolstered himself with the confidence in his charm...and other areas.

If Rafe wanted to benefit from the arrangement, then he needed to keep his wife satisfied. In that, he knew he could deliver. A sated woman was a happy woman, and if there was one thing he knew, it was how to satisfy a woman. He'd acted many a part in his life, and he would approach the role of devoted husband with the same mentality...no matter the slightly sick feeling that had occasionally begun to bloom in the pit of his stomach.

The truth was, he'd come to like Victoria over the past several months. He'd come to recognize her wit and humor, to appreciate her American frankness and understand the nuances of her mannerisms. If he were honest, then he'd admit he'd enjoyed all the events they'd attended together a great deal more than he would have otherwise. He'd always been a man who reveled in mirth and celebration—two things well absent from his childhood home—and who sniffed out the best entertainments, but adding Miss Rockford into the scenario had been unexpectedly pleasant. He enjoyed her company. He liked her as a person. And it almost made him regret how he'd approached her with ulterior motives under the guise of friendship. There had never been a moment he hadn't acted with the intention of wooing her and her family enough to win her hand. However, so much time spent in her presence meant he'd learned a great deal about her. He knew how she enjoyed the theater, how her nose wrinkled when she found something truly humorous, how she tapped the fingers of her left hand together when she was thinking. It made her seem less like a means to an end and more like an individual...one he liked spending time with and with whom he could conceivably spend many years.

But…was he possibly robbing her of a different future by claiming her out of desperation for money? Not that he placed much stock in the notion of love, but perhaps Miss Rockford did. Perhaps she might have found a love like Alice and her husband had; perhaps she could have found a man who did not take her away from America, her family, and all she'd ever known; perhaps she might have had a husband who didn't have three young wards whom he'd hidden from her on the chance that their existence might have deterred her. It was a blasted inconvenient time for his conscience to dust itself off and make itself known. Of course, it hadn't been loud enough to keep Rafe from going through with the wedding.

He spent the two hours since their arrival at the hotel taking his time removing his coat and waistcoat, sipping a glass of warmed brandy, stuffing that conscience back into its box, and counting the minutes until he would finally go to his wife.

It was a foreign thought, that. And, unnerving as it was, it wasn't enough to rein in his anticipation. After all, these last few months had been some of the longest of his life.

Determined not to offer Miss Rockford or her father any reason to back out of the arrangement, he'd gone without female companionship since before even speaking a word to the American heiress. His last mistress, Lady Dallow was only slightly more than two decades in age, and she was already enjoying the freedoms of a woman who had married a much older man and inherited the title of "dowager" relatively quickly. She hadn't taken kindly to Rafe's termination of their relationship, but it hadn't been anything he wasn't used to. Women were often distraught when it happened, but they eventually moved on. Since then, Rafe had remained as chaste as a monk, and now the drought was about to end. His blood began to hum in anticipation.

Victoria was undeniably attractive, so he fully anticipated a night filled with more than just mild pleasantness—even if she was an untutored virgin. He had lain awake many a night pondering all the things he could teach her, imagining the sounds she might make, and how soft her skin would be with nothing between them.

When he found her waiting for him, standing before the glow of the fire as it cast her willowy figure in silhouette, he knew the night would be no hardship at all.

He pressed the door closed with his back and approached her with the slow, even steps of a trainer bridging the distance to a skittish filly. In his hand, he held two glasses of the rich brandy he'd been enjoying, and he offered one to her. She hesitated only a moment before accepting it, like he knew she would. He found it unexpectedly arousing that she enjoyed a stiff drink now and again, but he'd determined it was less the fact that she enjoyed brandy, and more so that she knew what she liked and wasn't ashamed of it. He watched as she followed his gesture to take up the seat by the hearth.

If she was confused when he placed a dark glass bottle on the floor near the crackling hearth, then she said nothing; neither did Rafe acknowledge it.

The time for that would come later.

As much as he wanted to lay her on the nearby bed and finally begin exploring the gentle curves he'd spent far too long imagining, Rafe had never deflowered a virgin, and he wanted to do right by his wife. He knew the future of their bed play depended upon this night...so it was a good thing he was very confident in his skills.

First on his agenda?

Encourage his wife to relax with banal conversation.

"Have you settled in well? The room is to your liking?" he asked as he made himself comfortable in the chair beside hers.

"Yes, thank you," she replied in a voice much smaller than he was used to hearing from her. She was nervous, but he couldn't very well blame her for that, could he?

"Are you looking forward to the honeymoon trip tomorrow? I was going to warn you that the Channel crossing might be quite rough, but then I realized you've already crossed the Atlantic." He knocked the heel of his palm against his forehead as if to underscore how daft he'd been.

"I've been around ships as long as I can remember. Even before Rockford Shipping became what it is, my grandfather was a captain. Luke and I have always enjoyed the water, and we often traveled to the docks and shipyards." He loved watching her eyes sparkle when she spoke of her family.

"Then you will have to be the one to reassure and comfort me when we disembark tomorrow. I am afraid I haven't been aboard anything more turbulent than a rowboat on the Serpentine."

"Truly?" Astonishment dropped her jaw, and she leaned forward. "I thought all lords toured the Continent, or is that an ignorant assumption?"

He couldn't very well tell her that there hadn't been enough money in the Blackwood coffers to fund such a trip, nor had his father been inclined to allow him to go out of sheer spite. Instead, Rafe gave a negligent shrug and sat back in his chair as if missing out on that rite of passage hadn't bothered him in the least. "I found diversions enough here in London to occupy me."

She tipped her head in acceptance and finally sampled the brandy he'd handed her. She savored it with obvious relish, and her appreciative moan shot straight to his cock.

"This is quite lovely," she commented, examining the rich amber color of the drink in the firelight. Rainbows of light danced across her features, highlighting her elegant bone structure and drawing his eyes to the rebellious dark wisps of hair falling forward to graze her regal cheekbones.

"I am pleased you approve." He watched her sip some more. "Forgive me for noticing, but you seem versed in brandy. It seems I will need to be sure our home is well-stocked with it."

She had the good grace to blush a bit, and it made her already lovely features even more so. "It is unladylike, I know, but it is my favorite drink. Claret is off-putting, whiskey burns too strongly, I can tolerate some wine and a sip or two of champagne, but brandy—good brandy—can be delicious and complex." She moistened her full lower lip with her tongue, and the action drew his eyes like a flash of light in darkness in a beacon of eroticism. He wanted to lick the brandy from her lips; to nibble the plump flesh and taste her sweetness. He suspected he could become far drunker from that than from the drink in his glass.

"I agree," was all Rafe could think to say. He was so addled, his mind working only in fits and spurts. What was it about her that made him feel that way? Where he was normally so confident and composed, just sitting with her in that room was making his heart race. It must have been his lack of sex. He hadn't gone that long without a satisfying release in at least a decade. He'd never lacked for company, and his body was completely off kilter because of it. The low ache simmering in his every muscle made its presence known with undeniable heat, and try as he might, he knew deep down that his body would not have reacted that way for just any woman. His lust growled appreciatively over the angle of her shy smile; even the timbre of her voice hummed through his veins like the headiest of substances.

Despite his inner impatience, the two of them settled into a banal conversation about the pleasantness of the day, the quality of the food, anything to lull Victoria into a state of ease. Gradually, the evening wore on, the hour grew late, his wife had finished her brandy, and the time had arrived. Already, she was more relaxed than when he'd first arrived in her chamber.

Relax, Rafe reminded himself. *Relax and do what you do best. She is like any other woman; being legally bound to her does not change anything.* He'd practically made an art out of making women feel desirable and giving them orgasms. It was a skill he'd long prided himself on, and he'd relished exploring new and exciting ways to share pleasure. Now, it was finally time to share that talent with his wife.

"You looked beautiful today, Victoria," Rafe purred, intentionally using that tone when speaking her given name for the very first time. He witnessed the gesture's intended effect in the dilation of her pupils, the slight catch in her breath. "Utterly enchanting," he murmured.

Chapter Eight

RAFE SET ASIDE his glass and stood. Victoria watched his every movement with wide eyes as he took her empty glass from her fingers, set it beside his, and gently tugged her to rise to her feet. He ran the back of his hand down the downy curve of her cheek, allowing it to drag lower down the lace and ribbons of her nightshift. It was impossible for him not to notice the hitch in her breathing, the rise and fall of her breasts beneath the thin fabric. Her small, puckered nipples peaked against the garment, and he imagined they were begging for his touch.

All in due time.

She smelled divine—sweet and warm. It was all he could do not to bury his face in her hair. Instead, he settled for pressing his lips to her forehead and murmured, "You are even lovelier now." And it was the truth; Victoria had been a vision at the church, but there was something even more tantalizing about her virginal innocence, the uncharacteristic shyness in her voice and demeanor. It made him long to free her from her inhibitions and show her all the wonderful new intimacies to be had between a man and a woman. She'd been torturing him with her proximity all day, teasing him with her smile, arousing him with every one of her breathless laughs; now, it was time for him to return the favor. "That kiss following the ceremony was far from satisfying, though." She opened her mouth to reply, but anything she would have said was silenced as his lips fell upon hers.

The time for chaste pecks and tempering his urges was long past; the dam of Rafe's desire had broken, and he would not be the only one to drown in the deluge.

Their lips met with such force that their teeth clicked together. At first, she seemed startled and overwhelmed by his need, but she very quickly became responsive to his advances...much to Rafe's delight. He'd caught glimpses of this fire in their one and only stolen kiss, and it was very reassuring to learn that he had not imagined the potential flame that burned within her. Though tempered by life in the public eye, this was evidence that his wife could be wholly herself behind closed doors. Uninhibited. Unencumbered. In fact, Rafe preferred this glimpse of ferocious passion. He liked his women a little wild, a little unpredictable in bed. He enjoyed both the surprise and the sport, and he was a man who was game to try most anything at least once or twice when asked nicely. He couldn't wait to unlock her fantasies and make them their shared reality. He longed to hear from her lips all the wondrous pleasures she desired, once he provided her with a decent base of carnal knowledge, of course.

With practiced movements so subtle she hardly knew what was happening, Rafe backed her toward the bed and began undoing the fastenings of her nightshift. The fabric parted to bare the creamy flesh between her breasts but kept the globes tantalizingly hidden. The teasing would make the final revelation all the sweeter.

She must have felt the kiss of cool air because she started slightly against him, her fingers flexing in the front of his linen shirt.

"Do not be afraid," he purred reassuringly.

Her voice was slightly tremulous when she said, "I am not." There was shyness there, but also a great deal of bravery...and even a bit of excitement. He admired a woman with heart—especially one with such unexpected pluck and spark. And he was coming to realize that the woman he'd married was an uncharted wonder.

"Remove your nightshift and lie on the bed." Rafe's words were calm and even, but firm enough that there was no room for her to deny him. In fact, he strongly suspected that she liked it when he spoke to her in such a way. How thrilling, especially from a woman as untested as she was. His mind whirled with all the possibilities they might explore.

But every other thought fled his mind when she finally did as he demanded. Her eyes were locked on his as she slid one shoulder free from the gaping neckline, and then the other. Earth-toned fire glowed in her hazel eyes as she examined his reaction to each revealed inch of flesh. Her movements were deliberately slow in the way a seasoned seductress might move, and Rafe enjoyed it all the more knowing he was the first and only man to witness her (rather successful) attempts at sensuality. And then, Rafe's heart stopped.

He'd seen more than his share of naked women in his life, some more conventionally beautiful than others, but Victoria—his wife—put them all to shame. She was lithe and graceful, long of limb, and shapely in just the right places. Her flawless porcelain skin glowed in the flickering firelight as she sat on the mattress and lay back against the deep green coverlet. The stark contrast of her body against the fabric was as striking as it was delicious. She looked soft and delicate, but her eyes spoke to him of a deep anticipation.

The gloriously unhindered view of her body made Rafe's mouth go drier than hardtack. Her head lay in the cradle of her dark curls as she watched him from beneath the thick fans of her lashes. His eyes drifted lower to take in her slightly parted lips, puffy and still glistening from their fervent kisses. Her pulse undulated within the long column of her throat, the fragile wings of her collarbones gave way to the perfect swells of her breasts, tipped with tawny, delectably erect nipples. They were every-thing he'd imagined, and so much more. She had a shapely torso, simultaneously lean and feminine; graceful hips and lean, creamy thighs bracketed the downy curls guarding her sex. Her legs were honed from walking and riding; her feet were dainty and impressively delicate. His eyes drifted slowly back up the length of Victoria's form, savoring every detail more beautiful than the last. Half of him wanted to pounce upon the tantalizing buffet she presented, but the other half just managed to maintain his composure and remembered that he had very specific plans for that evening.

It took a godlike amount of self-control for him to merely instruct his wife to roll onto her stomach rather than commit every curve of her body to memory with his hands. She flashed him an unsure glance, but she complied, nonetheless. He barely stifled a groan as the perfect globes of her rear were revealed to him. The sculpted roundness of her bottom melded into the trim curve of her waist to form the most perfect shape in all the world as far as he was concerned. His breeches had already grown uncomfortably tight, and his situation was only getting worse with each second that passed. His cock gave an insistent throb as if to underscore his dilemma.

Quickly, Rafe retrieved the small vial of scented oil he'd placed near the fire to warm. Unstoppering it, he inhaled the rich scents of patchouli and vanilla before testing its temperature on the inside of his wrist. Victoria looked at him over her naked shoulder when the mattress dipped beneath his added weight when he knelt beside her. The sight stole his breath. It did not take a great imagination to picture her looking back at him like that as he claimed her from behind…

"Relax," Rafe rasped. "And trust me." Dimly, he recognized it was a lot to ask in this scenario, but he knew what he was doing. He wanted only to bring her blinding pleasure, if she would allow it.

He waited with inhuman patience until she rested her cheek on her crossed arms, and finally, he tilted the vial and poured a trickle of oil onto the concave curve of her lower back. Her hips lifted reflexively at the sensation, causing him to perform a full-body shiver that he felt all the way to the root of his throbbing cock.

He set the vial aside and began long, slow strokes of her spine and shoulders, the curve of her waist and the slope of her buttocks. Gradually, Victoria melted into his ministrations, going boneless and releasing helpless little purring noises from deep in her throat. Every muscle in Rafe's body trembled with restraint. He needed to focus on something else lest he spend in his breeches like a pathetic whelp.

He cleared his throat. "I once visited a very exclusive establishment run by a family all the way from the Ottoman Empire. It was modeled after their special bathhouses in opulent buildings where they perform these massages in steam-filled rooms." He conveniently left out how the golden-skinned women who performed the massages rubbed their entire bodies against the recipient, and the act often culminated in wild, sweaty, oil-slicked sex... "After one experience, I convinced them to sell me some vials of their oil imported from their homeland. The scent is lovely, is it not?"

A small moan was her only response, and it melted into a groan when he pressed his thumb into a sensitive spot at the base of her neck. He repeated his ministrations across her body, paying careful attention to her physical and vocal cues to allow her to guide his efforts. He liked to think this trick was what made him a lover whose skills were whispered amongst women of the *ton*. He listened to women. First and foremost, he dedicated himself to their pleasure. He had learned to obey their desires—both silent and spoken—because who could know better what a woman needed than that woman, herself? Of course, with his wife, it would take her some time to learn her own pleasure, but Rafe did not see their simultaneous education as too great a hardship.

When Victoria was sufficiently boneless, Rafe had her roll over once more. The content, slightly dazed look in her eyes was more arousing than he would have believed. Each stroke of his oil-slicked hands had worked to swipe away at her reservations—so much so that she seemed to care very little that her breasts were bare to him. It was perfect. She was perfect.

Slowly, he began touching her once again, beginning with her upper arms and shoulders before moving to her chest, massaging her petal-soft breasts in smaller and smaller circles, decreasing his pressure until his palms were just a whisper across the aching peaks. Whether she realized it or not, Victoria arched toward him, seeking more, and he had to bite back a smile. His fingers trailed down to the sensitive skin of her inner elbows, pressed between her fingers, painted glistening patterns down the graceful curve of her waist, dipped into the dainty hollow of her navel, her well-turned legs, and the ticklish arches of her feet. Her giggle died when her eyes met the dark hunger in his. It did not take a great deal of experience for her to recognize what was on his mind.

His restraint as close to snapping as it had ever been, Rafe leaned back to untuck and rip his shirt off over his head. He allowed her wide eyes a moment to peruse the newly revealed flesh. It might have been a touch of vanity, but he took deep pleasure in the darkening of her cheeks as her gaze raked him up and down…freezing only when he hooked his thumbs in the waistband of his breeches. He spent a great deal of time riding whenever his schedule permitted, and he spent at least one day each week at Gentleman Jack's with Swanleigh working on his boxing. He knew his body, toned and leanly muscular as it was, was considered quite pleasing. What really gave him pleasure, however, was witnessing how his wife enjoyed the way he looked. It couldn't possibly be more than he liked her body, but it was flattering, nonetheless.

His cock gave a powerful throb, further straining the tortured seams of the garment. His body screamed for freedom, but he took his time unfastening and sliding his breeches down his legs and kicking them aside, giving Victoria her first unfettered look at a naked man. She attempted modesty, but her curiosity won out, and he was glad it did. If the erotic pleasure of having her eyes on him was any indication, then he would enjoy her physical touch a great deal.

Though he ached to cover her body with his—to climb atop her and slake his roiling lust while teaching her the joys of the flesh—he held himself in check. He laid himself beside her on the thick mattress, inhaling deeply the mingling scents of the oil, Victoria's flesh, and a whisper of aroused woman. He was close enough that they shared the heat of their bodies, but he did not touch her except to gently, tenderly, press his lips to hers.

It took several soft passes of his lips on hers, but she eventually relaxed into him, melting once more into him. Her hand pressed tentatively against the center of his chest, testing its firmness and heat, tangling in the patch of dark hair between his pectoral muscles. With each pass of their dueling lips and tongues, she grew in boldness. Her fingernails traced gentle paths through the dusting of dark hair across his chest and tripped over his sensitive nipples. She explored the hard curves of his shoulders and the swells of his arms. He couldn't help the soft groan deep in his throat when her hands began trailing lower, spurring on his desire with a vicious whip.

When she leaned into him and pressed the hard tips of her breasts against his chest, Rafe took that as his invitation to move forward. His hands began another exploration of their own, tugging his wife close around her waist and finally feeling her delectable softness against the length of his body.

His hand slid between them, easily finding her weeping center, the molten core that begged for his touch. Her inner thighs were already coated with her desire as he stroked her there, gliding his oil-slicked fingers up and through her folds. Her breathy sigh of relief at the contact drove him further. Instinct took over, and Rafe listened to her cues, paid attention to each little tremor of her body to discover the pressure and rhythm that she needed. When her knee rose and she hooked her leg over his hip to grant him unfettered access to her sex, Rafe knew he'd won. One and then two fingers slid deep inside her tight sheath as his thumb worked the stiff pearl at her apex. It was a beautiful dance where her hips moved in tandem with his rubbing, thrusting fingers. Feeling her flutter around him, he knew the time was right to curl his digits inside of her and stroke firmly, demanding her body give itself over to his efforts.

Victoria gasped and mewled, clawing at his shoulders, the nape of his neck, his chest. He hissed in pleasure and pressed his forehead against hers so they were nose-to-nose. The blending of pain and desire was so delicious that it was nearly unbearable.

"Yes. Just like that. Mark me. Claim me as I am claiming you," he growled. His cock rose long and hard between them, stiff and reaching for Victoria. Still, he refused to allow himself relief until she experienced it first—a lady who lay with him was always guaranteed to reach her pinnacle at least once before he did.

Suddenly, Victoria's entire body tensed. Her head fell back on a silent scream, her thighs trembled, and her glistening cunny convulsed around his hand as she was rocked by wave after wave of all-consuming pleasure. Her gasps and whimpers mingled with the obscene sounds of his persistent strokes of her wet flesh.

"God, yes," Rafe panted, unable to tear his eyes from the plethora of emotions dancing across his wife's face. "You are glorious."

Then, it was as if a feral creature had been unleashed inside of his wife.

With a growl of her own, Victoria shoved hard against his shoulders. Fearing he'd hurt her, Rafe fell back to the mattress. Rather than clamber away, she pinned him beneath her and climbed to straddle his hips. Her hair fell in a dark curtain around their faces as she bent to kiss him, her tongue delving deeply into his mouth and battling him for supremacy. Her pebbled nipples grazed his own with every undulating rub of her body along his. It was like she wanted to touch all of him at once and didn't know where to begin.

Holy Hell...

Who was this woman he'd married?

She was wild and breathless with passion, infectious in her

ardor. As far as Rafe was concerned, she could do bloody well whatever she pleased with him. He was content to be a specimen at her mercy so long as she continued to look at him like that...to straddle him like that.

BENEATH VICTORIA, HER husband lay back with his palms resting on her smooth thighs, caressing the play of her lean muscles as she explored and rocked against him. Her body still tingled and glowed from whatever he'd done to her, but still, her body ached for more. She hadn't known such pleasure was possible—that her body could be so tense and so molten all at the same time. Every last nerve she'd felt had dissolved in the pink haze of ecstasy exploding from her core. She wanted more; she needed more.

Acting on instinct, she lowered herself atop Blackwood so the underside of his shaft caressed the slick slit of her sex with each pass. They hissed in unison. She realized there was little grace to her unfamiliar movements, but she liked to think she made up for it in enthusiasm. At least he allowed her to discover the sensations that pleased her and find a rhythm that stoked her arousal, applying pressure to help guide her only when she struggled. The sensations began to grow within her once more, rekindling the embers that remained from her earlier release.

It might have been minutes or hours, but his restraint finally snapped. Blackwood rolled Victoria beneath him. Her heart hammered in her ears as he spread her thighs wide with his knees and his gaze drank in the pink flush extending from her damp hairline down to the ripe buds of her nipples. He notched the broad head of his cock at her entrance and, before she had time to register what was coming and tense her body, he pressed forward in a single steady motion. Her hands clamped down onto his shoulders, her nails leaving crescent bites in the flesh as she grappled for purchase. Blackwood, however, did not stop. He could not—both for his sanity and her well-being.

Both of them were glistening with sweat and panting in short, ragged breaths by the time he was fully seated within her. She took him so well, spreading her legs wider still, asking for more with her dilated eyes and moist, kiss-plumped lips.

Well, he would give the lady what she desired.

Running his palms against her sensitive inner thighs, he pressed them wide. His eyes were riveted to the spot where they were joined, and the slow glide of his member as he claimed her all but drove him mad.

"Do you like it when I fuck you like this, Victoria?" he growled, his eyes leaping to her flushed face. "Do you like my cock inside of you?"

A low groan wilted into a whimper as he increased his pace, his balls gently slapping her rear with every one of his deep thrusts.

"I want your words, wife," he demanded, insisting that she say the words. The way she canted her hips for more, every sigh and gasp, the feline way she clawed at him to bring him closer were all affirmative answers for him, but he so desperately wanted to hear the words from her delectable lips. "Do you like my cock?"

"Yes!" she finally cried when he penetrated her deeply and held himself there. "Yes, I like it!"

"And you want more of it?" Rafe asked, giving her nose a teasing graze with his.

"Yes, damn you!" Victoria sobbed. "Please."

"What is my name?" His voice was barely above a growl.

"Please, *Rafe!*" she cried out, writhing beneath him.

With that, Rafe's restraint snapped, and he, too, allowed himself to be wild. He pounded into her, reveling in the way her body accepted his and embraced his invasion. She was so sweet, so wet, she felt like liquid silk. In turn, Victoria welcomed everything he gave her. It wasn't long before she began to throb around him, her body beginning its tremors of pleasure once again. Just three more thrusts and he had her screaming her release beneath him. She yanked him over that edge along with her, his own orgasm nearly crippling him in its intensity as he spilled himself over and over again against the lips of her womb.

Boneless and sated, they collapsed in exhaustion. Rafe rolled to lie beside his wife, and the two of them stared at the ceiling, chests heaving, hearts pounding, as they reveled in the afterglow.

VICTORIA'S HEAD SWAM as she slowly drifted back into her body. She was somehow drained and incredibly awake at the same time. How was that possible? How could joy like this exist in a world where anyone ever left their marital beds? More importantly, how could she survive if this was a taste of what her future held?

Surely, a woman's body could survive being broken in such a beautiful way only so many times before it gave out.

She listened to the heavy cadence of Blackwood's breathing beside her. The fire had died low, casting the room in deep shadows and cocooning them together. He was so warm beside her; he smelled so good. Heaviness gradually settled in, beginning with her fingers and toes, working up her limbs to weigh down every bit of her until she found it impossible to keep her eyes open.

IT WASN'T LONG before Victoria's breathing evened out and she curled against Rafe's side, fast asleep. She'd been drained by the emotions of the day and the physical relief of her orgasms. He hoped she would sleep soundly and rest, because she certainly deserved it. Lord knew Rafe hadn't expected their first night together to go like *that*. She was explosive in the bedroom, and he couldn't wait to see where that might lead them. In the warm aftermath of their intercourse, it was impossible not to enjoy his good fortune at marrying a woman who wasn't missish or painfully reserved. They could have some fun together, to be sure.

When he was sure Victoria was sound asleep, Rafe slipped from her bed, committed the rosy perfection of her naked body to memory, and gently pulled the coverlet over her. He gathered his discarded clothing before returning to his own bedchamber. He'd never stayed a full night with a woman—never allowed himself to be vulnerable enough to sleep beside one. His marriage was the beginning of a lifetime of compromises, but that was not a concession he was ready to make.

Chapter Nine

THE NEXT MORNING, Victoria awoke with a feline stretch and a languid sigh. As she moved and her consciousness grew brighter, she gradually became aware of small aches which could only have resulted from the previous night's activities. Her inner thighs twitched with the memories, and her core emitted a tender throb. Judging from the halo of warm sunlight peering around the room's curtains, she'd slept the entire night following her thorough introduction to the art of wifehood. She bit her slightly puffy lower lip and fancied she could still taste her husband in the whisper of brandy. It had been more than she could have imagined, and even more wonderful than Lady Morton had led her to believe.

The duchess had pulled Victoria aside toward the end of the wedding breakfast, saying, "I realize you do not have a feminine influence in your life, and I refuse to allow you to go into tonight without even the slightest bit of warning; therefore, I am taking matters into my own hands."

"Warning?"

Lady Morton had nodded. "It isn't really my place to have this conversation with you, but I will not allow you to be as unprepared as I was."

"Unprepared?" Victoria had squeaked.

"Oh, are we doing this now?" Lady Swanleigh flitted over and joined their private corner.

"Doing what?" Victoria had asked, her alarm growing by the second.

"As much as I enjoy both Mr. Rockfords, they are *men* and surely have not bothered to consider what this night will entail. I am certain I would have been brought in if they had."

"And how would that conversation have gone?" Lady Swanleigh had laughed airily. "Can you imagine?"

Having had enough of their banter, Victoria grabbed Lady Morton's hands and pleaded with her to just come out with whatever she needed to say. The day had gone so well up to that point.

"What Lady Morton is trying to say is that there is usually a mother or other close female relative with whom a bride might discuss the…mechanics of the wedding night."

The pang Victoria felt in the vicinity of her heart whenever her mother's absence was pointed out made its presence known once more, but then it quickly gave way to the realization of just what they wished to discuss with her. Instantly, Victoria's cheeks caught fire, and it was everything she could do not to turn toward her husband at the sound of his laughter across the room.

"I see," she'd rasped, then cleared her throat. "That is, I have a somewhat rudimentary understanding." Her mouth was parched, and her tongue felt suddenly too large for speaking; her cheeks had only burned more brightly. She'd prayed the ladies would not ask how she knew of such things, even if Lady Morton's books had been one of a handful of forbidden sources for her material.

"Good," the duchess had chirped with a smile on her pleasingly wide mouth. "Then you are already more educated than I was on my wedding night. I was told to lie back and allow whatever my husband wished to happen."

"My mother never spoke to me about any of it," Lady Swanleigh chimed in with a dismissive shrug of a shoulder. Victoria didn't know if it would be more damaging to pretend marital relations did not exist, or to be told they were something to be endured. Neither option had left her with a particularly pleasant sensation in the pit of her stomach.

"And…" Victoria paused and looked between the women. "You intend to step in?"

"Precisely!" Lady Morton had beamed before leaning in to speak so they would not be overheard. "First and foremost, it is not something to be feared."

"Not if you are with the right man," Lady Swanleigh had added thoughtfully, then rushed to say, "And Rafe, of course, *is* the right sort of man! I've known him for many years now and count him amongst my closest friends. He can be quite thoughtful."

"And his reputation precedes him," remarked the duchess. "I do not believe you have anything to fear on that front—not that either of us would know first-hand, though."

Lady Swanleigh rapidly shook her head in agreement.

"We haven't much time left, so let us begin, shall we?"

What followed was an only slightly mortifying account of the physical act of making love, described in hushed tones and only mildly vulgar gestures and subtle demonstrations. Victoria was certain her face resembled a beet by the time it was all said and done, but she had to admit that she was quite a bit more educated than she had been when she awoke that morning.

"The act itself is natural. Utilitarian. But what it *can* be is…transcendent."

"Life-altering," sighed Lady Swanleigh.

"Beautiful."

There was a pause as both women were briefly lost in their musings, and Victoria was able to recover herself somewhat before the duchess looked at her. Her crystalline blue eyes searched her face.

"You are nervous because you do not know what to do. That is entirely normal." Lady Morton squeezed her hand, and Lady Swanleigh took up her other.

"He will teach you and, before you realize it, you will be in charge. I promise."

"You likely already wield more power than you know…" Lady Morton lifted her chin in Blackwood's direction. Victoria glanced in the direction she indicated, only to find her new husband watching her intently. His dark eyes had been riveted upon her, as motionless and innately powerful as a statue of a god. As if instinctively knowing what lay in store, a delicious tremor ran up and down the length of her body.

Oh, how Rafe had proven their words right. He had taught her a great deal already, and Victoria looked forward to learning more.

She smiled sleepily and rolled over, expecting to find her sleeping husband lying on the pillow beside hers, but she was alone.

A frown immediately knit her brows together, only deepening when she sat up and scanned the shadows to find herself abandoned in the bedchamber. A quick touch to the vacant pillow told her he hadn't been beside her for quite some time—maybe even the entire night. The thought unleashed a ripple of unease deep in her belly. She knew it wasn't that uncommon for married couples to exist in separate chambers, but she'd thought their wedding night—of all nights!—would have been one to share.

She spent several minutes locked in indecision before deciding she would continue on with her straightforward personality. She would locate her husband and directly ask him where he had been and why he had left. The air was slightly chilly on her naked flesh as she slipped from the bed to locate her discarded clothing and dress herself. It was a stark contrast to the heat of the room and the sensual closeness of the evening before. The heady scent of the exotic oil Rafe had used still lingered in the air and on her skin, making her entire body heat all over again.

"Calm yourself…" she muttered chidingly and tugged the tie of her dressing gown a little more firmly than was necessary.

One cleansing breath later, and she was turning the handle on the door to the adjoining chamber through which Rafe had visited her. Her eyes were instantly drawn to her husband as if yanked by some powerful, unseen force. He sat at the small table set by the window. A china cup of steaming tea sat before him as he skimmed the freshly pressed newspaper. He sat with all the grace and dangerous allure of a jungle cat, legs splayed out before him, crossed at the ankle, feet bare. He wore only a pair of half-buttoned buff breeches and a deep blue dressing gown open to reveal the broad swath of taut naked chest beneath it. Victoria's mouth went suddenly dry as sand—especially when her eyes returned to his handsome face, and she was greeted with a blindingly beautiful grin.

"Good morning, wife. I trust you slept well?" His voice was warm as the summer sun on a beach.

Words were too difficult to locate in that moment when she was first faced with the man who had touched every intimate inch of her only a few hours before, so she settled for nodding in response. Where had her indignation at her abandonment gone?

Burned away like fog by the brilliance of her husband's beauty, she supposed.

"Care to join me?" he offered solicitously. "It is not a full breakfast, but the pastries are better than any I've had in recent memory." It was then that she noticed the platter of baked goods and various spreads laid out beside the tea service.

"Yes, thank you," she said to cover up the plaintive whine of her stomach. She had been too distracted to eat much of the supper the hotel had served them the night before—too preoccupied by Lady Morton and Swanleigh's hasty instruction only a few hours prior.

As she took up the vacant seat across from Rafe, she couldn't help but spare a glance at the nearby bed. The luxuriously large mattress was covered in a rumpled coverlet the same shade of green as the one beneath which she'd slept. She did her best not to dwell upon the evidence of just where her husband had chosen to sleep. Instead, she focused on overcoming the newness of the intimacy of sharing breakfast while in a state of undress with a man. Where was she supposed to look? She knew where she *wished* to look, but that likely wasn't very proper behavior.

His face was once again half-hidden behind his newspaper, but what she saw was still unnerving in its perfection. She could easily stare at him for hours, but she didn't dare risk being caught ogling him like that.

The enticing expanse of his chest peeking at her from between the open panels of his dressing gown was rather inviting, but it, too, was dangerous…oh, so very dangerous. It made her recall just how delicious the salt-tinged sweat of his skin tasted when she'd pressed impulsive, open-mouthed kisses against his flexing shoulder.

Not even her plate was safe territory; if she glared at it too long, then he might think she possessed a strange fascination with food…or cutlery.

Leave it to Rafe to put his disarming amiability to good use… Either because of or despite her unease, he launched into pleasant chatter about their upcoming honeymoon trip, their plans, the day's weather for their crossing to the Continent. Almost immediately, Victoria was transported back to their weeks of friendship, and she settled back into their comfortable habits of interaction. He became less the man who had used his wicked tongue and body to introduce her to pleasure and returned to the man who had used his easy smile and smooth words to earn her trust and make her feel more comfortable than she had since arriving in England. He had a way about him that made her feel as if she'd known him for years rather than a few short months, and it was pleasant to sink into that sensation.

"All said, I do not believe we will have an eventful crossing," Rafe said as she selected a jam-filled pastry made from flaky golden dough. "If you find it agreeable, we should depart for the docks in two hours' time. That should—" A small scratch at the door interrupted him. "Enter," he bade the newcomer without breaking his sentence's stride. "Two hours should be sufficient for you to prepare yourself for travel, should it not?" he finished just as a red-haired maid entered the room and bounced into a curtsey.

"This letter arrived for you, My Lord," she whispered, eyes appropriately downcast for three entire seconds before turning them on Rafe.

Victoria brushed a crumb from her lower lip as she watched the maid's saucer-like eyes take in every glorious inch of Rafe. It galled Victoria to no end that she could be annoyed by an appreciative glance at her husband from another woman—she was not a possessive or jealous woman by nature—but she was quickly discovering new aspects of her personality that had been heretofore unseen before her marriage. She'd have to explore this new facet of her personality, mull it over, and decide how best to move forward with this realization. Add that to the wild, uninhibited sensuality Rafe had somehow unlocked the night before, and her list of realizations was rapidly growing in length.

Rafe accepted the letter, and the maid excused herself. Victoria watched her leave—more slowly than necessary, mind you—until she felt Rafe's piercing eyes upon her. Her cheeks warmed instantly when she realized she'd been caught staring.

Rather than witness disapproval or amusement in Rafe's expression, however, she thought she saw interest and…was that appreciation?

Victoria quickly averted her gaze and shoved another bite of pastry between her lips, realizing immediately what a poor decision that was because her mouth had gone bone-dry all over again. She nearly choked, silently struggling to chew and swallow the morsel as Rafe broke the seal on the letter. Frantically, she poured herself a cup of tea and sipped it, not bothering to add any of the sugar set in the nearby silver bowl for that purpose. She nearly sighed in relief when the offending bit of food was finally dislodged but cringed when she wondered how much of that blunder Rafe had seen.

Hesitantly glancing up, she realized he wasn't paying attention to her in the slightest. His attractively bronzed complexion had weakened to a sickly pallor, so bloodless as to be quite alarming.

"Rafe?" she croaked, her throat still slightly scratchy from the pastry incident. He gave her no indication that he'd heard her. "What is the matter? What did the letter say?"

He stood up from the table so quickly that the chair he'd been occupying fell back to the floor with a startling crack. "We are no longer leaving for the Continent; we must return to London." The frantic roughness to his tone was more than a little alarming to her, especially when she'd only ever seen him as amiable and charming. "Home. We must return home."

"Why?" she asked, her tone rising with her unease. "What has happened?" What could have caused such an abrupt and dramatic change in him? One minute, they'd been wading into the waters of their first morning of marriage, and the next had made her normally composed, flippant husband so suddenly serious and, daresay, nearly panicked. Though she tried, she could not make out the address on the letter he still held in his hand. From what little he'd uttered, Victoria suspected its contents had something to do with the Blackwood estate or responsibilities—something dire.

Rafe had already removed his dressing gown and, now bared from the waist-up, was striding to the wardrobe to retrieve the clothing that had been prepared for that day's travels. He was too preoccupied to do anything other than command Victoria to ring for a maid so she might prepare herself. "We leave within the hour."

Heart thrumming, Victoria stood and did as he instructed. She attributed her silent acquiescence more to her confusion than subservience, hoping that all would be revealed to her as soon as they were in the carriage and on their way back to Town.

AFTER RETRACING THE journey they'd completed only the day before, their hired carriage slowed to a stop before a pretty Townhouse. Victoria had not amassed a substantial knowledge of

London addresses yet, but the neighborhood appeared to be tidy and safe. Though the homes were not the size of the ones she'd visited in Mayfair, the streets were relatively clean by city standards, and the small front gardens were well-kept. She suspected this was an area where politicians, second sons of lords, and other respectable men might reside alongside people like Rafe and his family—those who, according to what she'd gleaned from her brother and father, had a respectable title, but not the capital to afford the same lifestyle as other peers. Regardless, Victoria found the area charming.

Every hope she'd had of prying answers out of her husband during the journey had been very quickly dashed upon her ascension into the carriage. Rafe had remained anxious and pensively silent for the duration of their journey, which had only served to stretch Victoria's nerves so close to snapping that they trembled. She'd made several overtures at questioning him from various angles, but to no avail. He'd merely held up a few fingers in dismissal or ignored her words entirely in favor of staring unseeingly out the window while alternating between tapping his boot on the carriage floor, rapping his thumb on his thigh, and raking his hands through his thick, dark hair. It was a wonder Victoria's sanity hadn't been lost in a ditch somewhere along the way.

It was almost a relief when the bustle outside the window grew in intensity. The change in scenery gave her somewhere to focus other than her maddeningly tight-lipped husband. His steadfast silence had only allowed her mind to wander into unwelcome territory and explode her sense of foreboding. What had been in that note that was serious enough to cause him to cancel their honeymoon trip? A death in the family? She knew Rafe's parents had passed years prior, and she'd never heard him speak of any siblings. Perhaps it was something with his house or property? Englishmen could be quite odd when it came to discussing their business and wealth in the presence of a lady; Rafe had never displayed such an inclination before, but perhaps their new status as husband and wife had changed this in his mind. These and other possibilities had spun through her mind hour after hour, mile after mile, until they'd finally reached that London residence.

A tall, lean footman dressed in dove grey descended the stairs and swiftly unlatched the door before helping Victoria step down to the swept walkway. She didn't care to admit that it was a relief to be out of the close and heavy air of the carriage—even if it was for the mixed bag that was the atmosphere in London. Rafe followed so closely behind that his boot nearly caught in the hem of her raspberry traveling skirt. She'd had the garment specifically made for their honeymoon trip, but now she felt foolish for being so excited about the gold thread and whimsical buttons along the panel of her bodice, each crafted with nautical symbols to carry a bit of Rockford along with her. How quickly the tide of their future had changed.

"Have the luggage unloaded and brought in," Rafe barked without slowing. Immediately (and much to Victoria's dumb-struck astonishment), his long legs launched him up the handful of steps and through the front door, both confirming to Victoria that this was his home and leaving Victoria to enter alone. Her cheeks burned with embarrassment and confusion as she murmured her thanks to the footman who had helped her to the walk, shook the wrinkles from her heavy skirts, and finally climbed the front stairs.

Rafe's booming voice echoed through the foyer as she entered, but she could not quite make out individual words; his tone, however, rang with every speck of anxiety he'd kept bottled up on their journey.

Left alone and greeted by no one, Victoria took her chance to examine her surroundings. A slow turn in place revealed a space that, clearly, had once been grand but had suffered from years of neglect and lack of updating. More than years—perhaps decades. A pattern of black and white marble tiles ran along the floor. Yellow papering covered the walls from floor to ceiling and while it had likely been quite lovely when it had been hung, it was now faded so badly that she could hardly make out the design of exotic birds and tropical trees. The brass sconces were worn in places from age. The window to the left of the door was clear and polished, but the draperies adorning it were slightly sun-bleached and expertly patched near the hem. The not-unpleasant aroma of beeswax and lemon almost masked the slight scent of old wood, a hint of dust, and aged parchment. A subtle swipe of her finger along the polished banister leading to the next floor confirmed that the home was kept relatively clean despite its shabbiness. In all, it was a marked difference from the exterior of the residence, and not a condition that would have taken a single generation to achieve.

Victoria was so preoccupied with her surroundings that it took her several moments to realize she was no longer alone; a maid cradling a small girl had entered from a cleverly disguised doorway—a servants' passage. The woman was garbed in the serviceable grey wool of the working class, unadorned except for a white cap upon her head. She was rosy-cheeked and plump of form and perhaps at least two decades older than Victoria. The child she held in her arms was barely more than a toddler. Her wild black curls moved with a life of their own when she buried her pale face into the older woman's neck, and she wore a frilly white nightrail that made her seem like a Renaissance cherub painted in the bosom of a cloud.

The sight was baffling.

Victoria's confused frown deepened even more when Rafe appeared at the top of the stairs, at once harried and relieved to spot the maid and the child standing below. He practically flew down the stairs, his eyes only for the girl. Victoria hadn't realized she'd clenched her fists until her nails bit so deeply into her palms that she feared she might draw blood. It was a task to unleash the tension in her body—even more so when Rafe scooped the little girl into his arms and cuddled her close.

"How are you feeling, darling?" he crooned, heedless of the

child's wayward curls as they clung to his lips and caught in the slight stubble of the beard he hadn't paused to shave away that morning in his haste to return to London.

"It is only a little cough," answered the maid reassuringly. "Mrs. West insisted on sending that letter, but I told her 'twould only worry you. Dr. McCullom has already come and gone. 'E left a salve to clear her lungs and recommended rest and warm steam. Cook is making soup for supper, so we were sitting in the warm kitchen air for a spell."

Victoria couldn't stop staring at the girl who clung to Rafe so trustingly, so sure he would provide her with comfort as she released a cough so deep that it made Victoria cringe. Rafe did not so much as flinch as he patted the child's back and held her close.

Initially, the sight warmed Victoria greatly…but that quickly melted into terror. What were the implications of this familiarity and concern between them? Who was this child to Rafe?

Just as her mind began to spiral into an abyss, her thoughts were shattered as a young lad careened down the banister and ended in a leap, sliding across the marble-tiled foyer and forcing Victoria to lurch out of the way lest she be knocked into a heap on the ground.

"Dominic!" Rafe snapped, his eyes narrowing at the boy. "Haven't I told you time and time again not to do that?"

A sudden thud behind Victoria made her jump for the second time that minute. The footman lowered his eyes and apologized for dropping her trunk before ducking back from the house to bring in the rest of the luggage. The incident seemed to remind Rafe that he was not alone, that he had, in fact, a (very confused) wife. She'd followed him into the foyer, and was gaping at him like a landed fish.

"Apologies," he said, finally fully looking at her for the first time in what was quite literally hours. "The boy is as much of a hellraiser as I was at his age."

Victoria's panic began in earnest at that point. She stuttered,

"A—Are these children…they are…are these your children?" She should have been more tactful in her inquiry, but it wasn't something her mind and her tongue could accomplish when faced with the very real possibility that her marriage was tumbling down around her before it had ever been given a real chance to begin.

From her conversations with him, she knew Rafe had never been married before; however, she was not naive enough to believe marriage was required for a man to father children. A signed document was not a magical talisman of fertility. Could this boy and girl be his children? He was certainly familiar enough with them. And could he expect her to reside with all of them beneath the same roof as a patched-together farce of a family?

Rafe shocked her with a great bark of laughter. "Good God, no!" His voice boomed. Her relief was still hesitant and would likely remain so until she finally received the explanation she'd been craving for the better part of that day. "May I introduce you to my niece and nephew, May and Dominic. A third child—another girl—is up in the nursery as well, but she's rather a poor conversationalist since she does not speak just yet."

"And…all of them live here?"

He patted the girl on the back, his hand moving in soothing circles. "Yes, they do. They are my wards."

"Who's she?" the boy—Dominic—piped in loudly, disregarding the conversation being had over his head.

Victoria, her head still spinning from the situation, struggled to form words to supply an answer.

"This is Victoria," Rafe supplied for her as he looked down at his nephew. "She is your new aunt, and she has come to live with us from now on."

Dominic wrinkled his nose in a singularly childlike expression that was at once adorable and galling. "There are too many girls in this house as it is!"

"Dom…" Rafe warned in a low tone.

This finally nudged Victoria into action. Spurred by her desire to make this confusing situation even marginally less awkward, Victoria stepped forward and held out her hand to the boy. Smiling pleasantly, she said, "I am pleased to make your acquaintance, Dominic."

Addressed directly, the lad turned his full attention upon her. He shared his uncle's coloring everywhere except the eyes, which were a piercing pale blue. Spots of ink stained his hands and various places on his cuffs and collar. He stood up straighter with all the haughtiness of a child born to privilege.

"You should be addressing me as 'My Lord,'" Dominic said with a sniff. "I am a lord, after all."

Victoria didn't know what she expected the boy to say, but it certainly hadn't been that.

Taken aback, her eyes sought the only familiar face in the room. The roll of Rafe's eyes confirmed the truth of what the boy had said, as well as what he thought of his nephew's manners. Looking back down into the child's eyes—so much more mature than she would have expected from one his age—she realized this was a first impression that could very well carry for the rest of her life. As Rafe's family and dependent, this was someone who would be around a great deal; how their future relationship would play out was in her hands.

She smiled in a way that was placating though not patronizing, and she dipped into a curtsey. "My Lord."

Dominic looked down his narrow nose at her, stared for a heartbeat, and seemed to judge her offering sufficient.

Rafe, on the other hand, was not as inclined to capitulate. "You needn't do that." He jerked his chin in a motion for her to stand.

Dominic harrumphed his displeasure.

"I believe it is only polite," Victoria replied gently, though she did stand. "It is a pleasure to make your acquaintance," she added to the lad. His intelligent eyes looked from her face to her hand, then to his uncle and back.

"You talk funny," he finally said to her.

"Dom!" Rafe snapped, but his nephew was already speeding away toward the back of the house, leaving his admonishments to fall useless in his wake. This was clearly a situation that had played itself out many times over in one iteration or another between uncle and nephew.

Chapter Ten

RAFE SIGHED AWAY his frustration and refilled his lungs with a bracing breath, but it did nothing to buoy his dismal spirits.

The day had been a disaster.

After receiving the note from Mrs. West, his housekeeper, he'd been too concerned over May's health to be much for conversation on the carriage journey back to London. His head had been too muddled with horrible scenarios to be trusted to explain everything to his new wife adequately. Now, the time for the full truth had come far sooner than he'd anticipated, and he had to finish tearing open the wound so everything could heal and (he hoped) his marriage to Victoria might move forward on sturdier ground. The situation was not ideal, but maybe it would be for the best. He'd kept his wards secret for months at that point; revealing their existence to Victoria could only be a relief.

Couldn't it?

Rafe handed his niece back to Nan, murmured a request that he be notified if anything else was needed or if there was a change in May's condition, saw them off toward the back stairs, and turned back to his wife. They were finally alone in the sparse foyer, so silent they would be able to hear a mouse sneeze in the wall.

He cleared the unease from his throat before speaking. "This was not the homecoming I'd planned for you." And that was the truth of it. He'd hoped to spend the first part of their honeymoon trip just the two of them, naked more than they were clothed, and then, when she was sufficiently starry-eyed and sated, he planned on revealing to her that he'd inherited the care of his sister's children…and that he'd been struggling to provide for their care and maintain the lifestyle expected of him as Viscount Blackwood. He'd hoped to soften the blow with a home that had been renovated in their absence, and a full staff befitting the household of a viscount. All of that had been blown to hell with the arrival of that note.

He wished his reaction had been less extreme, but his life had been one tragedy after another as of late. He could hardly be blamed for rushing back to London when he learned of May's illness. Rafe ran a hand through his hair and wondered at how different his life was from what it had been less than half a year prior.

"No?" Victoria's tone was deceptively calm when she finally spoke. "Did you plan on having even *more* surprise children present?"

Normally, he might have been amused by her sass, but he found he couldn't muster it. He also did not think she would appreciate his making light of the situation. Even if her words might have been interpreted as levity, he knew her better than that. Despite her kindness in the face of Dominic's deplorable manners, the tightness of her full lips and the lack of sparkle in her eyes warned Rafe that he'd now trodden into dangerous territory. Then, a nauseating possibility struck him straight in the gut and demanded to be immediately voiced.

"You do not care for children, then?" Had he made a horrendous miscalculation and assumed she would enjoy their presence as he did?

Her brows twitched. "It is not that I do not care for children; I merely do not believe their existence should be sprung upon one as a by-the-by."

Rafe inclined his head. That was fair enough.

"The upstairs rooms have yet to be prepared, so let us go to the parlor to speak."

Rather than accept his arm, Victoria brushed past him and strode in the direction he'd indicated. When they entered the room, however, the back of Rafe's neck immediately heated with shame and regret. Like the rest of the home, the space was immaculately clean, but it remained undeniably worn and shabby. The papering had once been cream- and hunter green stripes, but it had yellowed and faded over the years. The frames of the furniture were polished and gleaming, but the once-emerald fabric of the upholstery had threadbare wounds nearly white from age and consistent use. The most pathetic part of it all was that this room was one of the better ones in the home. Generations of poor management of the estate, careless spending, and lack of foresight had left Rafe with the dregs of what it meant to be a titled lord. Land that could have been profitable had been sold to cancel debts; money was invested in industries that had been shaky at best; necessary improvements to holdings hadn't been made, causing tenants to flee for better circumstances. As for Rafe's father, the man had been so listless from grief that he'd paid no attention to the well-being of his estate, allowing less than scrupulous managers and solicitors to skim more than their share or make unadvisable financial decisions to run the Blackwood coffers nearly dry.

As Victoria's keen eyes danced over every surface in the space, he knew it was already apparent to her that he'd hidden the dire straits of his finances from her, as well as the existence of his three wards and last remaining close family.

Rafe cleared the emotion from his throat. "May I ring for refreshments?" he offered, but his wife declined with an immediate shake of her head. He inclined his head in understanding and took up a position near the hearth. Every one of his muscles was unbearably taut, poised for a potential battle he hoped was not in store. Everything about this was wrong. Guilt bubbled up from beneath where his heart resided in his chest—as unfamiliar a sensation as it was discomfiting. He told himself that he hadn't really done anything wrong. He'd had every intention of explaining his situation to Victoria, and he was far from the first lord to wed an heiress for a quick infusion of funds into a nearly destitute title.

Then why was he so bothered by the wariness flitting behind her eyes, the tenseness in her full lips, the pensiveness that had enveloped her demeanor like a shroud?

His only hope lay in her silence and willingness to accompany him into the room for an explanation. Whatever emotions she held in check beneath her deceptively placid surface, she thought enough of him—or, at least, their marriage—to give him this chance.

His expression more serious and sober than Victoria had likely ever witnessed from him, Rafe began his explanation. "I was the second child born to the fifth Viscount Blackwood. The first was a daughter, Alice." This was the first time Rafe had spoken his sister's name since her death, and the sound of it unleashed shards of glass to prick at his throat and behind his eyes. "She was already ten years of age when I was born, and our parents had given up hope of ever producing an heir. Alice stood in when she was no more than a child, herself, after our mother died from childbed fever." Victoria pressed her fingers to her lips in surprise at that raw revelation. "The old viscount never recovered from the loss of his wife...and he never stopped blaming me for her death." His conversational tone belied the harsh reality of the statement.

He could tell Victoria of all the times his father had called him a disappointment, struck him out of his own pain and frustration, blatantly accused a child of causing the death of his own mother, but he did not. He forced those memories back down his throat and shoved them behind the locked door of his soul.

"Alice did what she could to shield me from his wrath; she played buffer between us until she met Lord Croftburne and fell in love. I couldn't begrudge her finding her own happiness—not after she'd given so much of herself to me—but I knew her leaving would create more unpleasantness at home.

"I threw all my efforts into carving out my own life away from the grief within these walls. Generations of Blackwood lords made foolish investments and spent carelessly, but the fifth viscount…" His voice trailed off for a moment before continuing. "He was too blinded by his grief to see everything he owned falling around his ears. When he died a few years ago, I was left to pick up what few pieces remained."

"And Alice?" Victoria whispered, as if fearing she already knew the answer.

"Nine years of blissful marriage ended with the broken spoke of a carriage wheel," Rafe answered flatly.

The way he'd shattered at the news of her death and that of her husband far overpowered any modicum of grief he'd experienced at losing his father only a few years before that. His world had buckled around him; nothing had felt quite solid any longer. For so long, he'd protected the feeble spark of hope that he and Alice might one day live life as siblings without the pall of their father's grief enshrouding their existence and coloring their every word and calculated action so as not to attract the old man's misplaced ire. That hope had been extinguished with an unfortunate accident on a rutted road as she and her husband had been traveling to visit his dying mother. Alice had been recently out of childbed, but had insisted that the short journey wouldn't overtax her. More than once, Rafe had cursed her husband's inability to deny Alice anything; more than once, he'd bitterly and unfairly wished Croftburne had traveled alone in that carriage and had been its only victim. Rafe could have helped heal Alice's broken heart, but he was helpless against a broken neck.

"Oh, Rafe…" Victoria's voice cracked. Her glittering eyes jerked him back to the present.

"Were he still around, the old man would likely have blamed me for Alice's death as well," he commented sardonically, a bitter smile tilting the corner of his mouth. He resorted to inappropriate humor, as was his way when the subject grew too uncomfortable, and he nearly squirmed out of his skin when Victoria's eyes shut and a single tear slid free down the curve of her cheek. He forced himself to continue. "The will stated I was first in line as guardian for their three children; they would be deposited into my care or else fall into the hands of a great aunt whom I knew would stifle them. She and I were the only choices—the only family Alice and her husband had remaining, once her husband's mother died as well. There was only one option as far as I could see."

"You took them in," Victoria whispered, though there was no censure in the words. If anything, Rafe might have detected a note of respect there. He refused to place too much hope in the four words, though.

"I had to. They are my family." He cleared his throat and extracted a handkerchief from the inner pocket of his coat, handing it to his wife. Victoria accepted it and dabbed at the single mutinous tear that had managed to escape. "The adjustment hasn't been easy. For any of us. Dominic has struggled with his lessons and has been acting out. May is sometimes lost, begging for her mother and father. Faith, the infant, is, perhaps, the worst off, despite being too young to know what she will never have. Her health is frail, and she cries..." He sighed tremulously. "She cries *so* much. The physician calls weekly to check on her progress, but, even with the best care money can buy, the prognosis is not optimistic. Not when she refuses food and sleeps in only fitful bouts. None of us is unscathed by the change, but all of us are doing what we must."

RAFE HELD HIS shoulders impossibly tense. He was so immobile that Victoria might have thought him a statue had the muscle in his jaw not flexed so rhythmically. He was like a man on the scaffold waiting for the floor to drop from beneath his feet, and she had the distinct impression that she was the hangman, holding his fate in her hands.

Would she sentence him for his sins, or would she forgive him for the reasons behind his actions?

She certainly would have thought less of him had he turned away the children, but if he had only told her the truth of it all—about the children and about his financial concerns—could she say with honesty that she wouldn't have hesitated to move forward with the marriage?

This entire situation was far more pressure than she cared to weather, but there was no shying away from it now. This man was her husband. His wards were hers, as far as she was concerned. The care and well-being of these three small children became as much her responsibility as his once the ink dried upon their marriage documents. Her fate was sealed.

She took her time examining all he'd revealed to her as they sat within the weighty silence of that room. Much as she wanted to, she was no saint who could absolve her husband of all his ills because his heart was in the right place. He'd hidden the children's existence. Not once had he broached the subject of dropping her into a mothering role immediately after upending her life with a move from America to London and marriage into a Society whose customs and rituals were all still new to her. She wouldn't be herself without at least broaching her feelings on this.

"So…" she began, "you married me to have a replacement mother for them? Did you ever stop to think that my gender does not inherently mean I know anything about children?" Her tone was slightly snippier than she'd intended, but she was exhausted at that point. Emotionally depleted. She'd so believed this marriage had gotten off on the right foot, but now…

Rafe held his hands out to her, palm up in a beseeching manner. "Anything has to be better than the last few months."

Surrounded, as they were, by the worn elegance of the house, Victoria experienced another gradual realization she'd been attempting to ward off—a reality she'd understood was a likelihood, but it seemed hadn't been entirely prepared to feel a pang of disappointment for.

With some difficulty, she spoke through the tightness that

had gathered in her throat. "It is quite a lifestyle change for a bachelor to take on three small children; quite expensive as well, I suspect, to fund it all from what you have admitted is a poorly managed estate. Now you must consider hiring staff to care for them, clothing them, feeding them, educating them, eventually helping to launch May and Faith into Society." Rafe saw instantly where her thoughts were headed, and he had the good grace to allow a flicker of guilt past his careful mask. Victoria felt the dregs of her optimism retreat inwardly. "Why would you wait this long to mention the children? And you clearly intended to wait even longer if we were to travel away from England for several weeks."

He shook his head helplessly, a lock of his dark hair falling over his forehead. "I thought it would be easier."

"Easier? For whom?" She stood once again. "Certainly not me—not when we had months of 'friendship' during which this detail might have been revealed." Victoria paused to bite the inside of her lip in an attempt to regain control over her emotions. "You must think so little of me if you believed you needed to hide their existence until there was no possibility of me turning my back on this marriage. You have not learned a thing about me. You may have listened enough to ingratiate yourself, but that is no more than any swindler would. I care very little about your need for funds—I've never been under the illusion that it wouldn't be an enticing factor in any union—but the omissions are insulting...to assume that I was the kind of person who would end a courtship because you had three small wards is even more so." Victoria's words rang clear and true between them. Heart pounding in her ears hard enough to make her head ache, she knew she'd said her peace.

Finally, her husband inclined his head in understanding—a mute acceptance of her statements—and sighed resignedly. "I apologize for any hurt my actions may have caused you; I did what I believed I had to do for the children, and for all of our futures." Victoria resented him for that last statement. She did not wish to feel pity and understanding; she was not yet ready to relinquish her anger, but it was so difficult when faced with his mournful expression and fathomless eyes. The man could charm a nun to sin. "And I hope you will understand the necessity of postponing our wedding trip. Now that we will reside here in Town, I will have the housekeeper, Mrs. West, introduce you to the current staff and show you around."

"Thank you, no," Victoria declined coolly. "I would rather retire to my room alone to think on all that has taken place."

"The bedchambers are likely not fully prepared since we were not scheduled to return for more than a month."

"I am sure they are satisfactory," she maintained. "I do not feel up to interacting with the staff. Rest assured, I will do my duties…but it will not be today. I believe I am owed that much grace after all this. And, if you feel anything like the exhaustion I am experiencing, then you will understand and allow me this courtesy."

RAFE WATCHED AS Mrs. West followed Victoria out of the parlor door and into the foyer. He listened as their shoes crossed the foyer and ascended the stairs; he waited for the familiar creaky step near the top of the first landing. Only then did he slam the side of his fist upon the marble mantle with a hissed curse. He stepped away from the hearth, grateful that his outburst hadn't caused the blasted thing to collapse and crush his foot. It would be just his luck for such a thing to happen.

He should have known better than to walk into his marriage with Victoria Rockford with such naive optimism. Nothing had gone as planned—nothing ever quite did for him. While it had seemed to start off well, it was looking like his marriage would be as frustrating as the rest of his life had been.

So much of London viewed him as a carefree rakehell.

Precious few knew just how much he cared.

He did not deny that he spent a great deal of time in the presence of beautiful women; he'd never hidden his reckless behavior.

All of it, however, had been his escape and his way to explore who he was when all he'd been within these walls was a bitter disappointment. His life had started with the worst of luck of all, causing his mother to take her last breath with his first, and it had only followed him through the years. All the smiles, all the drunken parties, all the most beautiful women in the world could not make up for the hollowness he felt inside. He'd been foolish to hope that marrying a respectable woman and setting both his wards and his title up for better futures would place him firmly on a better path than he'd ever taken before, but it seemed he was incapable of not making a mess of things.

When one issue was resolved by the immediate influx of Victoria's wealth and the steady income her annual stipend of several thousand pounds would provide, he now had a wife who didn't trust him…and he'd be damned if he knew how to fix the muddle he'd made.

Because this truly was all his own doing; there was no one else to blame for his situation but himself, and that was perhaps the most irksome of all.

In the span of only a few hours, their marriage had gone from one of optimism to one of unleashed mistrust and injured feelings. Rafe was used to dropping women with whom he no longer saw eye-to-eye—women who were more trouble and effort than he wished to endure. None of those women had ever been vital enough to his life for him to try to work through whatever disagreement they'd experienced. He'd endured far too much rancor and animosity in his early years to willingly put himself through any more of it; now, however, he could not run away. Fleeing the marriage was not an option…not if he had any hope of the future he'd set out to achieve.

He knew Victoria's brother remained in London for the time being and, if he caught so much as a whiff of discontent in their marriage, Rafe did not doubt that he would do everything within his power to remove both Victoria and her wealth from Rafe's reach.

He felt entirely out of his depth, and he did not care for it one bit...almost as much as he hated the fact that he'd wounded Victoria's feelings.

A sudden screech and crash shattered his train of thought. Rather than wince, Rafe closed his eyes and tilted his head toward the ceiling as if seeking benediction.

"It wasn't my fault!" came the immediate denial of responsibility in a young lad's very familiar voice.

Rafe sighed and scrubbed his face before leaving the room to deal with the latest disaster.

Chapter Eleven

Victoria spent the rest of her first full day as Lady Black-wood pacing the viscountess's chambers. The rooms were surprisingly spacious given the relatively modest size of the home, and, given the delicate silk papering and ornate canopied bed, they must have been quite grand at one time. But her husband had been right, of course. The rooms were far from prepared to have a resident.

Upon being shown into the room, the poor housekeeper and two maids had apologized profusely for the state of it. They immediately scurried about removing sheets covering the furniture, opening windows, and unrolling the mattress, doing their best to air out a room that likely hadn't been used since Rafe's birth.

"Please do not fret," Victoria had tried reassuring them. "I realize we were not due to arrive for quite a while, and you had no notice that our plans had changed."

"We will have this room spick and span in no time, my lady!" the housekeeper, Mrs. West, reassured her. "Allow me to show you to another room better suited, and I will have some refreshments sent up while you wait."

"Thank you, no," Victoria said with what she hoped was a friendly smile despite her heavy spirits. The red-faced footman arrived, carting the first of her trunks. Her belongings were scheduled to be sent over while she and Rafe were on their honeymoon trip, but now she could send for them sooner since it seemed they would no longer be leaving England. "I will help unpack and organize my clothing. I promise to stay out of your way." Despite the housekeeper's protests, Victoria insisted upon remaining while the chamber was aired and clean pillows and bedding were fitted. When they were done, the scent of lilac drifted through the room, both pleasant and surprisingly calming. The space was gradually transformed into something with a great deal more potential than she'd seen on first impression.

She spent a couple of peaceful hours working alongside the staff. Their discomfort was palpable, but she made every effort to show them that she was not the typical titled English lady. These were people with whom she'd spend most of her days from then on. She'd grown quite friendly with many of the employees who worked in her father's household, and she did not see why that could not be the case in her own home. Besides, the last thing she wanted right then was to wander the halls of an unfamiliar house and accidentally encounter her husband. That moment would come sooner or later, of course, but she needed more time.

Victoria hoped time would help her come to terms with her new reality—not only was she a new wife, but she'd also inherited a trio of children...and her husband had, indeed, turned out to be exactly like every other man who'd ever pursued her. He thought little of who she was, seeing her only as a bank account.

A means to an end.

An improvement upon his own circumstances.

He'd done a remarkable job of concealing it beneath a veneer of friendship, she had to give him that.

She'd believed in him so fully; she'd stood up for him when others had disparaged him. And now she felt like the worst sort of fool.

But he did have his nieces and nephew to consider... It wasn't as if he'd married her to live a lavish lifestyle with no responsibilities; he had children for whom he needed to care and provide.

Victoria had only limited experience with London Society, but the cost was likely substantial if he wanted to perpetuate the façade of wealth by properly educating them and launching them into the rest of the *ton*. His aim had been more altruistic than—

No.

She would not forgive him for everything simply because May had looked so sweet and pathetic as he'd held her, and Dominic had been mischievously charming, looking so like his uncle that the familial resemblance was undeniable. Their adorable faces would not sway her…at least not this soon after the events of that day.

Victoria took a calming breath and asked if one of the maids might help her change before they left. Now that they were staying in London, she would have to make inquiries into hiring a permanent lady's maid sooner than she'd anticipated. She mulled over this and their abandoned honeymoon trip as she donned a more comfortable dress of sprigged cream and pale blue muslin. She tried not to sigh overmuch for all the missed adventures as her hair was unpinned, brushed, and twisted into a simple coil at the nape of her neck. As she waited for the tea she requested, she promised herself that she would stop her pining once it arrived. Despite what London Society might think of her, she was not the spoiled, vapid girl or ice princess they expected. She could allow herself to feel disappointment, but she could also overcome it and recognize that there were far more pressing matters requiring her attention.

Namely, three small children and a marriage teetering on a rather precarious ledge.

She considered how she might move forward as she prepared her cup of tea with a healthy serving of the fine sugar from the bowl. She noted with some curiosity that the service was mismatched. The difference in pattern was subtle, but there if one looked closely enough. The realization caused an unexpected dip in her stomach. Things must certainly be dire if the household could not even maintain a complete matching set of china. She set down her cup a little more forcefully than intended.

"Damn and blast," Victoria muttered and slumped back into her chair. It was one thing for a man born to privilege who allowed his greed to overshadow his conscience and lure a woman into marriage to deepen his own pockets; it was another for a man who was so desperate to claw his way up from ominous—if genteel—poverty that he would befriend, earn the trust of, and then marry an heiress to provide his title and the wards he'd inherited with the security necessary for any sort of future. If she looked at it objectively, was it really all that different from what her own family had done?

If one could sip tea begrudgingly, then Victoria had discovered that ability.

Her tea finished, she perused the room and sorted through the trunks that had been brought up. She made a mental note to add to the list of items to have carted over from America. Most of her things would be given away or donated at her instruction, but there were some books and other trinkets, as well as a fur-lined winter cloak, she desired to have with her in London. She ran her fingers along the spines of the books still so neatly tucked away in the smaller luggage. Selecting one, she curled up near the hearth to read. It was another of the books recommended by Lady Morton, and Victoria was quickly drawn into the compelling tale of a woman who disguised herself as a man to forge a new path for herself.

Before she knew it, hours had passed, and still Rafe had not come looking for her. The light in the room had grown lower than was comfortable for reading, elongating the shadows and closing in the corners of the room. The chamber was utterly, eerily silent. This area of London seemed less busy as well, making the noise in the street noticeably less frequent.

Was she more relieved or irked by the fact that her husband had left her in silence, not seeking her out to speak further? She could not decide.

The fact was, Victoria was a woman unused to so much

leisure and solitude. She knew she would lose her sanity if she stayed shut away in that room for much longer, no matter how compelling the book she held in her hand. She might have felt differently if it felt like home, but this place—this life—was still too new for her to feel settled in any way.

Finally, she crept from the room, glancing up and down the hallway and finding it deserted. She listened for several heartbeats, but there was not so much as the creak of a floorboard. She'd seen very little of the Townhouse, but she knew it was a fair size, even if it was not exactly a grand residence. Regardless, she did not think she'd become too lost if she attempted a bit of wandering. A quick count of the doorways reassured her that she would be able to find her own chamber later.

Her exploration of the second floor revealed several additional small bedrooms, as well as a family sitting room, which, unlike those bedchambers, actually seemed to see some use. It was interesting to her to note how the staff's efforts were concentrated on the spaces her husband might use. The entryway and parlor below, for example, were lovingly and carefully cleaned to make them as presentable as possible; the same could be said about that private sitting room. The unoccupied bedchambers were similar to the state her own had been in upon arrival: barren of fripperies, sparsely furnished, looted for any pieces which might be more beneficial elsewhere, and forlorn, cleaned just often enough to prevent them from smelling musty.

Victoria purposefully avoided the final bedchamber on the floor—the one directly adjacent to her own—suspecting she'd find it in fine repair and most certainly occupied. Instead, Victoria headed back up the hallway in the direction of the stairs, knowing there was a decision to be made once she reached them. She could either make her way downstairs to the main floor or up where she believed the nursery was likely to be located.

Rafe or the children.

The decision was not all that difficult for Victoria to make.

She ascended the carpeted staircase and found the nursery

door ajar. Tilting her head, she listened to the silence for several heartbeats before she nudged it open. The door swung on quiet hinges to reveal a bright, airy room that spanned the length of the front of the Townhouse. Several large windows overlooked the street and filled the space with the warm glow of the early sunset, making the sky-blue walls appear even more like the open air of the country. Along one wall were two child-sized beds covered in lovingly crafted quilts; a small lump in the middle of one indicated it was occupied. Opposite of those was a narrow iron bedframe for the night nurse beside a draped bassinet. The polished wood floor was covered in a thick rug woven in a pattern of warm colors. It had likely been quite vibrant at one time, but time and use had worn it into more muted tones. Despite the large size of the space, it felt cozy and brimming with love—far more comfortable and welcoming than what she'd seen of the rest of the house.

A masterpiece of a dollhouse sat in one corner. A variety of dolls—porcelain, wood, and rag—toy soldiers, carved wooden blocks, and a miniature wooden horse with what appeared to be a real horsehair mane and tail were scattered around the room. A small area for lessons had been set up near the door, with books and writing tools strewn across a small table. Additional books had once been neatly organized on the bookcase positioned nearby, but they were now stacked haphazardly, as if small hands had wrought destruction in a moment of curiosity.

A board creaked beneath Victoria's slipper. The nurse—Nan, was it?—looked up from her mending of the hem of a tiny pink dress. Her eyes widened, and she stood abruptly, sending the rocking chair swaying.

"My lady!" She greeted her a little breathlessly and dropped into a proper curtsey. She must have guessed Victoria had perused the space because she instantly launched into an apology. "The little ones only just went down for their naps, and I was about to tidy up as soon as I finished the mending."

Victoria brushed away the woman's anxious words. "I am

sure with three children and a skeleton staff, it must feel as if the work is never done—especially the laundering and mending." Nan accepted her offer of a warm smile and returned it with a grateful one of her own. "I did not mean to disrupt anything and only wished to look in on the children."

"Of course," Nan replied with a hopeful smile and set aside her work. For the first time, Victoria considered what these new circumstances must be like for Rafe's household staff. It was evident to her that they were all doing what they could, even though a home of that size required at least double the staff she'd already seen to maintain the minimum standard of living for a peer's residence. She took the obvious effort and care performed in the more visible and oft-used rooms in the Townhouse as evidence that the staff were trying their best and doing what they could, but so few hands could only do so much. Additionally, it was natural that they regarded her sudden arrival with a mixture of nervousness and optimism.

Would she view the home's shabbiness as laziness or short-comings on the part of the staff? Certainly, some women might, but Victoria was not one of those women. And she did not doubt that the staff were entirely aware of just what she brought to the marriage, even if they were not privy to the exact sum. More funds could mean more staff, better wages, and more comfortable accommodations for all. Servants such as Nan would have assistance and would no longer be responsible for a dozen tasks at once. Many hands would make lighter work.

Nan showed her over to the bed where the sick little girl was curled on her side, her curls a wild mess of reckless abandon. Victoria couldn't find it in herself to be disappointed with the cancellation of her honeymoon trip when faced with the child's cherubic features and pouty lips. May's tiny chest heaved in a barking cough, and she rolled to her side. The sound tugged at her heartstrings almost as much as recalling how distraught Rafe had been upon seeing the ill child. A wave of tenderness threatened to eclipse her annoyance with her husband once and for all.

"And the littlest one is over here," Nan whispered and walked Victoria over to the bassinet holding the child Victoria had yet to meet.

She didn't expect to find a swaddled infant, impossibly tiny and frail, her coloring even less healthy than that of her ill elder sister. There was no roundness to her cheeks and only sadness in what should have been a sweet curve to her lips. A lump instantly formed in Victoria's throat.

"How old is she?" Victoria whispered, barely able to keep herself from touching the sleeping baby to confirm she was real and not an incredibly lifelike and tragic marble carving.

"Nearly nine months," Nan replied and adjusted the swaddling. The answer surprised Victoria. She did not profess to know a great deal about children, but she'd have guessed the child was half that age. "She was such a happy child until her parents passed," the nurse continued. "Since then, she eats very little and does not sleep well. She is still so young, but that does not mean she hasn't felt their loss as keenly as the others—mayhap even more so, since they were all she knew." Tears began to burn the backs of Victoria's eyes. "It bothers his lordship a great deal," Nan added softly, sadly, tearing Victoria's attention from the sleeping child. "Sometimes, he'll come in in the middle of the night just to check on the babe…the nights are particularly difficult for her."

The mental image that was created was unbearably heart wrenching. "And where is his little lordship?" Victoria asked, forcing the words through her tight throat as she inquired after the third and eldest of her husband's wards.

The maid gestured to the corner near the door where Dominic sat facing the wall, hunched over on a tiny stool with his chin cupped in his hands. Nan led her away from the sleeping girls and explained, "He is in punishment for running through the hall and breaking yet another vase after Lord Blackwood specifically warned him against running so carelessly indoors." Nan crossed her arms beneath her ample bosom. From her expression and the shake of her head, it was clear that this was far from the first—or even the second—time this situation had occurred. "We'll be out of vases by the end of the month at this rate," she groused candidly. Nan's eyes widened as she remembered to whom she was speaking. "Apologies—"

Victoria offered her another reassuring smile. "I have an elder brother, and I know firsthand how destructive little boys can be. All that energy they possess is quite disproportionate to their deceptively small size, is it not?" This appeased the nurse, and the corner of her lined mouth twitched.

Victoria looked back at the sullen lad, the sight tugging at her heartstrings. He'd been so silent that she'd entered the room and walked right past him without noticing. Resolute, she crossed the room and bent at the waist, so their heads were closer. The boy eyed her warily. "How long are you to remain in punishment, my lord?" she asked with all seriousness.

"Forever," he grumbled and turned his eyes back down to the floor. Victoria tried her best not to smile at his dramatics.

"Well, how was that vase broken?"

His shoulders lifted in a brief shrug, but, when it was clear that Victoria would say nothing else until she received a verbal reply, he looked down at his shoes and gestured to them. "These shoes. They don't let me run well; they make me slip." He looked back up at her and indignantly demanded, "What good are slippery shoes?"

Victoria smiled that time despite her best efforts, but she sobered quickly and said, "Well, we will have to remedy that, won't we? Perhaps find you some better shoes?" Dominic's eyes widened as if the possibility of improved footwear had never occurred to him. "However," she added gravely, "you will have to promise me that you will only use them to their full advantage out of doors where no vases can be threatened." The boy sat up straighter and nodded enthusiastically. "Now, how much longer are you truly supposed to stay here on this stool?"

The boy frowned furiously. "My evil uncle said I must stay here until supper."

"That seems rather harsh," Victoria replied gravely. "It was only one vase, after all."

Dominic averted his eyes and, just as she'd hoped, he admitted, "It's because I was told several times not to run inside…and I've broken three vases now. And a tea service. And maybe a few porcelain figurines."

"Ah…" Victoria nodded with all the seriousness she could muster. Though inexperienced with children, even she knew that she could not undermine Rafe's authority by freeing the boy from his punishment early, but she made a mental note to speak to him about it. Instead, she straightened and said, "I look forward to seeing you at supper, then."

The boy frowned up at her again, his expression far more serious than what one would expect from someone his age. "Why would you eat here in the nursery with us? Won't you eat with Uncle Rafe?"

Victoria was taken aback by his question. "Do you not take meals with your uncle?"

"No—it is not how things are done." Dominic sounded mature beyond his years, likely repeating something he'd likely heard often from the adults in his life. "Besides," the boy added, "he is not usually home for supper."

Victoria emitted a thoughtful sound. It wasn't as if she were ignorant of the customs of the upper classes; even in America, young children did not take meals with the adults when there were guests. Her father, however, had always made sure to include his children whenever possible. If he was entertaining friends and colleagues, then Victoria and Luke would frequently share in the meal. There was never a question that they would all dine together as a family on quiet nights—much like the one they would be having that evening. She did not see why at least Dominic could not dine with her and Rafe, and it would certainly go a long way toward allowing them all to get to know one another. She made a silent promise that she would add it to her list of things she wished to address with her new husband.

"If not at supper, then perhaps tomorrow? I would like to have the opportunity to get to know you."

Dominic eyed her with a mixture of wariness and curiosity before finally lifting his shoulders in a negligent response.

That would have to do.

Victoria lifted her hand to Nan in a silent goodbye before exiting the nursery…and running straight into her husband.

It was like colliding with a brick wall.

She released a surprised "oof" as his fingers wrapped around her shoulders and steadied her stumble.

"Victoria?" Was it her imagination, or was his voice a little breathless when he said her name? "What are you doing here?"

It was impossible for her not to notice the heat of his body and his intoxicating scent. She'd been so confused and distraught that day that it had been relatively easy for her to set aside her newfound carnal knowledge. Now, however, as close as they stood in the narrow hallway, it all came rushing back to her. She could only pray the lack of windows would help disguise the sudden flush she felt creeping up her throat.

"I—I thought to look in on the children…" Her eyes flitted to the deepening furrow between his dark brows. "Or…do you not wish for me to know them?" She hadn't considered that possibility. He had certainly gone to great lengths to disguise their existence thus far; what if he actually desired to continue to keep these parts of his life separate?

Had the day not been so emotionally exhausting, Victoria might have laughed at the rapid shifting of expressions on his face—confusion suddenly morphed into pleasure. "No! It is quite alright. I would like very much for all of you to become familiar." He paused and cleared his throat, tempering his voice when he asked, "Were you speaking with Dominic? How is he faring?"

"Still in punishment. Still miserable." With each passing second, she was becoming more aware that Rafe still had not released her; in fact, his thumbs moved ever so slightly along the bare skin of her collarbone revealed by the neckline of her gown.

"And we really must invest in less-slippery footwear for him; it will probably save us a great many shattered vases and other damaged housewares." Her tone was serious, but Rafe knew her well enough at that point to catch onto her jest. His laughter was a relief—the evaporation of some of the built-up tension between them. It helped usher in some normalcy.

Victoria smiled softly and prepared to excuse herself but was stopped when his hands tightened ever so slightly.

"Victoria…" Rafe started and stopped, his eyes dancing over her features. "Victoria, please know how sorry I am that everything came out as it did." Her heart began to pound more forcefully in her breast. "I should have told you about the children, and I hope we might speak more on our situation and our future this evening."

It was Victoria's turn to feel a little breathless. She could only nod after a brief hesitation. She interpreted the softening of the tension around his eyes as an expression of relief.

"Are your chambers up to scratch?" he asked, changing the subject.

"They are fine," she replied, making sure to add that the staff did a remarkable job in such a short span of time.

While her words of praise seemed to please him, there was resignation in his tone when he said, "I will escort you on a shopping excursion tomorrow for anything you might need or desire for the space. It is the least I can do for canceling our honeymoon trip so suddenly." The caress of his thumbs began again, and it was all she could do not to emit a delighted shiver from the contact. Waves of warmth echoed out from those little points of contact, gaining heat and power as they rippled throughout her body.

"I understand it needed to happen," she said as steadily as possible. "I can hardly blame you when there was an ill child involved."

This seemed to unburden his conscience enough for the time being, and he was finally willing to allow her to leave. "Then you will join me for supper?" Pleased when she nodded in the affirmative, Rafe released her and turned to enter the nursery. "I must have one more conversation with my nephew before he is released from his prison sentence," Rafe said lightly, the most charming tilt to his lips. "Since you'll not be running off on us just yet, he needs a gentle reminder that he should not comment on a lady's manner of speech, no matter how odd and foreign it may be."

Victoria released an affronted gasp, but Rafe was already turning away. His parting chuckle unleashed another ripple of awareness to break out across her body. She did her best not to ponder how her skin tingled in the absence of her husband's touch, but she was also the first to admit she did a poor job of it.

Chapter Twelve

SUPPER THAT EVENING passed pleasantly enough, even if it was a bit of a slapdash affair with a cobbled-together meal thanks to the unprepared larder and short notice. Victoria did not blame the staff, however, recognizing that they'd done the best they could many hours after the markets had run out of their freshest wares. While the meal had been simple, it had been delicious—a sentiment that Victoria ensured was passed along to those responsible for its creation. Interestingly, she caught Rafe watching her as she'd said as much to the footman in charge of carting out the food and then clearing it away.

"Why are you staring like that?" she'd asked and quickly swiped at her face with her napkin. "Is there something on my face? Why did you say nothing?" she hissed.

Rafe's lips merely tilted in a soft smile, and he shook his head, turning back to his serving of rabbit stew. She narrowed her eyes at him, but no further response came.

As predicted, the children had remained in the nursery for the meal, so it was only the two of them at the table. It was absurd, really. Even though the room was far too large for the size of the table at which they sat, it could still have easily accommodated at least three times the number it did that evening. It had likely been pulled in from another of the rooms or a storage space and placed there along with its mismatched chairs once the dining room had been dusted and cleaned. It felt like far too much effort for the staff for just the two of them, especially when they were already spread so thin. Victoria couldn't help but think it might have felt more worth it had the children joined them—or Dominic, at the very least.

"I was surprised when your nephew informed me that he does not regularly dine with you."

Rafe's expression was so similar to the one Dominic had displayed that she had to bite the inside of her cheek to keep from smiling. "It is not the done thing," he answered simply, and Victoria learned precisely where the sentiment Dominic displayed had originated. Even if they butted heads like bison, uncle and nephew were two halves of the same coin. Though she had spent only a short time with the two of them, it was already evident to her that Dominic idolized his uncle. His every word, gesture, expression, and action were committed to the lad's memory and reflected back with a child's innocence. She wondered if Rafe noticed it, or if he was too blinded by the weight of his responsibilities to fully appreciate the honor it was.

"Might we consider having at least Dominic join us soon? I believe he would enjoy being included, and I would like to spend more time interacting with him." Rafe's lips parted to form a reply, but she spoke quickly to head him off in case he might put an end to her plans before they could truly begin. "When I was his age, I would often dine with my father—Luke as well. It was an opportunity for us to come together as a family, share stories, and feel close to one another."

She watched the thoughts pass behind his eyes, dragging out the seconds far longer than Victoria believed was strictly necessary, but he eventually inclined his head and said, "I will think on it."

Quite pleased with herself, Victoria tucked into her apple tart with a sigh of pleasure as the sugar crystals melted on her tongue.

Following the meal, Victoria retired to her rooms, and one of the maids who'd earlier helped her set up her chambers was already waiting to assist her in preparing for bed. She donned another white nightshift and her dressing gown, stretching in relief as she was freed from her stays and the layers of fabric. She looked forward to sprawling atop the mattress and falling into a restful, dreamless sleep. The past few days had been overwhelming, to say the least, and she looked forward to a quiet respite.

The maid had just finished gathering up Victoria's discarded clothing when, following a rapid double-tap on the door, Rafe entered her bedchamber. He carried with him two glasses of brandy and had stripped down to his breeches and his shirt-sleeves—just as comfortable and casual as she was. At her lord's arrival, the maid scurried from the room and shut the door behind her, leaving Victoria alone with her husband.

The hearth had been stoked, but the edges of the room were cast in harsh shadow. Rafe, only half visible in the poor lighting, was a specter of sensuality, beautiful in his harshness. Her core clenched with the memories of just how sensual a creature her husband could be.

He glided toward her with his innate grace and held one of the drinks out to her. The warmed amber liquid within the crystal glass sat comfortably in her palm and gave her something to focus upon other than the way her body reacted to her husband's nearness. Hadn't she been furious with him only hours before? Hadn't she considered—if only a moment—walking away from him because of his secrets and omissions?

However, faced with this Rafe—the impossibly charming man with the disarming smile and easy manners, the one who had made her warm to the idea of marriage to an Englishman—she nearly forgot how to breathe, let alone clutch tightly to the shreds of her retained animosity.

And now, aside from how beautiful he was, she also knew what he could make her feel. His talented hands and lips and body were even more intoxicating than the forgotten drink she held in her hands. Even if he might have only married her for her wealth and to fill a vacant position in his household, Victoria could feel every inch of her body straining to be nearer to him, as if she were a flower and he, the radiant sun. What was it about him that drew her against her will? His unique combination of charm, charisma, and good looks was surely deadly.

It was only with great effort that she was able to turn her eyes down to her brandy.

"I am glad the truth is revealed and we now have some sort of understanding between us, Victoria. I cannot begin to tell you how relieved I am," Rafe began. "The children mean a great deal to me, and I hope, in time, you will become fond of them as well."

Her reply was a small nod of her head. In truth, she hoped for the same. She could not hold the existence of these children against them—they could no more help placement in Rafe's household and under his care than they could the fact that they were orphans. Victoria's chest tightened, even more so when she pictured the infant in the bassinet. A part of her mind had not left the infant since she'd first laid eyes on her tiny form hours earlier. She'd been like a lost fawn in the woods, impossibly delicate and ethereally fragile.

"What about the baby?" she asked. "Does the physician know what ails her?"

A shadow passed over Rafe's features, and she realized she'd strode into sensitive territory. Nan hadn't been exaggerating when she'd said Rafe was very concerned with his youngest ward's frail health. The question hadn't felt intrusive when she'd posed it—were these children not now her nieces and nephew, and did she not have a vested interest in their well-being?—but the look he gave her made her think twice. In one swift move, he tossed back his drink and set the empty glass aside. In less than the span of a heartbeat, he closed the space between them and plucked her glass from her fingers. She did not see where he'd placed it because, in the next moment, she was swept up into his arms and held high against his chest. On instinct, Victoria wrapped her arms around his neck, and she was instantly enveloped in his heady, masculine scent.

Her eyelids fluttered.

It would be so easy to bury her face in his throat, to revel in the light scratch of his evening beard against her cheek.

No sooner had she been deposited atop the coverlet than Rafe was covering her body and her lips with his. There was no tentativeness in his touch that evening; his every move was bold and claiming. His tongue swept into her mouth with reckless abandon while his hips nestled shamelessly in the vee of her parted thighs. The intimate press fanned her desire, made her ache for more, urged her to spread herself wider for him so his thick, hard length rocked against her rapidly dampening flesh.

Victoria's carnal knowledge was limited, but she wasn't foolish. She knew her husband was silencing her with kisses…but she found she did not much care. Not when it ignited such sensations beneath her skin and within her body.

RAFE HAPPILY SANK into the kisses, devouring his wife. His tongue tangled with hers, licked, and sipped. She was sweeter than the dessert they had shared, headier than the brandy he'd imbibed, and more desirable than was reasonable.

Her pliant curves and gentle softness beneath him made him throb in anticipation. His blood hummed with remembered passion and the excitement of impending completion.

"You feel so good…and you taste even better…" he murmured against Victoria's lips. The tiny whimper torn from her throat was nearly the end of his control. He had to remind himself that she was still relatively untried—one night in his arms, a worldly woman did not make.

But it was a start.

"I look forward to doing this as often as possible," Rafe said, licking and nipping his way down her throat to her decolletage. "We seem rather compatible, you and I, and there is something to be said for physical compatibility." She trembled when his tongue dipped into the valley between her breasts. "This, I have found, can be a better foundation than anything emotional." She arched into his ministrations, her ripe nipples peaking the thin fabric of her night clothes. His mouth watered from the desire to taste them. "How wet you are for me…how hard I am for you…? Those are more necessary to any attachment than false words of affection. Of the lie of love."

Victoria froze beneath him so thoroughly that she even stopped breathing.

He lifted his head to discover her wide, disbelieving eyes looking down at him.

"What?" she whispered.

Rafe cocked his head. "I was trying to offer you a compliment."

"By saying you are grateful there are no emotions between us?" The slight rise in her tone should have warned Rafe that he'd made an unfortunate misstep.

"Well, no. The compliment was in the fact that I find you so enticing…that we have physical attraction and compatibility. That is more than a great many couples in our situation possess. The truth is that this was not a love match." Though nothing he said was a lie, it all seemed to increase the shadows in her hazel eyes. "I am incapable of love, Victoria. I do not believe in the emotion. I have never experienced it, nor do I plan to."

Rafe had, rather unfortunately, misjudged his bride's sensibilities. Used to speaking with more worldly bedmates, he'd made a grave mistake.

Victoria displayed a surprising amount of rage-induced strength and shoved against him with all her might. He was sent, rather gracelessly, tumbling off the bed with one leg caught up in the air, tangled in the bedding. His back and shoulders thudded heavily to the floor. He was dazed from the unexpected change in his position, so he hadn't yet reacted by the time Victoria peered over the edge of the bed while clutching the faded coverlet to her chest.

"Leave!" she snarled. Otherworldly flames of fury danced in her irises, which had so recently been hazy with desire. The stark contrast was stunning. "If you have no notion of how insulting your words were, then I do not know what to do with you. You are beyond help. Beyond redemption. I may not be as experienced as you are, but even *I* know that lasting relationships cannot be built upon physicality, alone; they cannot survive if two people do not strive for more. Your assertion that you do not believe in deeper emotions—that you cannot feel them and will not even try—why, that is perhaps one of the most damaging revelations of the day. And *that* is saying something." Rafe was struck silent by the vehemence of her words, the raw pain dripping from every syllable. This was certainly not the response he'd anticipated. "Perhaps this marriage was a mistake."

Catching his breath, Rafe clambered to his feet. "You misunderstand—"

"I think I understand perfectly well. Despite what you believe, I am not naïve enough to have ever assumed that ours was a love match, so do not insult me by trying to explain that it was not. If I hadn't been certain of it before today, then your obvious need for funds has now made that abundantly clear. And you do not need to insult me further by telling me to my face that there is nothing emotional between us, and that there never would be." Rafe tried to shake his head in denial, but stopped. That hadn't been what he meant, but he could, begrudgingly, see how it might be interpreted that way. He liked her well enough; he was attracted to her, but he had already lied to her far more than he should have. He'd thought it would be a kindness to both confess to his undeniable attraction to her and to let her know that she should not hold out hope for love from him. He would care for her, see to her needs, but wasn't it cruel to allow her to hold out hope for more?

Perhaps his timing hadn't been the most fortuitous, but none of it had been a lie.

He'd never felt love, and he never planned on feeling it.

He refused to allow such a destructive emotion into his soul. Anything that could turn a man into a hateful, abusive father who cursed his son and heir was not something he wanted to ever give himself over to.

"And what about me?" Victoria added. "Don't you think I would rather spend my life with someone who appreciates me for more than what he would earn from tying himself to me? I suppose that foolishness lies with me, because I was blind enough to think that we might at the very least have a foundation of friendship between us. Now I can see it was all a ruse. I gave up on the fantasy of marriage for true love a long time ago but thank you for reminding me of that. You have your money and your wife. You have shattered any illusions I might have had about forming an amiable marriage upon a foundation of fondness, and you might as well leave right this moment because you are certainly not welcome in my bed."

Rafe wanted so badly to have his chance to rail right back at her, but how could he when she was right? How could he fight the truth? He'd lured her in with contrived friendship, married her for her money, and had always planned on continuing life as normal once he and his wards were on more stable ground. She had been treated as a means to an end, and he'd insulted her horribly by insinuating that there was nothing sacred about their union—a union barely more than twenty-four hours old.

He shoved his hands through his hair and, with a growl, he stormed from the room, slamming the door behind him. A haze of frustration clouded his vision. He was frustrated with Victoria for her reaction—even if it might be a little bit justified. He was frustrated with himself for his idiocy. He was frustrated with his lot in life that this was what he'd become.

His furious pacing froze mid-step when a thin wail floated down from the floor above.

Heart sinking, he threw on a pair of breeches and lashed on his dressing robe before stepping out into the hall.

Chapter Thirteen

T HE NEXT MORNING, Rafe felt as if he'd been trampled by a horse. Exhaustion wrought havoc upon his visage; dark circles sat beneath his eyes, and he could have so very easily slept the day away.

Just a week ago, he likely would have done just that.

Now, however, he had an irate wife upon his hands. The fumes of her fury lingered in the air around him, clinging to him with all the unpleasant, cloying stench of smoke. His normally glib and gilded manners had fled him last night along with the blood from his brain and left him in a sorry state, to be sure. To make matters worse, he could hear Alice's admonishments bouncing around inside his skull as if she were alive and well in the room right there with him to reiterate repeatedly what a perfect bastard he was. As much as he hated to admit it, she was right. While he'd much rather have hidden away in his darkened rooms for the better part of the day, the echoes of his sister's voice prodded him awake and out of bed like a hundred furious wasps.

As he dressed, his ears perked for any sound from Victoria's chamber, but none came. She was either already away and belowstairs, or she was still asleep. He would find out soon enough. Inhaling a bracing breath, he left his chambers and descended to the main floor...only to find not a single sign of his wife.

Rafe poked his head into every room—even the ones occupied only by dust and the remaining pieces of sheet-covered furniture not decent enough to sell—and went so far as to duck down to the basement kitchens. The maids had blinked owlishly at his unexpected arrival, and he'd beat a hasty retreat with a muttered apology when his appearance had startled Mrs. West into dropping a freshly washed cast-iron pot with an unholy clang.

He made his way back up the stairs, continuing upwards toward the bedchambers and, on a whim, he decided to check the family parlor. The door was ajar enough where he could see inside without being immediately detected, and what he saw caused him to blink several times to be sure that the scene before him was real.

There, Victoria sat on the floor in the center of the room, her skirts a pool of cerulean and cream stripes around her. Faith was asleep in her arms, a silent bundle of white muslin and pale pink flesh, as Victoria asked Dominic, "What about your left-flanking cavalry technique?" Dom sat back on his heels and eyed the array of tin soldiers spread out before him. "The Americans will win, regardless," she teased lightly.

"My soldiers will win!" Dominic argued as he gestured vehemently toward his red-coated toys to indicate they would prevail against the blue. "No one can best the British military!"

Rafe watched Victoria's unabashed smile in awe as she and Dominic exchanged a few more amiable verbal parries. Warmth bloomed from his breast at the domesticity of the scene—something foreign and unexpected in many ways, to say the least.

That was, until her eyes fixed on him and she realized he'd been watching her. A stony mask slipped over her lovely face, and it felt to Rafe as if all the heat had been blown from the room on a gust of animosity.

Accepting his fate, Rafe cleared his throat, pressed the door open fully, and entered the room. Pasting a smile upon his face, he asked, "And what are we up to here? Waging a bit of war?"

Victoria turned her eyes down to focus on the child in her arms. She spoke as she adjusted the wrapping more tightly around her. "With May still abed with her cough, I thought I would take Dominic and Faith off of Nan's hands for a spell." Her tone was as chilly as the Thames in winter.

"Victoria thinks the Americans can beat the British," Dom complained with all the righteous indignation of a child convinced of his own knowledge as law.

Rafe smiled regretfully at his nephew. "She is correct in this instance. It happened. Once. And it'll never happen again." He finished it with a cheeky wink and strode over to where Victoria sat on the floor. He crouched down to look into his niece's face to see for himself how she was faring.

He'd spent the better part of the night pacing back and forth with her, striding through the halls of the Townhouse like a lost specter of yore, speaking to her in hushed tones and telling her nonsense tales concocted from sleep-deprived fantasies. The motion and sound of his voice seemed to soothe her somewhat— to calm whatever part of her heart that ached so deeply from the loss of her parents that it refused to allow her any peace or solace. He could have left the inconsolable child to Nan and the wetnurse they also employed to help out in the kitchens, but that felt cruel to Alice's memory, and that was the last thing Rafe ever wished to do. Instead, he habitually took it upon himself to console the child as best he could, listening to tips provided by Nan and the other maids, and making up some techniques along the way. His weeks had been filled with trial and error, but he'd do it for eternity if it meant giving Alice's ghost peace to know her children were well cared for.

While Faith was quiet in Victoria's arms and her eyes were closed in slumber, the child was far from peaceful. Her pert little nose was wrinkled, and her smooth brow was furrowed in discomfort. Rafe's heart ached powerfully at the sight. He stroked a gentle finger along the child's forehead and she relaxed slightly, some of the tension leaving her frail body. If only it were that easy to banish whatever ailed her innocent soul.

VICTORIA WATCHED HER husband intently, taking her opportunity to examine him in such proximity. Even his high cheekbones, the aristocratic slope of his nose, the sensual curve of his mouth, could not detract from just how beleaguered he was. It was irksome how he could remain attractive in such a state. What was worse...he smelled *divine*...like leather and mahogany. She injected steel into her spine and valiantly resisted the urge to sway toward him.

Remember what he said last night, she reminded herself over and over like a fortifying chant.

She turned her attention back to the weary lines bracketing his eyes and mouth. She wasn't vain enough to hope Rafe had lost sleep over her and the argument they'd shared the previous evening. The infant in her arms cooed, and Victoria recalled how Nan had told her he would often check on the babe during the night. Was it possible that was what had happened after Rafe had left her chamber? She did not want to picture him sitting up all hours of the night with the child; she didn't want to feel her heart softening toward him all over again.

How could he do this to her time and time again?

What was it about him that made her do this?

Because, even for all his mistakes and faults, there was a heart beneath the polished façade that was so much more complex than he was given credit for. And, even if he believed himself incapable of love, she just couldn't believe it.

There was no doubt in Victoria's mind that this child and her siblings meant a great deal to Rafe, and, as much as she wanted to loathe him, his heart was not a part of him she could force herself to dislike.

Everything else...well...that was another story entirely.

Seeming to realize where he was and what he was doing, Rafe retreated a step and straightened. "Have you broken your fast?" he asked, his voice deep and rough. Victoria could only nod in reply. "I have not forgotten my promise to you. Would you still care to do some shopping today?" When Victoria hesitated, he heaved a sigh and leaned back in, so Dominic would not overhear. "We do not have to if you do not wish to, but I would like to do this for you." When she remained silent in indecision, his mouth flattened into a line of resignation and he turned to leave.

Just before he quit the room, Victoria piped up—against her better judgment, of course. "I should be ready to leave shortly, just as soon as I have the children settled once more with Nan."

A dramatic groan floated up from where Dominic was sprawled on the nearby floor, and Rafe's attention turned toward the lad. "Unfortunately, it seems as if you are not going to escape your studies for the entire day. Your tutor should be arriving soon anyhow," he said lightly before swiftly stooping and scooping his nephew up beneath his arm like a sack of flour. Victoria couldn't hide her smile when she listened to the boy's giggles as he was carted down the hall and up the stairs to the nursery.

IT DID NOT take Rafe long to regret his offer of shopping. He was rather quickly reminded of the reason he'd avoided it at all costs in the past. In fact, he'd grown quite adept at concocting excuses with no notice whenever a woman attempted to coerce him into escorting her to the shops. He loathed sitting around like a puppy waiting for his mistress's attention.

However, he also knew better than to say anything to that effect as he watched Victoria select new papering for the walls, fabric for draperies and bed hangings, and even furniture for her bedchamber. Biting his tongue was likely the safest thing he could do since his marriage was precarious at best; the disaster of the last forty-eight hours needed to turn around lest it set the tone for the rest of their lives. He didn't think either of them would survive a future beneath such a pall.

So, he did his best to swallow his distaste for the activity and dutifully escorted his wife through one after another of London's premier shops. He had to admit, the speed with which Victoria spent money was astonishing. To place such large and extravagant orders was a new experience for Rafe, who, while he'd always had the relative safety of an old title and credit upon which to fall back when it came to necessities, had been forced to choose a priority rather than spend indiscriminately. He'd needed to decide whether it was more important to spend his limited funds on the image he presented to Society, or an excess of comforts behind closed doors. So, the staff had been whittled down to the bare necessities, unnecessary rooms had been closed up, he'd quietly sold off whatever holdings were not entailed, and he'd opted, instead, to keep up on his outward appearance. Rafe had purchased the best clothing he could afford, kept the most elegant carriage, and maintained a membership at Duke's, the most exclusive gentleman's gambling club. The generations of estate mismanagement had left him in dire straits, and it was a never-ending task to disguise. This shopping excursion was proof that Victoria had never experienced such concerns or deprivation. She was like a fairy who simply had to point at something she enjoyed and knew without a doubt that it would materialize in her home.

Knowing what he did about the increasing number of impoverished peers desperately grasping onto old ways while struggling to maintain unattainable façades, Rafe wondered if women such as his wife were the way of the future for the English aristocracy. In a world gradually beginning to shift away from the old agrarian ways of tenant farmers, ancient titles with undiversified holdings were not accruing the same income they had in prior decades. Rafe was far from the only aristocrat in need of a rich wife, but his needs had been made more immediate by the adoption of his wards. Lord knew Rafe would have been in serious trouble in a matter of weeks had he not convinced Victoria to wed him.

Victoria said little to him as she made her purchases, never once bothering to question a price or haggle with a shopkeeper. In fact, she hardly looked in his direction. At first, he'd been content to watch the sway of her hips, the tilt of her head, the shape of her bosom and arms beneath the blue spencer she'd added to her outfit, but, as pleasing as she was to behold, he found he missed the sound of her voice and the curve of her smile when she did converse with him.

Oh, yes, he'd wounded her.

Of course, Rafe regretted damaging her feelings, but he was unsure how to make things right. What he had said had been the truth.

Theirs had not been a love match.

Victoria may not have known just how much money and dowry had played into his proposal at the time, but neither of them had ever professed to be in love with the other. Her notions of fidelity in such an arrangement were simply unrealistic in today's Society. He could count on a single hand the number of men he knew who were still faithful to their wives. And call him cynical or whatever you would, but those marriages had not been all that long-lived as of yet. He did not wish them ill, but he believed himself a realist. There was plenty of time for both those husbands and wives to seek pleasure outside of their marital beds when the novelty of explosive emotions wore off. He never understood why people prided themselves on honesty, but only when it pertained to the admission of such impermanent and damaging emotions as love. Why was it any less welcome when he attempted to set realistic expectations for the future of his marriage? He'd always felt Victoria was more levelheaded than most Englishwomen, so why had she taken such exception to his words? Love was not in his repertoire. Love was not something to which he ever aspired. He'd only ever seen the wreckage left in the wake of those who claimed to feel love. Even if he believed himself capable of experiencing the emotion, why in God's name would he ever wish to? As he saw it, he was saving both of them a great deal of pain and heartache.

Rafe remained contemplative and complacent as they strolled through the streets, shadowed by their footman who carried the smaller packages and occasionally ducked back to the carriage to deposit them. The rest of the purchases would be delivered directly to the Townhouse later that day or would arrive in the coming weeks, after they had been crafted to Victoria's specifications.

Though she touched him as little as possible, she could not refuse to link her arm with his as he guided her along the street. He had to admit, he enjoyed her nearness more than was reasonable. She was lovely that day—even beautiful. She was effortlessly graceful and elegant, confident in her place, and he found it enchanting.

Suddenly, there was a tug on his arm as Victoria's steps halted in front of a shop. The glass-paned windows presenting displays of children's toys had caught her eye.

"The children have enough toys," Rafe said not unkindly, both because it was the truth and because he, too, had often fallen prey to the desire to bring gifts home to them nearly every day— even when his purse had been pitifully light. "They are quite spoiled," he added as a warning. One area he'd refused to skimp upon was the children's happiness. If he went without fresh beef that week, then he would gladly do so, so they might have new clothes for their ever-growing bodies or a few new toys to bring light back into their eyes.

Victoria stared determinedly through the window, her eyes dancing over the wares with interest. The evidence of her warming up to his nephew and nieces so quickly despite their unconventional meeting did curious things to Rafe's insides. Was that a flutter?

"I think it might be a nice gesture to give them something from me. They've endured enough change in their short lives that I would like to make this transition as simple and as welcoming as possible."

Rafe could not argue with that logic, so he guided his wife into the shop without further protestation. He watched silently as she touched and examined some of the displays, fingered a colorful fabric-covered papier-mâché sphere with a basket suspended beneath it like a balloon he'd once witnessed in Hyde Park. She reverently petted the dark curls on a porcelain doll's head and adjusted another's impractical, pristine white pinafore.

"I thought you said you did not know much about children," Rafe commented idly as she bent at the waist to look into the face of a carved wooden soldier dressed in red wool.

Victoria lifted one shoulder and continued her perusal. "I do not. I have only common sense." A miniature horse cart, complete with mule and driver, caught her eye next. "I longed for comfort and normalcy after my mother passed, and I would have resented anyone who attempted to step in and disrupt it. This might go a long way toward building a bridge between us." Again, Rafe could not argue with the logic. He had never known life with his own mother, and he'd been relieved at his father's passing, so he had never been in the situation Victoria described; however, he could see how it might make sense if one felt a modicum of affection both to and from one's parents—especially as a child. These weeks had not been a comfortable transition for any of the children, like donning a pair of boots cut incorrectly and being told they were meant to fit. He hoped this gesture from Victoria would help ingratiate her with the children and mark the beginning of her finding her niche in his life.

Eventually, Victoria thoughtfully selected a toy for each of the children—a wooden sword for Dom, a new doll for May, and even a silver rattle for Faith. Rafe requested that the shopkeeper have them wrapped and delivered to their address that day, before they exited the shop and stepped back onto the street.

"Dominic is quite high-spirited, is he not?" Victoria mentioned lightly as they resumed their stroll through the crowds.

Rafe scoffed. "That is one way of putting it." His house had been a great deal lonelier without the children, but there had also been a great many more fragile items in one piece.

"Why do you believe that is?"

"Likely because he is only a boy. That is how they are," he

replied matter-of-factly.

She made a thoughtful hum. "I may be wrong, but I wonder if it might be in part because he is hurting and does not know how to express it. He lost both parents less than a year ago, and he is old enough to feel those losses quite keenly. My brother was around his age and suffered similarly after our mother's death."

He'd known Victoria's mother had passed of lung congestion following a particularly bitter winter, but he hadn't considered it as a way to afford her beneficial insight into the children's temperaments, as morbid as that was. He covered her gloved hand with his and applied just enough pressure to reassure her that he heard her and appreciated her opinion. He remained silent and contemplative as they continued walking.

The afternoon began to wane by the time they entered a shop where Victoria might order a few new pairs of warm gloves and have them made in plenty of time for winter. She had nothing in her current wardrobe to carry her through the colder months, and it had been decided that it would be more efficient for her to have most of those items made rather than ship them from America.

While Victoria's hands and fingers were measured by the shopkeeper so a template could be made, Rafe examined a display of buttons and examples of embroidery one might request to have added to his or her order. It was then that an all-too-familiar tittering reached his ears.

A trio of young women was eyeing him from across the length of the display, fluttering lashes and whispering in one another's ears. Coy tilts to their heads and practiced nibbling of lower lips were designed to entice, but they only made him feel a wash of weariness. This display was something he had grown used to over the years—especially after he'd begun garnering a reputation as a charming rake and a fantastic, generous lover. Even women who were afraid he would corrupt them simply by casting a smoldering glance their way were drawn to his magnetic smile and personality.

"Does that happen quite a lot?" Victoria had come up beside him and blatantly gestured to his admirers.

"It does," he replied without conceit and adjusted the ribbon on her bonnet for her.

She glanced at the women and then looked back at him once more. "Why?"

He smiled, careful that it was not one she could interpret as condescending. "You do not place much credence in rumors and reputations, do you?"

"If I had, then I would have listened to my brother and never accepted your proposal," she replied flippantly. The barb stung, but it was softened when she spoke again. "But, for argument's sake, how much should I believe in them?"

He leaned in very close to her ear and said, "It is brave that you still married me, knowing what is said about me. I am either a shameless flirt without morals, or a heartless Lothario, depending upon the source."

She placed a firm hand on his shoulder and pressed him back. Though her face was serious, the crests of her cheeks were growing pinker by the second. "How much is true?" she demanded.

He tilted his head and lifted a shoulder. "Knowing the *ton* as I do and having heard some outrageous whispers myself, probably less than half of what is said. Do not misunderstand me, I am by no means lily-white; I have rightly earned by reputation as a rake, and I am not ashamed of it. I would not insult you by denying who I was before I met you."

She narrowed her eyes at him for a moment before tilting her chin back at the women, who, at that point, were whispering furiously as they attempted to sort out if Victoria was his new American wife or another mistress. "Well, if I wasn't here, which of those women would you have chosen?"

"Victoria…" he said in a low, warning tone. Why did she wish to torture herself?

"Rafe…" she said, mimicking his tone. He knew she was

displeased with him, but that logic did not speak to his eager body. Even her ire was arousing to him.

With a sigh of resignation, he looked the women up and down, which only caused them to blush and titter even more. It did not take him long to provide his wife with an honest answer.

"None of them," he said with finality.

Victoria cocked a disbelieving brow at him.

"They are not to my taste." The words came out flippant, but it was clear they had spurred some possibilities and curiosity behind his wife's eyes.

"And what are those?" she eventually asked. "Your tastes?"

Rafe pretended to give this thoughtful consideration when the answer was already on the tip of his tongue. "Bold," he answered in a sensual rumble. "Elegant. Confident." He paused and cocked a brow at Victoria. "Each of my paramours was those things, if you wish to have the bald truth…but now my wife is all of those things at once." The statement finished with such sincerity that he shocked even himself.

Victoria scoffed lightly, and he recognized in the angle of her slim shoulders that she was preparing to leave him behind. Acting quickly, Rafe cupped her elbow to prevent her from doing so. "I can tell you do not believe me, but I speak with all honesty." He leaned in until his breath stirred a loose curl near the delicate shell of her ear. "You are very different, Victoria. And, for all the money in the world, I would not have married you if you'd been one of those three women across the shop." He didn't think he imagined the minute shiver that traveled the length of her body when his thumb pressed against the pulse on the inside of her arm. "Please believe that I am sorry for wounding you with my comment last evening; I only meant to lay bare the truth."

"This is neither the time nor the place," she hissed tremulously, her eyes scanning their surroundings.

A master of private assignations in public places, he'd already judged how far they were from the shopkeeper and any other customers, and he knew the risks of an eavesdropper were very low. While a few glances were being cast their way, the ladies across the space had finally read Rafe's disinterest and moved on.

"Neither was last night for what I said, but I thought I would keep the trend." This was, by far, one of the least titillating conversations he'd had with a woman, but it was one of the most important. It could not wait if there was any hope for their future.

Victoria nibbled her lower lip in indecision. "I do not understand how you can be so certain that you will never feel more than…a physical attraction in this marriage." Every bit of skin from her hairline to the top of her throat above the embroidered neckline of her spencer turned pink. "You are adamant that you have never and will never feel love; help me understand why that is."

Rafe braced himself for the truth. "Some people are built for deep emotions; I am not one of them." Her brow furrowed, and he turned his body to block her from the rest of the shop. "My entire life, Alice has been the closest I've come to love. In offering you this truth, I saw it as a way we might move forward with proper expectations. I did not mean to insult you by underscoring the fact that ours was not a marriage of love, but I wanted you to be aware that my inability to love was not due to any shortcoming on your part. I never want you to feel as if it is your fault."

"So, it was meant to be a kindness?"

"It was meant to be realistic." His words were flat, but not cruel. He was merely reciting a fact. "You may never have love with me, your husband, but you might eventually find it elsewhere. And I will be happy for you if and when that happens."

Something flickered in her captivating eyes, and it made him pause, his resolve in the rightness of his convictions stuttering ever so slightly. He watched the column of her throat tighten and opened his mouth to speak, but the shopkeeper chose that moment to return with Victoria's receipts. By the time Rafe turned back to his wife, she was already headed out the door and back into the street.

Chapter Fourteen

V ICTORIA AND RAFE received their first visitors after tea that day in the form of Mr. Simon Stratford and his wife, Odette.

"I was sorry to hear your honeymoon trip had been cancelled," said Mrs. Stratford. "We have not had the opportunity to travel further abroad than Edinburough; a holiday on the Continent would be such an adventure."

"I am certain we will find time to plan another someday," Victoria replied with a smile that was less genuine than she hoped. Though she'd tried, she hadn't been able to shake Rafe's earlier words—his admission that love was not something he could feel or even desired to experience—had shaken her. He'd effectively destroyed any hope she might have held that they might one day develop a depth of feeling for one another; she did not know if it was better or worse that he believed it was a kindness to speak so bluntly to her. It was, she supposed, some consolation that he'd made it clear that it was nothing against *her*; it was just how he was. She gave herself a little shake and did her best to focus on their guests rather than the state of her fledgling marriage that had already been tested far too many times. "Besides, you would have to leave your little one behind for far too long. How old did you say Alexandra was?"

"We celebrated her first birthday last month," Mrs. Stratford beamed from the opportunity to discuss her daughter, and then she positively glowed when she turned toward her husband. "It would be rather difficult to leave her, wouldn't it?"

Mr. Stratford made a thoughtful sound of agreement before looking back at Rafe. "Why was your trip cancelled?" he asked bluntly.

Rafe brushed crumbs from his fingertips and set aside the plate Victoria had prepared for him. "Business."

The answer was so far from the truth that Victoria's head whipped around to face him. Could Mr. and Mrs. Stratford be unaware of the children's existence, or did Rafe simply not wish to admit that the reason they'd canceled their trip was due to May's illness?

"Business?" Mrs. Stratford asked; one of her brows lifted in skepticism. "I've never known you to handle business of such import that it would hinder your more enjoyable plans." The words were spoken in a sweet tone, but there was an edge to them. Victoria bit the inside of her cheek and watched the interaction play out.

"Well, dearest Odette, I am a changed man." Rafe sprawled backward negligently, gesturing to the barely suitable room around them. "I am no longer the ne'er-do-well you've come to know and love, but a man who is both a husband and a responsible lord."

Mrs. Stratford gave a little disbelieving shake of her head before she took another sip of her tea. She set it aside and said, "I am certain the *ton* are breathing a collective sigh of relief. After all, you've left a string of broken hearts in your wake—many of them my friends."

"Do you really think it is appropriate to bring this up in front of my wife?" Rafe asked.

This seemed to chasten Mrs. Stratford some, but the blue spark in her eyes did not dim. "Apologies, Lady Blackwood. I am sure this is not the visit you were anticipating. And I *did* promise to try to set aside my differences with the viscount, so this was not particularly sporting of me." She had the good grace to appear abashed.

"Pardon?" Rafe interjected with a small frown. "When did you have that conversation?" His question went unanswered.

"By all means, I am the last one who will support a man who is in the wrong—whether or not I happen to be married to him." She shifted her eyes toward Rafe. "I am under no misconception that he was quite the scoundrel before we were wed." *And it seemed that she was not the only woman who'd been optimistic in her future with him.* She swallowed past the lump in her throat. It was one thing to hear the rumors about Rafe; it was another to be confronted with their fallout.

Mrs. Stratford tapped her fingers on the arm of the chaise. "Very well," she huffed. "I hope that both of you will be able to join us at the theater for the closing performance of 'The Folly of Dreams'." She looked at Rafe. "But know that I am doing so because I quite like your wife and I believe she will be the only woman unwilling to tolerate your antics."

VICTORIA AND RAFE followed the Stratfords to their private box at The Mask & Lyre in the West End. Victoria had been to the location before with her father and brother, but this time was vastly different because it was her first outing with Rafe as husband and wife. She was now the subject of interested stares for a new reason: She was the woman who had brought one of London's most notorious rakes to the altar.

In the carriage on the way to the theater, Mrs. Stratford had explained to her how she'd grown up entrenched in the bustle of the theater. Her mother was one of the principal actresses at the location and regularly drew full houses for her brilliant and moving performances. To say that Victoria's interest had been piqued was an understatement. While she'd already witnessed a few performances during her time in London, it was another experience entirely to say that she had a distant connection to someone in the performance—someone lauded for her talents. She wondered why Mrs. Stratford had never taken up a role on the stage, but she did not have an opportunity to ask.

"If you'd like, I am sure I can arrange for us to visit backstage one of these days," Odette had offered. Then, her eyes flicked to Rafe before she added, "Perhaps, just you and I shall go. There are too many ways to accidentally kill a man with a prop or piece of scenery."

THE PERFORMANCE TAKING place on the candlelit stage below held everyone in the audience rapt…except for Rafe.

He was busy taking advantage of the shadows and his position sitting behind his wife in Simon and Odette's theater box to watch her. Every thoughtful tilt of her head, each time her slim shoulders leaned forward during a moment of tension, the graceful arch of her neck…he'd been held rapt by all of it since she'd descended the stairs dressed in that artful concoction of iridescent sapphire silk. The gown was not one he'd seen on her before—he certainly would have remembered it. The cut accentuated her porcelain bosom and trim figure; a sheer swath of the fabric was draped below her collarbone to draw the eyes, and made Rafe nearly desperate to nibble her just there.

He marveled at how easily she'd charmed Odette, how she'd even managed to wrest a small smile from Simon, how beautiful she was when she was free. This was the first time out that she hadn't been swarmed by a passel of hangers-on and would-be fortune-hunting suitors. Without all those men vying for her attention (and Rafe working to prevent any of them from garnering her favors), Victoria was more relaxed than he'd ever seen her in public.

During intermission, it was everything he could do not to pull her into the rear of their sheltered alcove and taste every inch of her. He didn't know how much longer he could stand being so close to her and not touching her. Unfortunately for him, his friends had impeccable timing.

"I thought I'd heard you'd returned to Town!" Dorian Poole, Marquess of Kempton, said by way of greeting as he entered the private box. He was a tall man with chestnut hair and ice-blue eyes, known for his intense moods and love of expensive horseflesh. A woman dressed in a low-cut gown of navy and black lace was on his arm. Her ebony hair was studded with pearls, and around her neck dangled a sizable sapphire. Kempton was known for being quite generous with his mistresses. Rafe had yet to meet this one, but she had a worldliness about her sultry eyes which, thanks to his years of experience, would have intrigued him enough to inquire as to her availability once his friend moved on to another paramour. That was, if the woman wearing his ring hadn't so thoroughly infiltrated his mind that evening. "I saw you from across the way when the lights came up and couldn't allow the night to pass without gracing you with my presence." He glanced over his shoulder. "Swanleigh and Caro came as well. It was a beast trying to pry them from their home—they've practically become shut-ins."

Kempton greeted the ladies, then warmly extended his hand to Rafe and then Simon. Though Simon was not generally considered a part of their close-knit circle of rakes and hell-raisers (one needed to step away from his books if he was to accomplish anything that would earn him such a title), he was welcomed, regardless, thanks to his long-standing friendship with Rafe.

"You'd heard correctly," Rafe replied and took his opportunity to slip an arm about his wife's waist. She stood there stiffly, though she did not recoil. He decided to take it as a positive. "Unfortunately, we had a change in plans."

"That *is* rather unfortunate," Kempton tsked.

"Such is life," Victoria replied airily just as Odette and Simon politely excused themselves to join another conversation into which they'd been beckoned from the hallway outside their box.

Rafe raised a brow at the fact that she did not reveal the real reason for their canceled trip. She'd questioned him after Simon and Odette had left the other day, wondering why he hadn't divulged to them the true reason for their canceled trip.

"I cannot destroy my image and let Odette know that I would overreact over my niece's health rather than galivant off to the

Continent," he'd replied flippantly, but recognized her skepticism instantly. Sighing, Rafe had admitted that, while Simon and a few select close friends knew of his recent status as guardian to the children, he was uncomfortable revealing just how much he'd allowed his life behind closed doors to change. It wasn't that he resented the children in the slightest; he simply didn't want to invite pitying looks or inquiries into his suitability. Victoria seemed to find that reasoning much more satisfactory and had nodded along with offering a promise to maintain his secrets for as long as he desired. He hadn't expected her to do so with such ease and earnestness.

He wouldn't have minded that she brought up the children—Kempton was among his close friends who knew the circumstances of his guardianship—but what he found most interesting was how she didn't lay the blame at their feet. Nor, as it happened, did she blame *him*. How interesting.

"Marriage seems to suit you both quite well," Kempton complimented them charmingly. "How goes the marital bliss, then?"

"Marital and blissful," Victoria replied with just a dash of wryness in her tone. Rafe was certain only he knew her well enough to pick up on it.

Just then, Odette gestured for Victoria's attention. "Lady Blackwell, I've someone here I wish for you to meet."

Victoria politely excused herself, so Rafe was left with Kempton and his lover, who seemed far more preoccupied with being seen in the private box than taking part in their conversation.

"Now that the wedding is through, I can finally tell you about the betting books," Kempton said, full of nonchalance.

"The what?"

"The books." His friend gave a negligent lift of his shoulder. "You know? The ones with wagers in them?"

"I'm not daft, you tosser." Rafe knew bloody well what books he was discussing. Duke's held extensive records and odds for betting on everything from prizefighting to how long it took a man to wind up drunk in the gutter with his purse missing.

Earlier in the year, there had been wagers about how long it would take for two of their friends, Gideon Bray, Marquess of Swanleigh, and Caroline Wells, to admit to their feelings for one another and marry. Rafe had won that wager. He should have suspected that there would have been bets involving his own marriage. "What were the bets?" he demanded.

Kempton held up his hands in mock defense. "I did not start them."

"But I am certain you partook," Rafe said with a roll of his eyes.

"There were some wagers about whether or not your wedding to Miss Rockford would actually take place. Then there were the spectacular odds that you would be the one to cry off."

Rafe was instantly disgusted. "You realize how vile all of that is, don't you?"

"Come now," Kempton chided, clapping a hand on Rafe's shoulder. "Were it anyone else, you know you would have participated."

Rafe emitted a noncommittal grumble.

"Thank you for the win, by the way. I'll have you know, my faith in you won me a tidy sum."

"Do not pretend at altruism," came the playfully chiding voice of the Marquess of Swanleigh a moment before he clapped Kempton on the back. "You only bet that way because the odds meant the payout would be larger."

"That, I can believe," chuffed Rafe.

"Can you blame me?" Kempton chuckled. Before he could say anything more, his mistress gestured to him and indicated that she wanted to walk about before the intermission concluded.

"She likely wants to be seen on his arm a bit more," muttered Rafe as he watched his friend leave.

"The woman is a bit much," Swanleigh said with a cringe.

"She isn't the one for him, then?"

"Not even close."

The Rank of Rakes had a longstanding consensus that Kempton, for all his easy ways with the fairer sex and thirst for entertainment, was truly the only one in their group who had ever desired a wife. The man had nearly made it down the aisle almost a decade earlier and would have been blissfully wedded to the woman of his dreams had fate not intervened and made a jaded man of him. They'd all watched Kempton spiral into a life of debauchery and pain-honed anger, but none of them was particularly equipped to offer any sort of advice. Instead, they stood by as he went through mistress after mistress and tried to convince everyone that he was managing quite well without the woman to whom he'd given his heart.

"Poor bastard."

Rafe nodded in agreement and then turned his eye toward Victoria's elegant profile. His skin actually tingled when she laughed. Was Kempton the poor bastard for having loved and lost, or was Rafe, for having been locked into marriage with a woman to whom he was drawn with inexplicable force? Which situation was more disastrous?

Rafe was unsure.

FOLLOWING THE FINAL bows, Odette excused both herself and her husband to disappear backstage and offer their congratulations on the well-done performance. "I would invite you to attend, but I fear Lord Blackwood may not make it out alive." She leaned into Victoria and added conspiratorially, "As I mentioned the other day, I do not put it past some of those women to orchestrate an accident for the viscount."

Victoria chuckled and shot Rafe a glance. "I shall keep that in mind. That knowledge may come in handy one day."

"Plotting my demise?" Rafe asked as he tucked Victoria's arm through his and escorted her from the box and into the milling crowd. All around them, bejeweled and perfumed patrons were chatting, blocking the way, and weaving through the throng toward the stairs and their awaiting carriages. It would be at least an hour before they were on their way back home, but Rafe did not mind—not when his wife looked up at him with mischief glittering in her eyes.

"If I tell you, then where will the fun be in the surprise of it all?"

"Leave it to me to marry a murderess," he groaned dramatically, earning another small laugh from Victoria. "You will drop a curtain weight upon my head and flee back to America!"

"Of course not." He could tell she was trying to stifle a smile. "I would ask the opinions of the hordes of ladies you have wronged, and I am certain we will come up with something far more creative than merely bludgeoning you."

He chuckled in response and decided it was time to steer the subject away from his untimely death.

"Did you enjoy the performance?"

"Very much so!" she replied animatedly. "I was impressed with the beauty of the scenery. I wonder how much like an Italian villa it was."

"I've never been, so I cannot comment on the accuracy."

Victoria made a thoughtful sound and then inclined her head to a passing acquaintance. "I think I would like to travel to Italy someday. I read a journal detailing an extensive trip from the southernmost tip to the Alps. The range of climates and terrain, the food, the people, the customs…they all seemed so beautiful and remarkable."

"Perhaps we might travel there in the future," Rafe suggested without thinking. "I do still owe you a honeymoon trip."

The genuine smile she gave him made his stomach perform some unfamiliar acrobatics. God, how he wanted her again…though he sincerely doubted she would welcome his advances. It was still too soon after their arguments, their accord, still too tenuous. He liked to think they understood one another better, but that had not come without its own issues and injuries.

He could appreciate how Victoria didn't wish—nor did she deserve—to live in the shadow of the ghosts of his past. He would not pressure her to open her bed to him and make her feel as if she were merely stepping into a generic role. If he had any hope of a peaceful future, then Victoria needed to be a part of it, one way or another.

Chapter Fifteen

Victoria and Rafe found routine in those early weeks of their marriage. When Rafe wasn't busy meeting with his men of business to secure and delegate the use of his new funds (provided timely by the elder Mr. Rockford, of course), and Victoria wasn't occupied receiving visitors and curiosity seekers, or redecorating the house to her specifications, they spent time with the children.

May had recovered from her illness, and Victoria was quickly introduced to her true, exuberant self. The girl was a whirlwind of dark curls, squealing laughter, and pouting pleas for "just one more game." While Dominic's outbursts and troublemaking weren't eradicated, everyone had admitted that he seemed to be turning into a new lad with Victoria around…and with his uncle's more consistent presence.

Victoria wondered if Rafe had any idea how much his nephew hung upon his every word and action. How he would mimic his speech patterns, his negligently elegant way of moving and standing, the way he narrowed his eyes when he was about to say something serious. It was idolatry at its finest. Witnessing the two of them together was like gaining a window into a younger version of her husband, and watching them was quickly becoming one of her most enjoyable pastimes.

Though he could sometimes be stern in his efforts to provide discipline, Victoria knew Rafe was acting only out of good intentions and trying to do the best he could without a decent example of his own. What tempered it was Rafe's willingness to relax around the children. He would wrestle with Dominic, read stories to May in a multitude of amusing voices, participate in endless games and tea parties, and cuddle with Faith as if it were something he genuinely seemed to enjoy. As she watched him teach his nephew to play a game of cards—the two of them laughing and throwing good-natured verbal jabs—Victoria realized this was such a different side of her husband than Society knew. Before her very eyes, he was feeling out his new identity, and it suited him.

However, whenever Rafe caught her watching, he would temper his behavior. It was almost as if he was embarrassed by his boyish enjoyment of these idyllic moments he'd likely never enjoyed when he'd been a child, himself. For a man who seemed the least self-conscious person alive, it was a fascinating difference to witness. So, lest she ruin the children's time with their uncle, she would often pretend to be very invested in whatever correspondence had arrived that day. That, at least, was not difficult to feign.

It felt to Victoria as if she was constantly fielding the latest influx of correspondence. A steady stream of it had come pouring in since she and her husband had been seen at the theater with the Stratfords. She'd been forced to have their newly-hired butler turn away a great many housecalls until she could perform a hasty and sufficient remodel of the more public rooms of the Townhouse; however, the *ton* was nothing if not resourceful and had resorted to writing and extending invitations. For the most part, this routine was familiar to her; she'd done much of the same when she'd lived with her father and brother. Now that she was entrenched within London Society as "one of them", however, she had more insight into who was genuine and who was merely seeking the latest gossip or tidbit to share at the next event.

In addition to the purchases she'd begun to make, her father had gifted her with some outstanding pieces of furniture. With careful organization and planning, she estimated she would be able to receive more than just Rafe's closest friends in the next week or two after the papering was finished and the fixtures were updated. The repairing, updating, and decorating of the main public rooms was proving to be an enjoyable task—and one she enjoyed, sitting with May as they selected from color samples together.

"Bwue!" May chirped and pointed excitedly at the paper sample Victoria held in her hand. The little girl's penchant for swapping her l's with w's never failed to melt her heart.

"Yes, darling. That is quite a pretty shade of blue, is it not?"

"Finally, something other than pink," Rafe groused as he strode into the drawing room. The furniture had been cleared, and every inch of the space had been cleaned and prepared for new papering and fixtures. Victoria and May sat in a puddle of mint green skirts and ivory pinafore in the center of the polished floor.

"Only one of the rooms has been decorated in pink," she refuted as Rafe stood over them, hands on his lean hips, his powerful thighs level with her eyes made her tongue feel too large for her mouth.

"If that one has her say, then the entire place will be a frothy concoction of pink." He lifted his chin at May, but the glitter in his eyes revealed his mirth.

"Don't say you would deny this little angel anything!" Victoria gasped dramatically and held the giggling girl aloft. "Tell her to her face that you would not paint the world pink just to make her smile."

Rafe narrowed his eyes a moment before he snatched May from Victoria's hands and swung the child in a circle. "She knows I can deny her nothing."

Victoria watched as he pretended to waltz across the room with May held close to his chest, and her heart throbbed with almost painful intensity.

Despite the closeness they were beginning to achieve, their marriage remained guarded and distant. They hadn't shared a bed again since that first night. Despite her ongoing annoyance with him, there was no denying the way her skin tingled whenever Rafe was near; nor could she deny the way she woke up damp and aching almost every night. She craved his touch; she yearned for his taste. Every accidental brush of his hand on hers, each time she caught his intoxicating scent in a room, she would burn anew.

The blasted man.

She was softening to him more and more each day. Watching him prove himself to be caring, responsible, and silly in addition to the glib, charming, witty man she'd come to know…well, that was hazardous to her sensibilities. He was wearing her down without even realizing it.

A few times, Victoria had lain awake wondering how he thought himself incapable of love when he so clearly loved the children—he was, in fact, a big child himself. Could it be that he actually believed himself unworthy of *receiving* that love? Could the scars left behind by his father's rejection have cut him so deeply to shape who he was? She thought it was entirely possible, and it was also entirely fascinating. Whether she wanted him to or not, her husband drew her in, and she knew she was in serious danger of losing her control.

DURING A QUIET period in the early evening while the children were ensconced in the nursery prior to supper, Victoria was attempting to drown that simmering desire in mundane correspondence when she sensed a flurry of activity in the hall. Footfalls and rushed, muted voices passed back and forth outside of the room. The stairs leading to the nursery creaked as they were traversed again and again.

Frowning, she set aside her work and went to see what the fuss was about. As soon as she stepped into the hallway, however, she was nearly knocked to the floor by her husband. A deep line of worry creased his handsome brow; his hair was uncharacteristically mussed and his eyes were wide with concern.

"I've sent for Dr. McCullom," he said hurriedly. "Faith has not eaten, and she will not cease her crying. No one knows what to do anymore; nothing is helping or consoling her." The naked concern was as torturous as a flame being pressed to Victoria's skin.

Without thinking, she grasped Rafe's hand and held it so tightly that both of their knuckles blanched to bone white. "We will go to the nursery and await the physician together."

After that, Rafe did not release her hand for what felt like hours. He clutched her to him as they waited for Dr. McCullom's arrival. He did not relinquish her when the Scottish physician was finally shown into the nursery. He kept her beside him as they stood by and watched his examination of the poor, miserable infant. Each of the pathetic, hoarse cries chipped away at Victoria's heart until she felt less like she was providing support to Rafe than the other way around.

Her husband was proving to be a difficult man to read. Despite the tenseness of his every muscle, he maintained a stoic expression throughout the duration of the physician's visit. Still, she'd come to know him well enough to recognize the flaring of his nostrils, the subtle flexing of his fingers on hers, that his anxiety was steadily growing with each passing minute that McCullom did not provide them with a solution.

"You say she has not eaten?" he asked the nursemaid, a hint of his Scottish brogue evident in his vowels.

"No," Nan said with a vehement shake of her head. "The wetnurse is tending to 'er own infant now or else she'd be 'ere. She said the babe 'as not taken to the teat once today, and not for lack of trying." Worry and fear had deepened the creases around her weary eyes. Victoria had witnessed firsthand how deeply Nan cared for her charges; seeing one of them in such distress must have been agonizing for her.

"Has she been soiling her cloths?"

"Not as frequently."

"And she has been this restless since when?"

"Since after supper last evening."

Victoria was surprised when Rafe answered the last query himself. Had he spent the night helping care for the child? That would explain why she hadn't heard a sound from his bedchamber all evening, why she hadn't seen him all morning, why he looked so weary and worn.

"Is there aught that consoles her?"

"Only when His Lordship carries her," Nan supplied.

McCullom nodded once and began closing up his bag. The child's wails faded to whimpers when Rafe moved forward to place a gentle hand on her abdomen. She was so tiny and his hand so large that it looked as if he could scoop her up as if she were a kitten.

"I fear this may be difficult to hear…" the physician began in a low, gentle tone that immediately alerted Victoria to the dire nature of the news—it was the same tone the physicians had used when they told her family her mother would not recover from her illness. She gripped Rafe's hand even more tightly. "All the medicine in the world cannot help someone who does not possess the will to live—no matter their age." Victoria's breath froze in her lungs, turning into a block of ice in her chest. "There is nothing medically wrong with the child—nothing that I nor any of the other physicians you have hired have been able to find— that would explain her failure to thrive, or why she goes through fits of listlessness and colic. Her unwillingness to explore like every other child of a similar age, or even to take sustenance."

"There must be something that can be done." Rafe's voice was brittle, as if the words were as painful as passing shards of glass through his throat.

"I am sorry." McCullom shook his head with earnest regret. "I wish there were something more that could be done—"

"That is unacceptable," Rafe hissed. He attempted to take a step toward McCullom, but Victoria placed a staying hand in the middle of his chest. It proved instantaneously effective.

"Thank you, Doctor," she interjected. "We appreciate your arrival on such short notice. Please, allow me to show you to the door." She moved to escort him out of the nursery, but it took Rafe several seconds to compose himself enough to finally release her hand. "I will return as soon as I can," she whispered to her husband. The only acknowledgement of her words was a slight tightening around Rafe's mouth. He stared down at his niece as if the intensity of his gaze might transfer to her some of his own will to live.

Throat tight, Victoria turned to join the physician in the dim hallway.

"I know this is not the news you desired, Lady Blackwood; for that, you have my sincerest regrets."

Victoria could only nod in response to his words.

"I would have suggested this to Lord Blackwood, but he is understandably distraught." McCullom stopped walking, forcing Victoria to do the same. His green eyes, brimming with regret and empathy, met hers. "Hold the baby, let her know love. If it is something that brings her comfort, then all the better. It is the best and only thing to do anymore. We have tried every other known medical intervention, but the child has never recovered from the loss of her mother. She is grieving in the only way a child that young knows how."

Burning tears rose to Victoria's eyes, and she nodded. She was so consumed by sorrow over the baby's condition and worry for how Rafe would manage it all that she hardly registered that they'd descended to the foyer. Silently, respectfully, McCullom took his leave. She was in a haze of grief and worry when she returned to the nursery and found Rafe standing above the bassinet, staring down into it as if it held his entire world.

RAFE'S MIND SPUN furiously. He wanted to rail and roar in response to McCullom's pronouncement that his niece was—

No.

He did not want to think the words.

However, that did not stop him from feeling as if he'd failed at yet another thing in his life. Alice had trusted him with her most prized possessions and he'd let her down.

He stared as the inconsolable infant and felt a part of him shatter—a part that had never fully healed after his sister's tragic death.

And now, he'd have to lose this baby, too.

His grip tightened on the edge of the bassinet.

He was so bloody angry at the unfairness of it all. How could this child be made to suffer so much in the wake of losing both her parents? In what sense was that right?

Rafe didn't know how much time had passed, but he looked up at the sound of his wife saying his name. She stood with her hands crossed before her, her knuckles twitching as if she was clenching and unclenching her fingers.

"I am so sorry…" she whispered, and it nearly broke him.

He unleashed a great, whooshing breath he hadn't realized was wedged inside his chest; it ended on a broken sob. His eyes screwed shut, and he desperately strove to regain control.

Bracing himself, he stood a bit straighter even though his body screamed to be allowed to crumple.

Witnessing his struggle, Victoria moved as if to wrap him in her arms, but he held her off with a single croaked word: "Don't." He did not wish to collapse.

She retreated a step and closed her eyes as if she were recovering from a verbal blow. Later, he would appreciate her desire to comfort him and be there for him, but, in the moment, he could not handle having her touch him. He wasn't ready to break. Not yet.

"Would you like me to sit with you?" she offered gently.

Rafe shook his head. "I cannot ask that of you." He could not request that she sit by his side as this innocent life wasted away before their eyes.

"You are not asking; I am offering. And I would like to."

"No, Victoria," he rasped, almost desperate in his determination to remain as strong as he could be given the circumstances.

Several tense minutes of silence passed before his wife finally respected his wishes and she retreated.

Suddenly weak and boneless, Rafe fell into the nearby chair and dropped his head in his hands.

He'd never felt so helpless in all his life.

Chapter Sixteen

VICTORIA COULDN'T SLEEP that night.

The hours following Dr. McCullom's visit dragged on with all the speed of caramelized sugar. Time was slow and sticky, unpleasant in its sheer quantity. Even if she hadn't been able to comprehend it, she respected Rafe's need for distance, and she settled for caring for him from afar. No longer able to concern herself with something as trivial and mundane as correspondence, she spoke to the kitchen staff to ensure food was brought to the nursery. Even when it returned untouched, she knew at least she'd tried.

Much like his niece, she could not force her husband to take sustenance.

She spent the hours following a solitary supper pacing her chamber, moving from the chair to the bed to the window in a random cycle of restlessness. Sleep was impossible with the pall that had been draped over the house after news of Faith's condition had spread throughout the staff. Each time Victoria closed her eyes, she pictured Rafe's raw heartbreak, the tortured helplessness she'd read in his expressive eyes. She would have given anything to take away that pain, to heal the child so wounded by grief that life was more a trial than a gift. Her innards were contorted with sorrow and impotence—if she felt this poorly, then how awful must her husband feel?

When she could stand it no more, Victoria donned her dressing gown and crept up to the nursery. She couldn't stomach the thought of Rafe spending the night standing silent vigil over the babe, solitary in his grief. Whether he wanted her there or not, Victoria cared for the child as well. Faith was her family, too. It was unthinkable that she would not be allowed to offer comfort and love when and where she could.

The door to the nursery was slightly ajar, so she pressed it open on its silent hinges. Watery moonlight streamed through the parted curtains to reveal Dominic and May asleep in their respective miniature beds. May's curls were a wild and unruly creature, obscuring her face as she snored lightly. Dominic had fallen asleep clutching a cherished toy soldier. The exhausted Nan was asleep in her own bed nearby.

What Victoria did not see was her husband.

Or the bassinet.

Heart clogging her throat, Victoria's mind began to run through the worst possibilities. Had something happened to Faith? Why wouldn't Rafe have sent for her if it had? Was he even now weathering the tragedy alone somewhere in the house?

Victoria gathered up the fabric of her nightclothes and dashed back down the stairs, heedless of the noise she made in her haste. She headed toward the first place she could think of to find her husband. She turned the knob to his bedchamber without knocking and opened the door.

There, she found Rafe lying atop his mattress, naked from the waist-up, his skin glowing golden in the warm light from a single low-burning candle and the flickering hearth set into the wall near the foot of the bed. The room was warm, but not uncomfortably so, and it smelled of her husband…woodsy and masculine.

He cradled Faith against his chest with her cheek pressed to his heart. The bassinet was set near the bed. The child was still and silent.

Hearing her enter, Rafe turned his head toward the door and made a small motion with his fingers to bid her to enter quietly. Victoria did so, pressing her fingers to her lips. She felt as if she stood on a precipice between hope and unimaginable sorrow. She almost did not want to ask the question on the tip of her tongue, so she might continue to exist in ignorance. In the end, her need to know won out.

"Is she…?"

"Sleeping," Rafe whispered.

Victoria choked on a sob of relief. She was forced to steady herself with a hand on the back of a chair lest her knees give way completely.

"I did everything I could think of," Rafe explained, his voice even and soft, low and comforting as the steady drum of summer rain upon the roof of a cozy house. "Nothing consoled her. She would not stop crying, so I removed her from the nursery so Nan and the children could sleep. We paced the main floor. I spoke to her. None of it helped. I thought only to bring her here so I might change my shirt, and her hands were so cold." Tears blurred Victoria's vision as she continued to listen. "I stoked the fire and picked her up. Once she felt the warmth of my skin, she calmed down. When she heard my heartbeat, there was a change in her. She even ate a little." He lifted his chin to the pewter bubby-pot and rag on the nearby table. Dr. McCullom had previously offered it as an alternative to assist Faith in obtaining enough sustenance, but he'd also cautioned that the device needed to be thoroughly cleaned after each use because he'd seen far too many infants fall ill. Rafe shifted slightly so he might gaze down at the top of the baby's downy head. Victoria could not force the words through her tight throat, but she knew McCullom had been right—holding the child close had, indeed, helped. "Her skin on mine seemed to buoy her condition the most, so here we are."

The sight of the tiny baby on Rafe's broad chest, watching the infant breathe in the steady, even rhythm of sleep, of finally experiencing a glimmer of hope, made Victoria's tears spill over. She collapsed to her knees at the side of the bed, burying her face in the crook of her elbow as her body poured forth its relief and gratitude. Rafe's large, warm hand took hers; his knuckle stroked her thumb in a gentle motion of comfort and support.

She would gladly accept all of it.

VICTORIA AWOKE IN the warm circle of Rafe's arms. It took her several bleary moments to recognize her surroundings, but, as her senses stirred one by one, she realized where she was and how she had come to be enfolded by her husband's warm body and cradled in his intoxicating scent.

In the wee hours of the morning, she'd drifted off to sleep while holding his hand, sitting as she had been with her head resting upon the mattress beside him. She didn't know how long she'd slept, but her knees had been numb, her neck ached, and no morning light peeked around the edge of the bedchamber's curtains. Stretching her protesting muscles, she'd looked up to find Rafe had drifted off to sleep as well in a half-seated position, propped up with pillows. She'd found it unreasonably charming that he, like his niece, was prone to light snoring. The infant remained still and sleeping on his chest. Rafe's neck had been bent at an awkward angle, but he looked so worn and weary that it hadn't mattered when a relieved sleep finally claimed him.

Not wanting the baby to fall, Victoria rose to her feet and, very carefully, picked up the infant and transferred her to the bassinet beside the bed.

Rafe startled and stirred when he realized the child's slight weight was no longer resting on him, but Victoria had calmed him with a gentle hand to his forehead, her nails combing back his thick, dark locks of hair. When she would have retreated to her own bedchamber, his hand closed tightly around the edge of her dressing gown. Loath to disturb him from his exhausted slumber, she'd very carefully climbed atop the mattress and settled in beside him, curling up against his side and resting her cheek against the deep, steady rhythm of his heart—much like Faith had done. And, also like the babe, the sound had lulled her into a deep, comfortable sleep.

She'd woken that morning with Rafe fitted perfectly against

her back, his even breathing tickling the nape of her neck, his body curled protectively around her. It was warm and secure. Though she was still clothed and he, mostly so, it almost felt more intimate than lovemaking. This was a different sort of vulnerability for both of them.

Victoria indulged in several minutes of simple enjoyment of their situation. He was so solid against her; his arm slung over her waist was pleasantly heavy, his bedding was sinfully soft beneath her cheek, and their closeness suffused her with an unexpected degree of warmth. After the drama of the day before, it was grounding to take the time to pause and simply feel.

What would it be like to wake up each morning like this?

To do so without the barrier of clothing between them?

Unnerved by the turn of her thoughts, Victoria turned her mind to more important things. She should check on the baby. Slowly, she began to try to extricate herself from her husband's grasp. Still sleeping, Rafe protested with a low groan. His arm tightened its hold and pressed her against the length of his body. He buried his face in the nape of her neck. Victoria smiled until she felt the unmistakably hard, persistent throb of his arousal nestled against her rear. Instantaneously, a spark ignited low in her belly; she began to feel her pulse between her thighs. It took everything in her not to press her hips back into him, to reacquaint herself with the impressive size of his member, to beg him to do to her what he'd done all those weeks before—to make her weak and trembling with pleasure, to unleash in her that wild freedom only he could coax from her body and soul.

As he dragged a sleep-languid hand along her side and traced her curves, she was torn between bolting and wanting to see what would happen if she rolled to her back and welcomed him into her arms...if she forgot all the secrets and history between them and moved forward as man and wife.

RAFE WAS ENJOYING the most delicious dream filled with tender curves and the sweet scent of lilac. He made a tentative thrust with his hips and was thrilled when they encountered the soft cushion of a woman's body made for pleasure. His cock throbbed in delight, heat pooling in his loins and growing at a steady rate. It had been so bloody long since he'd had a dream so vivid, felt so content; he intended to take full advantage of the fantasy.

His fist twisted in soft, thin fabric, dragging it up and over the gentle hills and valleys he'd traced. Lithe thighs. Graceful hips. A trim waist. He couldn't wait to explore the wetness between those legs and test the weight of what he suspected were utterly perfect breasts.

A soft gasp made his eyes snap open.

His pulse stuttered.

This was no mere dream or fantasy.

Rafe blinked dazedly as the woman in his bed shot up, her dark hair falling loose and wantonly around her shoulders, as she hastily readjusted her nightrail and dressing gown. She moved so quickly and his mind was so exhausted that it took him a few seconds to decipher the situation.

He was most certainly in his own bed.

The woman scurrying out of his grasp was Victoria.

And he'd been sleeping with her.

Just...sleeping.

Never in his life had he spent the entire night with a woman. He would spend as many hours pleasuring them as they both liked, but, in the end, he'd always retreat to sleep on his own. Always.

He'd always felt the act of sleeping beside one's bed partner to be too intimate, too vulnerable, and it had ever made him feel such a powerful sense of discomfort that he'd avoided it at all costs.

But he'd just woken with his wife in his arms with no recollection of how she'd come to be there, and—he did a mental check of his body and realized he was still wearing his breeches—they had not engaged in intercourse.

He tried to feel disappointment in himself for compromising

on his beliefs—even if it had been subconscious—but he couldn't bring himself to do so. In fact, drinking in the sight of Victoria's flushed cheeks, her drowsy, sleep-leaden eyes, her hair falling free from the plait she'd once worn, Rafe could not entirely recall why he had made that rule for himself in the first place…

His cock twitched, doing everything in its power to convince him to draw Victoria back into his arms, back into his bed, and beneath him. What he wouldn't give to be inside his beautiful wife right then.

Rafe cleared his throat and subtly (or so he hoped) adjusted his breeches to make more room for his rampant crisis.

"Good morning," he muttered, his voice rough from sleep and need.

Victoria made a little sound of acknowledgement but did not provide much more in the way of a reply. Then, he caught sight of Faith's bassinet around Victoria's shoulder.

All at once, the previous night returned to him with all the force of a landslide. He remembered attempting to console his niece for hours, fully expecting her to waste away before his eyes. While most men might have turned to God in the pits of despair and grief, Rafe was not a religious man. Instead, he'd prayed to his sister.

For hours, he'd paced and walked, alternating speaking to the whimpering baby in his arms and the sister who had so unfairly and unwillingly left her behind. He'd begged for guidance, assistance, and then mercy as the night wore on—anything to give the baby some relief. Placing her on his chest had been like a balm to her soul-deep wounds. She'd calmed enough to eat. The rhythm of his heart had lulled her into sleep like nothing else had in days, if not weeks. And slept, she had. It was nothing short of a miracle. Rafe could hardly recall a time when he'd seen her so peaceful; he could have wept with relief. In fact, a tear or two may have escaped his eyes when Victoria held his hand.

He remembered his wife arriving in his rooms, her tears when she found out the baby was showing signs of improvement.

Her genuine joy and relief had touched him deep, deep inside, moving him in a way he hadn't known was possible. Her reaction had been more than someone grateful for another life; it was that of someone who cared deeply for another. His body had ached to hold her, but he'd had to settle for taking her hand in his and hoping it would convey his gratitude and everything else he was incapable of putting into words.

Now that he knew she'd remained beside him throughout night…he was moved all over again. His niece was not her child or her blood—not to mention, Rafe had made an ass of himself as of late. Still, she'd remained.

He tried not to read too much into it.

"How is the baby?" he asked instead.

Victoria's shoulders seemed to slump with relief when the focus shifted from her and the fact that they'd woken in one another's arms. She peered into the bassinet. "Still sleeping soundly," she whispered after a few heartbeats of observation. "I can take her and ring for Nan and the wetnurse. She should probably eat again, and you can get some more rest."

Rafe declined her offer with an immediate shake of his head; he doubted he'd be able to sleep with the memory of his wife's curves still lingering on his fingertips. "I will rise and send a note for McCullom if she eats again. He will want to know of her condition."

Victoria nodded and stood, holding her dressing gown tightly around her body like a shield as she turned to retreat to the door and, likely, the safety and privacy of her chambers.

"Thank you," Rafe said gently. "Thank you for staying with me."

To his surprise, Victoria halted her steps and offered him a small smile. "Of course."

"You did not have to remain all night."

"Whyever not?" she asked with a frown.

"She is not your family, and I do not wish for you to feel obligated to care for her and her siblings as you do, but

I…appreciate it. Sincerely."

Was he mistaken, or was that an amused tilt to one side of her lips? "As far as I am concerned, we all became one family the moment our marriage was finalized. Your wards are now mine. I have and will continue to treat them as such, and nothing will convince me otherwise. The children have been through enough already. I am determined to show each of them that love and stability remain in this world. Now, if you'll excuse me, I am going to speak with Nan and prepare for the day."

As she finally left, Rafe stared after her and wondered at the woman he'd married.

Chapter Seventeen

MUCH TO VICTORIA'S relief, Faith began to eat with greater frequency in the coming days. Though she still suffered from fits of colic, she calmed when held close to Rafe's chest. He seemed to be the only one able to comfort her in her worst moments.

Victoria secretly loved watching that large man carry that tiny baby against the broad expanse of his chest. Often, he carted her from room to room throughout the better part of the day, even writing letters with her securely nestled against him. She suspected his arms had become so used to holding her that he sometimes forgot he was toting her around; she'd become another part of him.

Bit by bit, the color returned to the child's cheeks. When McCullom visited twice since that first morning after Victoria had woken in her husband's arms, the physician seemed hopeful—if still cautious. He recommended the continued comfort and physical contact with the babe, stating he'd taken the liberty of corresponding with a few colleagues and all agreed that such action likely served to provide the child security when she floundered.

"She has improved, there is no denying it," McCullom said one afternoon after examining the baby. Her cheeks had begun to fill out somewhat and take on the pleasant plumpness one expected from a child her age. She was becoming more interactive and attentive to her surroundings, which were both very good signs, according to the physician. "Should your schedule allow, I might suggest taking some fresh air in the country if she continues to increase in stability and strength. A stay away from the thick London air could further her progress. A change in scenery might entice her to try to explore, to learn to crawl, and eventually attempt to walk."

This sparked a light in her husband's eyes, the likes of which she'd not witnessed before. He appeared almost boyish in his hopeful exuberance, and it was infectious. He'd looked at her after McCullom took his leave; it was clear he was trying to maintain his composure, but the emotions were welling up inside of him.

"Did you hear that? She is doing well," he said with a grin so broad it was almost comical.

"Yes, I was standing right beside you," Victoria replied, unable to completely stifle her giggle.

"What do you think?"

"About?"

"A stay in the country."

"You desire my opinion on the recommendation?" She had been unprepared for him to do so, as if she had an equal say in the well-being of their household—a group of people slowly beginning to feel more and more like a family.

"Of course. Why wouldn't I?" His tone was incredulous, as if he'd not once considered *not* asking after her thoughts. Whether or not his aim was intentional, it made Victoria feel like a partner in their marriage. It was also another example of how something in him had switched since the morning she'd woken in his arms, as if he'd slowly realized that he no longer had to shoulder every decision, every hardship, alone. That he did not have to be the only one who cared. He couldn't have known how much that meant to her; it felt as if she was being allowed into her proper role. She felt appreciated. She felt respected.

Victoria swallowed hard. "I think it is a brilliant idea."

So, together, they agreed to rent a country house in Kent where he knew some of the families in the area. In fact, Mr. Stratford's family's country seat was only a few miles away from the house they and the solicitors selected for their stay. The home itself was chosen carefully. Though funds were no longer an issue, neither of them felt the need to waste the money and effort to rent out and staff a grand estate.

Rafe desired just enough space for a small loyal staff in addition to them and the children.

Victoria requested enough land for the children to roam and explore freely, perhaps some gardens where May might pick some flowers, and a pond where Dominic might learn how to fish.

They both felt it would likely be beneficial to all the children to take the country air and enjoy the freedom. London had parks, but they were not the same as being outside the city's boundaries.

In the end, they selected a property called The Cottage, though its dimensions lent themselves more to a small Tudor-era estate than a quaint cottage. Four bedchambers and plenty of property for outdoor air, bordered by sheep fields and a manmade fishing pond that was stocked each season, meant all of the requirements were met.

With McCullom's final approval of Faith's health, the household was packed up, and they traveled to Kent.

The children, unaware of the catalyst, were thrilled to have a holiday. Rafe had confided, somewhat abashedly, that the children had not left London since coming into his care. As a bachelor, he'd had little reason to abandon the delights and entertainments of the city.

"And there had been the little matter of your need to find a wealthy bride," Victoria had added drily, not thinking about the words before they sprang from her lips. She'd been distracted by selecting some reading materials from what remained of the sparse Blackwood library. Her eyes flew to Rafe. She hadn't meant the words maliciously; her irreverent sense of humor had merely slipped out. She'd spent the better part of the previous weeks considering that there were more important things than worrying about how her marriage had come to be and feeling sorry for herself. She was well and truly wedded, she was quickly falling in love with the children, and she was quite liking the new sides to Rafe she was experiencing. He'd married her for her fortune, but she didn't think even he was as good an actor as to continue to perpetuate a façade in even his most vulnerable moments. They enjoyed each other's company.

Following her assertion, two terrible, tense heartbeats passed where she and Rafe merely stared at one another.

Then, he laughed.

Any remaining strain left his beautiful face and his bark of laughter was like music to her ears, lightening the air in a house that had been too long fraught with unease. She was relieved that he hadn't interpreted what she'd said as a snipe.

"I suppose that is the truth of it," he replied with a smile. "There aren't many heiresses frolicking through the Kentish sheep fields." He closed the space between them until his front was so close to her back that Victoria could feel the warmth radiating from his skin. He stretched up and plucked the book she'd been eyeing from the shelf just out of reach above her head before dangling it before her face. He leaned forward until his cheek was nearly pressed to hers and murmured, "Irreverent minx." He dropped the book into her hands and stepped away. "We leave in two hours; will you be prepared by then?"

Victoria's skin rotated through a cycle of heat and chills; she was rendered mute, and all she could do to reply was execute a jerky nod.

She was still trying to compose herself when the butler arrived bearing a sealed letter for her. Handing him her selection of books and requesting that they be added to the luggage that had yet to make its way to Kent, she accepted the letter and was pleased to recognize her brother's bold handwriting.

She'd previously written to her father and brother advising

them of their movement and her hope that she would see them in person again before her father's return to America. In reply, Luke had reassured her that their father would not leave without saying his goodbyes in person. As it happened, Luke would also be traveling in the vicinity of their rented home on his way to the southern coast for a meeting. Without a moment's hesitation, she dashed off to her rooms to pen a hasty reply. Knowing her brother, he was deeply entrenched in work and she'd likely not receive a reply by the time they departed for the country—the letter she held in her hands was already in response to a note she'd sent him days earlier. She scrawled a hasty invitation for him to join them at The Cottage, telling herself that Rafe would not mind.

She looked forward to showing Luke how her life had evolved, of proving to him that—despite its bumps—her marriage was working out. She was also excited for him to meet the children. Purposefully omitting their existence from her note, she did not wish for Luke to draw any unfavorable conclusions before meeting them in person and hearing their story from her mouth. She finished her message telling Luke that, though she missed him terribly, she knew business would come before all else with him. If his schedule permitted, she hoped they might at least have a short visit because he was long overdue for a bit of needling from his younger sister.

"IT'S AS PRETTY as a painting!" Victoria sighed in pleasure as Rafe helped her down from their coach. Her blue eyes were wide with joy and wonder as she drank in the sight of their rented country home for the next couple of months.

It had been a long while since Rafe had traveled this far outside of London—not only because he hadn't had the need to, but also because he hadn't had the funds to do so. As they'd strayed further from the city, he'd been reminded of how beautiful bucolic scenery might be. The colors were astonishingly vivid, the air was noticeably clearer, and the excited chatter of May and

Dominic was as infectious as their heightened spirits when they pressed their faces to the small carriage windows and drank in the passing scenery.

The bulk of their luggage had been sent ahead of them so the house might be prepared for their arrival. Rather than travel with Nan and the other servants, Victoria had suggested keeping the children in their coach for the duration of the journey. This had resulted in two crying tantrums from May, one unfortunate mess from Faith, ceaseless questions and movements from Dominic, and hearing the phrase, "How much longer?" no less than three dozen times.

It had also provided the opportunity for a great deal of laughter, guessing games, riddles, and blissfully silent naps, during which Rafe suspected he'd been caught staring at his wife. When the carriage fell silent, it was difficult not to be drawn to the domesticity of the scene before him, with Victoria cradling Faith in her arms and running her fingers through May's mop of curls as she slept cushioned by a pile of her teal traveling skirts. As they'd swayed gently with the motion of the carriage, Rafe had been hard pressed to look anywhere but at Victoria. He could have watched her care for and adore the children for hours on end, examining the way the afternoon sunlight cast golden streaks and unexpected flares of red in her ebony hair, the curve of her full lower lip as she smiled down at the sleeping girls.

This strange phenomenon, where he froze and simply stared at her, had happened with increasing frequency. He'd been attracted to women before, drawn to them, entranced with them, but those had been but fleeting moments...waylays in his meandering existence. This felt somehow different. Perhaps because the scenes playing out in his household were so unfamiliar to him. Not only because he was still growing accustomed to having a wife and children, but because of how they all interacted with one another.

While he could still be standoffish and brimming with trouble, even Dominic had warmed to Victoria's efforts. She never grew weary of his barrage of questions about her sea voyage from America, about what her life was like in her homeland, whether the borders of civilization were really as wild and untamed as the stories said they were. She was always keen to cradle Faith, and he'd found her on several occasions just speaking to the child of stories and anecdotes from her childhood in Boston. With May, she was never too busy to host a pretend dinner party attended by only the most cherished of dolls and toys, or to spend an hour or two practicing drawing with pencils and paint. Rafe was often asked to judge the outcomes of their artistic endeavors, and he hadn't the heart to tell his wife that she was no more skilled than May.

Never had Rafe been exposed to such quaintness.

In fact, he hadn't even realized such a thing was possible.

The first time he'd experienced that thought, he'd felt supremely disloyal to Alice. His sister had done the best she could with him, but she'd been a girl who had lost her mother, too, and they'd both lived beneath a man who'd turned frigid with the pain of loss. By the time Rafe had been Dominic's age, Alice was out in the world experiencing Society and finding her own place. Gradually, warmth had seeped from Rafe's life, through no malicious fault of Alice. He could hardly fault his sister for seeking out her own joy.

But, in a few short weeks of marriage with Victoria, Rafe had begun to feel his world warm once again. Like the early morning hours in the height of summer, he could sense the potential for heat the likes of which he'd never known.

It made his skin tingle in anticipation.

"I must agree with that assessment. It is pretty," Rafe replied, continuing to hold onto Victoria's hand even though she'd successfully descended to the crushed gravel drive. He joined her in gazing up at the impressive façade. The two-story building had been constructed from heavy timbers and bleached plaster, a slate roof in excellent repair shone silver in the sunlight. The leaded windows consisted of an artful arrangement of dozens of smaller diamond-shaped panes, lending an air of charm and whimsy to the architecture. Hundreds of years prior, skilled hands had built this home to last, and it was a sight to behold. Manicured gardens flanked the courtyard and sides of the house, so rich and full of blooms that Rafe could smell roses mixed with other unidentifiable, heady floral scents drifting on the breeze. In the distance, rolling green hills flowed like the undulating waves off the coast.

Nan had immediately swept the bouncing children away to stretch their legs, have something to eat, and then explore. Forgotten in the wake of their excitement, Rafe and Victoria were left alone in the drive while the last of their belongings were unloaded and carried inside.

Rafe heaved a sigh of relief. "It is a relief to have some peace after that journey," he said. "Now I know why people usually send their children in another carriage."

Victoria swatted gently at his chest with the back of her hand. "Do not be such a grouch," she chastised him lightly.

He caught her hand before she could pull it back. Even through their gloves, his skin tingled from the contact, the sensation of having her delicate fingers in his. He couldn't resist raising her hand, inhaling her scent, and pressing a kiss to her knuckles. He savored the widening of her eyes and the barely perceptible catch in her breathing. He liked knowing she wasn't as impervious to him as she pretended.

"Shall we explore the grounds? Become acquainted with our home for the time being?"

Victoria only nodded mutely and he escorted her up the pair of steps and into the house. Was it his imagination, or was there a hint of color cresting her cheeks? The corner of his mouth lifted in a self-satisfied smile, but he had to quell his drifting thoughts lest he become too excited by the prospect of tasting the lower lip she was busy nibbling.

After handing off their hats and gloves to the waiting butler who had come with the house as part of its permanent staff, Rafe and Victoria began to wander the home. A close dining room with dark paneling offered a long table with carved wooden chairs. Twelve could be comfortably seated there for a dinner party, though they had no immediate plans to entertain.

The parlor was cozy, and the tall, narrow windows offered views of the distant verdant fields. The kitchens were situated in the back of the house in a stone building nestled against the same lush vegetable and herb gardens that had likely been supplying the residents with sustenance since the home had been built.

There was no dedicated nursery, but the second floor of the home had ample bedchambers to accommodate Rafe, Victoria, the children, and their caretakers. Nan had already settled them into the room on the far eastern corner. Not as big as the lord's chamber, it was still well-sized for a home of that age. Dominic and May would share the oversized bed, and Nan would occupy a cot that had been brought in, and Faith would sleep in the bassinet they'd toted from London.

Finally, Rafe and Victoria made their way toward the Western side of The Cottage and the rooms which had been prepared for their own use. Rafe watched as his wife wandered the room containing her belongings. The bedframe was surprisingly large for the narrowness of the mattress; the entire thing was dwarfed by the thick curtains draping from the ceiling to hang around it. A trio of small windows admitted warm late afternoon light, making the polished wood paneling glimmer with golden light.

"Is everything to your satisfaction?" Rafe asked, but the question was more a way to distract himself from admiring the trimness of her figure and her graceful movements, the way her fingertips stroked the fabric of the coverlet as if to test its texture.

"It will do quite nicely," she replied with a genuine smile.

He wanted her to invite him to stay with her.

He wanted her to join him in his bedchamber.

He wanted her to walk into his arms and hold him with the same care and devotion she showed the children.

But none of that happened.

Rafe nodded. "Very good," he said stiffly. "I'm sure we are all fatigued from traveling. Perhaps supper in our rooms is in order."

A hint of surprise shone in her wide eyes, but it was masked quickly. Before she could respond, Rafe forced himself to turn on his heel and cross the hallway to the final bedchamber and shut himself away.

Leaning back against the door and closing his eyes did nothing to erase the knowledge of just how tantalizingly close Victoria was.

Chapter Eighteen

V ICTORIA TOOK A detour through the kitchen gardens after speaking to the cook about that evening's meal. She was determined that Dominic's ninth birthday supper would consist of all his favorite foods, bountiful desserts, and a special surprise. The idea had been planted in her mind weeks earlier, but now she had an excuse to act upon it. Following a day filled with all the outdoor adventures a boy could imagine, presents hidden away in trunks carried from London, and lovingly crafted decorations she and the staff had made from patterned wallpaper remnants, Dominic would join her and Rafe for a meal in the dining room.

Indeed, it had been confirmed to Victoria that children did not typically join adults at the dinner table, but he really had been remarkably well-behaved as of late, and it was his birthday, besides. What better way to celebrate than to make him feel special and grown up?

She hadn't bothered asking Rafe's permission for her plan, but it was less out of fear that he would naysay it, and more so because she enjoyed keeping her own confidence and witnessing the reactions. She wanted to believe her husband would welcome the change on this special occasion and bend tradition for his nephew's sake.

She hoped Rafe would not prove her wrong.

Victoria was so lost in her plans that she did not realize she was no longer alone until she nearly collided with Rafe at the end of a row of turnips. The solid wall of male muscle was as immovable as the ancient garden boarder. She would have fallen back to her rear had his hands not caught her shoulders and steadied her.

"That must have been quite the wool you were gathering." Rafe's chuckle sent a thrill of awareness dancing from the head to her toes and then settled beneath the warmth of his hands on her. "I said your name twice as I approached. I did not mean to catch you unaware."

"I—I did not hear you," she stammered lamely.

"So I've learned." His smirk was maddeningly attractive.

Victoria gave herself a little shake, but it was ineffective at resetting her equilibrium because he had yet to release her shoulders. "Is there something you needed?"

"I was going to invite you for a walk, but I can see you're already enjoying one. Unless I can convince you to prolong your outing?"

The tilt of his head.

The glitter in his eye.

That blasted charming lock of dark hair falling across his forehead.

The closeness of his warmth.

The woodsy scent.

Those hands on her shoulders.

The thumbs gently stroking her collarbone.

How could she resist?

"I might."

The pleased grin he gave her weakened her knees so swiftly, they might have buckled completely had he not been so swift and smooth in pulling her arm through his and tugging her into motion.

"I did not realize you had such an interest in vegetables," he remarked, toeing a drooping cabbage leaf out of their path.

"It's less about the gardens and more about the fresh air. I was waylaid on my way back from the kitchens," she explained.

"The weather seemed far too fair not to enjoy."

"And you decided to walk amongst the peas and the…what are those?"

"I believe they are onions."

Rafe eyed the tall green stalks dubiously and, seeming to come to terms with her statement, made a thoughtful sound, and they continued on their way. "So, a walk amongst the peas and onions was the perfect thing for a day such as this?"

Victoria plucked a pod from the vine and shelled it, popping one of the sun-warmed peas between her lips. It burst with sweetness, reminding her of summers in her grandmother's kitchen. "Flower gardens are lovely, but a treat while you stroll is so much better." She held up another pea between her thumb and forefinger. Rafe's eyes flicked between the pea and her face until he finally registered what she was offering. His lips parted, and she popped the pea between his lips. A gasp escaped her throat when his teeth grazed the pad of her finger. Somehow, an invisible string was drawn directly from her finger to the spot between her thighs that suddenly began to throb with every beat of her heart.

"It's a shame that strawberries aren't in season," Rafe murmured. Victoria was unable to tear her eyes away from his lips. "They're much more satisfying to feed to your lover than shelled peas."

Victoria's cheeks caught fire and she resumed walking, inadvertently tugging him along with her as she did so. She cleared her throat and determinedly changed the subject. "How did Dominic enjoy fishing?" Rafe had spent the middle of the day with his nephew at the fishing pond. The groundskeeper had provided all the necessary equipment for a day of angling, much to the lad's excitement. Victoria had helped the cook organize a picnic of sorts for them to enjoy while they were on their outing.

"I learned something quite interesting," he replied drily.

"Oh?"

"I am quite atrocious at catching fish."

An unladylike bark of laughter burst free from Victoria. She couldn't help it—she hadn't expected that declaration. "I was under the impression that you were going to be a sufficient tutor."

"Apparently not."

"So your over-inflated sense of masculine confidence proved faulty then?"

Rafe narrowed his eyes at her. "I've done it a few times. How difficult could it be to show someone else?"

"Too difficult, apparently," Victoria sniggered.

"It takes a great deal more patience than I remember," he groused.

"Exactly how long has it been since you last went fishing?"

He lifted his head toward the sky and squinted his eyes in thought. "Kempton and Brinley dragged me along because they hadn't believed my father had never taken me. I think it was before University."

"So at least a decade ago?" She laughed incredulously. "Whyever did you believe that qualified you to teach Dominic?"

"Listen here, you little minx…" Abruptly, he turned her and caged her body with his against the stone wall of the gardens. Victoria hadn't realized they'd traversed the length of the garden and exited the grounds protected by a wall that reached just over her head. With Rafe craning his neck and leaning into her as he was, both of them would have been hidden from view of the kitchens and any of the rear-facing windows in The Cottage. "I've had just about enough of your teasing," Rafe said. His voice was a low rumble that reverberated through his chest, across the scant space between them, and into hers. It sank into her heart, her lungs, her blood, her very bones. She might have been intimidated by his size were it not for that mischievous glimmer in his eyes. Despite his words, he was enjoying her teasing…and he was teasing her back.

"I wouldn't tease if there wasn't an occasion for it," she replied, only slightly breathlessly.

"Oh?" His silken tone made her skin prickle with awareness. His face was so close to hers; his body, so intoxicatingly near. She felt his knee and thigh brushing the fabric between her legs. If she tilted her pelvis even a little, he would be pressed against the damp, sensitive flesh screaming for his attention.

The demanding ache had only grown worse with every brush of his hand on hers, every tender moment she witnessed between him and his wards, each smile he shared with her. If Victoria were honest with herself, she would admit that her physical desire for her husband had never wavered since their wedding night; if anything, it had simmered beneath the surface, growing stronger with each new piece she learned about him, and bided its time until just such a moment when they were alone…and he had her at his mercy. She pressed her palms into the weathered stone wall at her back, cursing its lack of purchase after the surface had been worn smooth from centuries of nature.

"I used to fish every summer," she said a little hoarsely. "I am confident that Dominic would flourish beneath my instruction."

"You think you know more than I do?" he asked, not unkindly. He was continuing their game.

"At least in this regard." Her breath hitched when his nose grazed her cheek. Was he smelling her?

No.

Scenting her was a better description of his deep, slow inhalation—like a hound and his ill-fated prey. Her body trembled in anticipation rather than fear.

How many nights had she lain awake wondering what it would feel like to have Rafe devour her again? To make her world shatter into a million glittering pieces, only to put her back together and do it all again…and again…?

Nearly every night since their wedding.

Whether she wished him to or not, her husband visited her nearly every waking and sleeping thought. He'd charmed his way back past the rudimentary defenses she'd rebuilt since learning of his steadfast aversion to allowing deeper emotions between them.

The rake had that way about him, and Victoria could well see how so many members of London Society were consistently won over by him.

"S—Surely, there are a great many things you might teach me, even if fishing is not one of them," she finally added.

She watched as the black of his pupils nearly swallowed the deep, striated blue of his irises entirely. The flaring of his nostrils and parting of his perfectly formed lips were evidence of his interest in her words. Though she hadn't meant the words solely as an entendre, she'd deeply intrigued him.

"I am certain…" he began and paused before starting again. "I am certain you are correct in that regard, Victoria." He bent his head and ran his parted lips along the column of her throat so gently it felt as if a butterfly's wings had left gooseflesh in their wake. She wanted to hear him say her name in that deep, husky tone at least once a day for the rest of her life. "And, should you desire it, you need only ask, and I will gladly tutor you in any subject you deem fit." His teeth caught the lobe of her ear for only a moment, sending a jolt of pain-laced pleasure arcing through her. It was done so swiftly that she almost believed she'd imagined it.

Victoria had been so lost in Rafe's words that she hadn't realized her eyes had slid closed until they fluttered open, nor was she aware that her hands had moved from the wall behind her until she had to force them to release their white-knuckled grip on the navy-blue lapels of Rafe's coat. She hastily wiped her damp palms on her butter-yellow skirts and forced herself to take a bracing breath of country air. Unfortunately for her, it was tinged with more than a hint of Rafe's masculine scent. She nearly whimpered from weakness.

And, of course, Rafe could see how he affected her.

Without any regard for her aching body or her pudding-soft knees, he tugged her arm through his once more and practically dragged her into motion. He guided her back onto the worn dirt path leading from the back gate of the kitchen gardens toward the fields sprinkled with blue and white wildflowers she could not name.

"Where are we going?" Victoria demanded weakly, still more than a little off kilter from the abrupt shift in tone and activity.

"I thought we were taking a walk?" he asked, feigning surprise. "Were we meant to do something else?" He turned his head to look at her, and she felt the suggestive caress of his gaze as tangibly as if he'd run his large hands over every inch of her naked body.

"No. Well, yes. I mean—" Victoria released a puff of frustration through pursed lips. "Yes, we are walking together."

He nodded decisively. "Very good. I believe we should have ample time to reach the distant sheep field and return before we need to prepare for supper."

She stepped on a pebble and winced as it bit through the thin soles of her slippers. "I am hardly wearing the proper shoes for such an outing such as that. Had you given me notice, I might have changed."

"I much prefer spontaneity." He was so lighthearted and cheery—so different from the velvety seductiveness she'd so recently experienced from him. "Besides, I shall carry you if you require it."

She laughed again. "Carry me? All that way?"

"My dear, I would carry you to the moon and back if you asked it of me."

Victoria's eyes flew to her husband, but he offered her only his impassive profile.

Do not read too much into what he said, she reminded herself. *He is a habitual charmer.*

And, while his intentions may not have been malicious in the least, she did not doubt that such sweet and solicitous words often passed his lips without a second thought. It was in his nature to flirt. That did not mean he felt anything deeper than friendly affection and physical attraction.

It did not.

It did not.

It did not…

Chapter Nineteen

RAFE WAS STILL mulling over his unthinking comment to Victoria in the kitchen gardens when he descended the stairs for supper that evening. Whatever had possessed him to make such a fanciful offer? Furthermore, why had he meant the absurd declaration?

She addled him.

He'd spent far too long pining after, contemplating all the ways he found her attractive, pricking his ears waiting for just the sound of her laughter. And all without ever again enjoying the heaven that was her body.

He had, indeed, dragged her on that ill-advised walk that afternoon, though they hadn't made it nearly as far as he'd intended before Victoria's slippers began to trouble her. In truth, he'd had no desire to explore the expansive fields surrounding The Cottage and had only wanted to expend some of the energy she ignited within him.

He could have gladly taken her right there against the kitchen garden wall—just hiked up her skirts, pulled her leg over his hip, and thrust into her until they were both screaming in release— but he'd managed to hold himself in check. Barely. He'd reminded himself that that was how a man treated his mistress, not his wife…unless she asked for it.

The instantaneous image of Victoria begging him for just such treatment was quite possibly one of the most erotic imaginings of his life, and Rafe had had more than his fair share of them.

Victoria hadn't complained about the walk; however, as soon as he saw a hitch in her gait, he was true to his word and immediately scooped her into his arms. With an about-face turn, they headed back the way they'd come, and he steadfastly ignored every one of his wife's protests that she was fine and more than capable of returning home under her own power.

"I do not doubt your determination in the slightest," he'd replied, trying his best not to become overly excited by the feel of her wrapping her arms around his neck and pressing her body more closely to his where he held her high against his chest. "But I'll not be accused of abuse when you are unable to walk properly for the next few days." There were far more pleasurable ways to hinder a woman's ability to walk comfortably. Or sit. Or ride a horse.

He'd barely stifled a groan at the possibilities.

Once back at The Cottage, they'd gone their separate ways to bathe and prepare for the evening meal. Rafe may or may not have taken advantage of the solitary time to abuse himself to his mind's creative images of Victoria... Who was he fooling? Of course he had pumped into his tight fist until the image of his wife's parted lips and passion-glazed eyes sent him over the edge.

All pleasant musings evaporated as soon as he entered the dining room and saw not only Victoria, but Dominic already seated and waiting for him. The sight of his nephew wearing his best clothing and seated across from Victoria was so unexpected that his steps stuttered.

The boy turned to him, his face utterly beaming with pride. His smile was so wide that it revealed the tooth in the side of his mouth that had come loose only the week before. His clothing was a perfect miniature replica of what Rafe wore—a dark coat, a patterned brown waistcoat, breeches, and a starched white cravat knotted simply beneath his chin. Even his shoes—the ones Victoria had purchased for him shortly after their first meeting—

were polished to an impeccable shine. He was turned out in the highest of fashion for someone his age, and Rafe was confused.

"What is going on here?" he finally asked, looking between his nephew and his wife. Unfortunately, this caused his attention to snag on the vision that was Victoria. She was dressed in a sky-blue gown more suited for a ballroom than a quiet supper at home. The cut exposed the delicate curve of her shoulders, a tantalizing hint of her decolletage lifted to delectable perfection, and accentuated the trimness of her form. Gems glittered at her ears and were draped from her throat, cascading in a waterfall to her cleavage. She was clothed to stun and impress.

His mouth went dry so suddenly and so fiercely that he could not form a protest when Victoria stood, made a quick excuse to Dominic, and wrenched Rafe from the room. She whirled on him as soon as they were out in the hallway, but he could think of nothing past the gorgeous contrast between her ivory skin and sable hair.

"This is the country," Victoria began in a low hiss. "I thought the setting would be informal enough that it would not be an issue if I invited Dominic to join us at the table for supper."

He could not form another thought beyond, "Children do not usually dine with adults." He knew it was inane, but how could he possibly concoct anything more coherent with her looking as beautiful as she did?

She pursed her lips and made a rather rude sound so incongruous with her elegant appearance that he actually jumped. "It is his birthday," she whispered more loudly. "And the boy desires nothing above being just like his uncle. Do not shatter his joy by sending him away. If you do, so help me—"

"Very well!" Rafe's chuckle masked just how unnerved he was by Victoria's powerful vehemence. He snagged her wagging finger and brought the back of her hand to his lips. "How can I resist when it is clear you've put such thought into planning this evening?"

She replied with a sniff and regal nod of her head before allowing him to escort her back into the dining room, where Dom waited for them. He was busy kicking his feet back and forth, watching the repetitive motion with downcast eyes. He looked up at their entrance, and the slump of his shoulders was evidence of what he expected to happen next. It twisted Rafe's heart in his chest that this boy—the one who, if Victoria could be believed, idolized him even though he possessed very few redeeming qualities—thought he would send him away. He was shaken by the faith both Dom and Victoria had in him, unnerved by the power he held in their lives. He wasn't certain he could live up to whatever image of him their minds possessed. He wasn't sure he was worthy.

Taking a few precious seconds to regain his composure, Rafe guided Victoria back to her seat, saw her settled, and then took up his own chair at the head of the table. He could feel Dom's expectant eyes upon him, gauging his every move to see when he would be sent back up to Nan and his sisters.

Rafe cleared his throat and raised a hand to the footman in the corner. The man ducked away to begin retrieving the dishes Victoria had planned with the kitchen staff. Rafe turned his attention to Dom and asked, "So. What was your favorite part of today?"

Immediately, the boy sat up straight in his chair and launched into a detailed account of how much he'd enjoyed his gifts and, much to Rafe's chagrin, how Rafe had been forced to wade nearly waist-deep in the pond to retrieve the pole that had slipped from his hands…while Dom had caught no less than five fish.

Victoria's giggle was unmistakable, and Rafe shot her a look that promised retribution.

The comfortable, upbeat chatter lasted throughout the meal. From the potato leek soup to the fresh trout landed by the lad of honor just that day, to the herb-crusted roast and on through to the sticky toffee pudding—which everyone agreed was delightful and the highlight of the delicious meal—Dom was elated to be treated like the little lord he was. His manners were remarkably impeccable, if a bit exaggerated. Every polite request, each time he refrained from slurping or dropping his food to the tablecloth or his clothes, Rafe grew more and more impressed with his nephew—how had the boy learned and grown so much without him noticing? Furthermore, more than once, Rafe caught Dom mimicking his posture or timing his bites to match his own, further underscoring Victoria's belief that the lad idolized him. It was humbling.

His heart swelled watching Dominic and Victoria interact and converse. There was respect in every one of her queries and comments. A wave of contentment washed over him as he sat there with his family. He couldn't stop staring at the scene Victoria had curated, the care she had placed in every detail that entire day. What had begun as a hunt for money had somehow wound up leading him to the one woman the children needed most…that *he* had needed most.

How had that happened?

How had she come to mean so much to all of them?

A grinning Victoria turned to him, and he suddenly knew the answer.

Because she was *Victoria*.

No other woman could have moved so seamlessly into their lives and made them all brighter. No other woman could have tolerated what he'd put her through and remained as strong and self-possessed. No other woman could have made him feel like he could turn his back on everything he'd ever believed was important and reconsider what his life could be.

FOLLOWING THE MEAL, their trio adjourned to the sitting room for a game of charades spearheaded by none other than his wife.

Normally, Rafe would not have participated in the game for all the gold in the world, but he was apparently pathetically weak when presented with Victoria and Dominic's hopeful faces. He'd felt quite absurd pretending to trot around the room like a horse, but experienced redemption when Dominic was forced to pantomime a cat and Victoria was at a loss over how to mimic a frog with any sort of grace or dignity during her turn. Rafe did not believe he would ever forget the sight of his wife attempting to hop across the room in an evening gown—something he knew every other woman of his acquaintance would have sneered at or simply refused to participate. The uproarious laughter echoing off the wood-paneled walls of the room made it all worth it.

The clock chimed the late hour and, with impeccable timing, Nan appeared to whisk Dom off to bed.

"I don't want to go," Dom groused, arms crossed over his chest. For all his mature behavior throughout the meal, this was a reminder that he was, indeed, still a boy, and it was hours past time when he would have been asleep. Despite the excitement glittering in his eyes and the joy radiating from his body, Dom's exhaustion was evident in every one of his features.

"Lord and Lady Blackwood were extremely kind to invite you to dine with them and then allow you to stay up so late tonight. Do not be ungrateful and demand more of them still," Nan chastised gently.

Victoria held out a hand to the boy and Dominic barely managed to stifle a yawn. He rounded the low table set before the sofa and she patted his arm. "I am so pleased you enjoyed your day of birthday celebrations, Dominic. It was lovely to dine with you, and I hope we will have the opportunity to do it again soon."

Sensing that his time free of the nursery was growing short whether he liked it or not, Dom whirled on Rafe. "I will go to bed, but only if you promise I'll be able to join you for after-dinner drinks one day."

The request was so unexpected, so specific, that Rafe couldn't help the slight chuckle of disbelief that passed his lips. He went silent when he saw the fierce determination on Dominic's face. "Very well. One day," he said.

"Promise." Dominic leveled his most intimidating stare at him. "Promise me."

"I promise, Dom."

Finally, he allowed Nan to guide him away and up to the bedchamber where his sisters were already sleeping soundly and had been for several hours.

Rafe shook his head. "Wherever did he learn such a thing?" he asked incredulously as he strode over to the sideboard and prepared drinks for himself and Victoria. The staff had quickly learned they preferred to enjoy their brandy warm, so the supplied decanter was already at the proper temperature. He strode over to where Victoria sat and handed her one of the glasses.

She gave a nonchalant shrug and said, "He *does* have a consummate rake for an uncle. God only knows what else he's been exposed to." The flicker of humor in her eyes reassured him that there was no bitterness in her words. Impulsively, Rafe bent and pressed a kiss to her temple. He took an inordinate amount of pleasure in the shocked widening of her eyes as he moved only a few feet away to stand beside the mantle.

"Thank you for everything you did for Dom today; you truly went above expectations, decorating, planning activities and meals, and arranging supper." He looked over and met her eyes. "I do not wish to make a habit of having the children join us for supper—however selfish it makes me; I quite like our quiet evening meals together—but I would not be opposed to continuing the tradition on special occasions."

"You seem surprised to admit that you enjoy when we take our meals together," Victoria remarked over the edge of her glass.

"I only mean that I am accustomed to eating outside of the home or visiting friends for meals; I never pictured myself pleased to remain at home without any grand plans." He'd never had a reason to want to be there before.

Victoria's grin was radiant. "Take care, or you might become domesticated, Mr. Tomcat."

"Fear not," he replied with a laugh. "I will likely always be just wild enough to keep you on your toes. It is in my nature."

"I do not doubt that."

They sat in comfortable silence for a few minutes before Rafe asked, "Are you happy, Victoria?"

She hummed and nodded affirmatively. "As happy as can be expected." It wasn't the glowing response he'd hoped for, but at least it was better than a *no*.

"I do hope so, because your happiness is important to me," he admitted, a part of him feeling quite raw when he did so. "I know this marriage has not been everything you expected, but I have been happy to find some peace in it. I hope you have as well." The words were difficult for him to say, but it felt important to him that she heard them—that she knew she deserved all the support she'd shown to him and the children over these past several weeks.

Chapter Twenty

IT TOOK VICTORIA a few moments to process what Rafe had said, and in the end, she was touched by his words. He might have claimed to have an aversion to love…but there he was, telling her he cared and appreciated her (as much as his sensibilities and insecurities would allow him to). He desired to make her happiness a priority, and hearing him admit as much to her made her feel like he was beginning to let her past the defenses he'd built.

But what if he was right?

What if his upbringing had damaged him too deeply for him to ever be capable of loving her? Victoria liked to think she could be content and secure in the knowledge that he cared for her—that it would be enough in her marriage—but could she forever settle for these tidbits of affection? How could she prevent herself from believing, from hoping, each scrap meant more than it did? That felt like perhaps the most impossible task of all because she come to yearn for it.

Victoria wanted Rafe's love.

After watching him with his nieces and Dom, after seeing how warm he could be, after witnessing the side of him that made her melt, Victoria's heart ached for it…almost as much as it ached to admit aloud that she was beginning to feel so much more for him.

"And you, Rafe?" Victoria asked instead. "Are you happy?"

He looked down into his glass, examining the fractured light bouncing around within. "Happier than I've felt in recent memory." Victoria's heart stuttered at his gentle admission. "For the first time in my life, the pieces seem to be falling into place." He looked up, and his smoldering eyes met hers, almost searing her with their heat.

Suddenly, Victoria was exhausted. She was worn down from fighting her intense attraction to her husband. She was drained from hiding how moved she was by his kindness, his tiptoeing around the notion of hope. He made her want to enfold her in his arms and never release him—not because he was pathetic and in need of coddling, but because he deserved to be held and cherished and shown what he'd been missing most of his life. Whether he realized it or not, he'd been searching out just that in every one of his casual relationships. He was a man who needed physical touch and comfort. It was evident in the way the tenseness melted from his shoulders each time she held his hand, each time he accepted her touch. There needn't be anything sexual about it, and it still brought him peace. She ached for her husband on every level, and she was tired of pretending she did not.

Taking a long sip of her brandy, she savored the rich burn of it trickling down her throat and curling sensuously in her stomach, allowing it to bolster her nerves for the next words she spoke. "Will you come to my bed tonight?"

Rafe's reaction was at once subtle and intense. She knew him well enough by then to recognize the tightening of his jaw, the slight blanching of his knuckles where he propped himself against the marble mantle, the slow way his eyes swept her seated form and drank her in. While her choice of dress had been mostly intended to lend an air of formality to Dominic's birthday supper, she'd have been lying if she'd said she hadn't considered how Rafe might react to the daring cut. Currently, he looked as if he were barely holding himself in check when he'd rather toss her to the sofa and take her right then and there.

The image of him throwing up her skirts and having his wicked way with her made Victoria clench her thighs together; however, it was ineffective in staunching the dampness blossoming there.

He nodded easily enough, though his naked need was there in his soulful eyes, as palpable as if he'd declared his desire right then and there like a town crier in the middle of the room.

Hear ye, hear ye! Lord Rafael Hart, Viscount Blackwood, wants nothing more than to tup his wife until she is a quaking mass of raw nerves and pleasure!

Victoria barely resisted the urge to fan her face and, instead, offered him a polite nod in gratitude, as if he had just agreed to accompany her on a walk through the park. Though her fingers trembled in anticipation, she continued sipping her warmed brandy and watched as he did the same. The minutes passed slowly, but the delay only stoked the banked desire flaring to life within each of them. It drew out the anticipation until it was a chord that might snap with a twang, launching them together until they crashed in a heap of writhing limbs and ecstasy. It gave them both the time to picture with vivid intensity the last time they'd shared a bed, and all the occasions since then they'd longed for the other's touch.

When she could no longer handle her body's insistent throbbing, Victoria tossed back the last of her drink, set the glass aside on the low table positioned between her seat and the hearth, and she stood. As steadily as she could, she shook the wrinkles from her skirt and murmured, "I believe I shall retire. It has been a long day."

She watched a muscle in Rafe's jaw tic a moment before he nodded. "Very well," he croaked. The evidence that she'd weakened his façade just by inviting him to her bed shot a thrill throughout her body. Her tongue darted out to lick her suddenly dry lips, and her husband's eyes were riveted to the sight. She felt sensual and powerful. She felt like a goddess.

With measured steps, she departed and climbed the angular

wooden staircase to The Cottage's second floor. Her mind was consumed with the possibilities. She wondered how long she might have to wait for him to come to her. Would he partake in another drink before knocking on her door? How should she wait for him? Should she undress and don her nightshift, or was she bold enough to wait for him nude beneath her coverlet? Which might he prefer? Her skin began to tingle, and that persistent ache between her thighs roared into a full-blown throb. If her desire wasn't quenched soon, then she feared she might collapse.

Victoria was so overwhelmed by her thoughts that she didn't hear the heavy footsteps rushing to catch up to her. She didn't sense her husband's presence until her upper arm was caught in a large hand and she was pulled into the room across from hers.

Rafe's bedchamber.

She gasped, both from shock and the sensation of having his hands on her. In one smooth move, he closed and locked the door behind them before pressing her back against the barrier.

"M—My maid must still assist me in undressing," she stammered and panted. Her heart was pounding against her ribcage like a trapped bird demanding the freedom of unencumbered flight.

In response, Rafe's mouth slanted over hers in a kiss that was nearly bruising with the force of its intensity. Without hesitation, he licked his way into her mouth, parting her lips and teeth with such skill that she hardly realized she was at his mercy until it was too late. He caught her as she sagged against the door and continued kissing her until they were both breathless from it.

"Forget the maid," Rafe growled against her lips. "I haven't yet had the pleasure of undressing my wife…layer…by…layer…"

Before she could catch her breath, Rafe spun her around and proceeded to impress her with his skill and knowledge of ladies' garments. With nimble fingers, he deftly undid the long row of tiny buttons along her spine, so the bodice fell around her upper arms; the laces of her stays followed closely behind. She was nearly boneless by the time he pushed down her chemise and slid her arms free, and she emitted an involuntary whimper of excitement as his lips touched every inch of skin he revealed. He kissed and nibbled all the way down her back to the curve of her waist and helped her drop her garments in a puddle around her feet.

Victoria's voice was shaky when she said, "What a talent you have."

His chuckle reverberated through her every nerve. "I am not a patient man, and waiting for a maid takes far too long for my tastes."

Her skin prickled beneath his gaze as she was left standing in nothing but her silk stockings and heeled slippers. She could feel his eyes as they trailed down the nape of her neck, the slopes of her shoulders, the curve of her back, the indentation of her spine before her hips rounded out into her bottom. She could hear him breathing, rough and harsh like a man who had just sprinted to protect his life.

Victoria was overwhelmed with the need to see his face, to witness what she did to him while he knelt behind her, but his hands grasped her hips and prevented her from turning.

"No," Rafe rasped. "Place your palms on the door. Yes, like that. God's wounds, you are beautiful."

Her heart skipped in her chest as she did what he instructed. She felt exposed and vulnerable to his perusal. And it was thrilling.

Rafe's fingers began to burn a trail from her ankles up her calves to press against the tender backsides of her knees. He found the edge of her stockings and their garters, and then his large palms were cupping the rounded mounds of her rear.

"Absolute perfection," Rafe whispered, kneading the muscle, pressing it, spreading it, and groaning in appreciation. She rested her forehead against the door, feeling her face catch fire as she arched back into his touch.

"Please," she breathed.

"Please, what?"

"Please…touch me…"

"Where?"

Victoria's tongue couldn't form the words. She tried again and again, but no sound passed her lips.

"Here?" Rafe asked, gripping her bottom so tightly she wondered if he might leave a mark; then she hoped he would, so she might carry a part of him with her everywhere. "Or here?" His hands slid around her waist and up, up to cup her breasts. He caught her nipples between his fingers and pinched them lightly, making her squirm and moan. "Or…" His voice drifted off as he dragged his hands back down to her rear and nudged her stance wider with his knees. Then, his fingers were parting her dripping sex from behind, stroking incrementally deeper between her swollen folds as she gasped. "Perhaps, you mean here?" he purred, his face so close to her rear that she felt his hot breath on her skin. Gooseflesh rippled across her body; her thighs trembled.

"Yes," Victoria hissed. She arched back into his touch further, effectively presenting her rear to him and giving him more access to her sex.

Rafe moaned in appreciation. "This is what you wanted, isn't it? You are already so wet for me."

"Yes," she moaned nonsensically. "Yes, yes, yes, yes, yes…" she repeated over and over as one, two, then three of his fingers invaded her, stretched her wide, and thrust with such tantalizing slowness that she thought she might expire from it. He worked his hand in deliberate undulations, as measured as the tide lapping at the shore. His wicked hand glided through her slickness and caressed her in just the way he knew would drive her mad.

He made a low moan of approval. "I think you are ready for more."

"Hm?" Victoria was already half-lost in a haze of pleasure when he spun her around so her back was now pressed to the cool wood of the door. Before she realized what he was doing, he'd hooked one of her knees over his shoulder and bent his head to kiss her mound. Her cry of surprise quickly gave way to a gasp of delight when his tongue parted her there, and he began to taste her. His tongue speared through her folds, lapped up her nectar, and flicked and swirled the sensitive, erect pearl of her sex. A thousand colors exploded behind Victoria's eyes. Never in her wildest imaginings had she considered this was something he might do to her—that he might *want* to do to her—and now that she had this knowledge, she knew she could never go back to life as it had been. This was awe-inspiring. This was rapture. This was the glorious perfection of lovemaking, the all-consuming delight that people lived and died for. This was…bliss.

Every practiced pass of Rafe's tongue plucked at her senses; it drove her higher until the air felt too thin to properly breathe. She gulped it in great heaving gasps and fisted her fingers in Rafe's dark curls, holding him in just the right spot to finally grant her the blinding release she'd been chasing.

She sobbed and trembled, tearing at his hair, clawing at his shoulders, pulling him closer with her heel digging into the back of his shoulder. She wanted him inside of her so badly that the emptiness pained her. Still, Rafe did not stop his ministrations with his wicked tongue. No matter how she fought and writhed, he forced her to ride out every last quavering thread of her orgasm until she was limp.

Only then did he carry her to the bed, kiss her soundly so she could taste her own sweet musk on his lips and tongue, and then lay her in the center of the bed. He ripped the clothes from his body and joined her, his hot skin sliding smoothly against hers.

"You are so beautiful," he whispered against her lips while his fingers gently plucked at her budded nipples. She felt every touch all the way to her core. He continued touching her as if memorizing her every curve and hollow while he told her how much he'd longed to be with her once more, and how hard she made him. The evidence of that throbbed heavily against her thigh, making her breath catch in her throat.

Victoria began an exploration of her own. She tested the breadth of his shoulders, the lean muscles of his arms, the perfection of his chest and stomach with its fine dusting of black hair, the mouthwatering globes of his rear, the hardness of his thighs, and, finally, the turgid column of his sex. He seemed quite content to allow her to peruse him at her leisure with her greedy hands and mouth. She learned the musky, salty tang of his sweat, how sensitive his earlobes were, that his nipples reacted much like hers did to stimuli, that his member was impressive in both length and girth, and she could hardly believe he had fit himself inside of her. She bit her lip at the thought of doing it once again.

As if reading her mind, Rafe guided her to sit astride his hips. "Now, guide me inside of you," he instructed gently. It wasn't an order; she knew she could decline…but she'd be damned before she stopped.

Grasping his length, she fed the thick head inside of her body and slowly, carefully, lowered herself onto him. The position was so different from what they'd tried before. He felt larger, and it took her several thudding heartbeats to acclimate. Once she did, however, there was no stopping either of them.

What began as tentative lifting and dropping of her hips quickly devolved into frantic rocking as he thrust up into her. Their bodies worked in unison to stoke the flames of their passion. Each one of his grunts and groans drove her higher as her senses were nearly overwhelmed by everything Rafe was. She was swimming in sensations, so only a flick of his thumb on the pearl of her sex sent her tumbling into another release. As she climaxed, Rafe's hands sank into her hips, holding her still as he pounded up into her with relentless force. He possessed her, claimed her, made her his own, until, with a guttural roar, he filled her with his seed.

Victoria collapsed onto Rafe's sweaty, heaving chest, and all she could hear was the deep pounding of his racing heart.

As THEY DOZED, Rafe realized he couldn't have removed himself from that cocoon of contentment had he wanted to.

Chapter Twenty-One

THE NEXT WEEK spent at The Cottage passed in blissful peace, where Rafe, Victoria, and the children existed in a little sphere of their own making.

Without the constraints of London Society, Victoria felt more relaxed than she had in recent memory. Even back home in America, she'd felt somewhat on display as part of Boston and New York's version of the upper class. In the Kentish countryside, however, she could traverse the fields with the children chasing grasshoppers and butterflies; she needn't worry about nosey callers and curiosity-seekers, and she did not feel so judged. In America, she'd been scrutinized as an heiress and an example to Society; even after her marriage, she'd been an object of interest to those English who were either jealous or looked down upon her for the match she'd made with Rafe. This time spent away from prying eyes also allowed her to sit with the feelings she was developing for her husband, and helped her to remember that there was more to both of them than met the eye.

Rafe, too, was far more relaxed. Though she suspected his sense of fashion would always lean more toward dandified than rugged—not that she minded, of course—he'd worn his coats less often and tended to spend his days in well-cut breeches and linen shirts. The expert tailoring and interesting patterns of some of his garments prevented him from looking too much like he belonged out in nature, but that only lent to his charm as far as Victoria was concerned. She'd be watching the horizon for Rafe and Dominic to return from another afternoon of disastrous fishing and spot a flash of robin's egg blue or a slightly unnatural green and know that they were on their way home.

She didn't know if it was relief over resuming their marital relations, but her husband was freer with his affections, he laughed more easily, and the lines around his eyes softened some—likely because sleep had been more pleasant for all of them the past few nights. Victoria and Rafe had taken to sharing a bed each night since they'd come together after Dominic's birthday supper. To say they were both pleased with the arrangement was an understatement; more than once, both had considered how fortunate it was that the children's room was located on the opposite side of The Cottage when their cries and groans of pleasure were too powerful to stifle. Rafe did request one concession from Victoria as recompense for sharing his mattress with her: He demanded she stop wearing her nightrails, claiming he did not care for all the tangling fabric. But Victoria knew better. He enjoyed rolling over to find her nakedness waiting for him. Still, she'd obliged, quite content to experience the near-feverish heat of his flesh against hers. Even at rest, he was lean, taut muscle, solid and warm. Often, he held her in his sleep as if he were afraid she would dissolve. Victoria did not mind, though, because it made her feel all the safer and more cherished.

Some nights, Faith still craved Rafe's arms to lull her to sleep with the rhythm of his heartbeat and the warmth of his skin against her cheek, but those times were growing less frequent. When they did happen, Victoria had taken to sitting up with them, occasionally reading to her husband in a peaceful whisper by the light of a single low-burning candle.

The baby was also beginning to gain some weight, so much so that Nan and the staff had needed to sew her some new garments. No one minded the extra work because they were so relieved that the child showed improvement. Woefully terrible with a needle and thread, Victoria had, instead, offered to go into town and purchase the materials they required. She picked a fine day with plenty of sunshine, donned an appropriately comfortable dress of dark green striped muslin and her walking boots, gathered her bonnet and reticule, and stepped out of The Cottage and onto the front drive.

Much to her surprise, Rafe had pulled up in front of the house, manning a smart gig and an elegant chestnut horse. He was dressed for London with his black beaver hat, ebony coat with gold buttons, patterned silver-and-purple waistcoat, impeccable buff breeches, and polished hessians. He transferred the long reins to one hand and tipped his hat to her jauntily.

"What are you doing?" Victoria had laughed as she finished pinning her plum-colored hat atop her head and checked to ensure she hadn't forgotten her reticule.

"You required conveyance to the village; I happen to be available. The gig and horse were in the stables and are available for our use as part of the lease." He grinned down at her and held out his gloved hand.

"How could I resist such an escort?" she asked, ascending the steps into the gig. No sooner was she settled than he snapped the reins and they were off.

Victoria squealed in surprise at just how quickly they were able to travel down the empty country lanes. Her husband was clearly a skilled driver, deftly avoiding ruts and divots as he drove them toward the village they'd passed on their way to The Cottage. One of her hands clutched the seat and the other scrabbled to hold onto Rafe's bicep.

She felt him chuckle against her side. "Do not fear, I've a fair amount of experience driving one of these."

"I do not doubt your skill as a driver," Victoria said a little unsteadily as she tried not to flinch when they steered closely to the bushes growing along the side of the path. "I am unused to traveling at such a high rate of speed. Carriages and hacks do not travel this quickly in New York, Boston, or London."

"A carriage wouldn't," he explained patiently and guided the horse through a turn. "This gig is sprung differently. It is lighter and nimbler."

"I can see that."

"Would you like me to slow down?" Rafe asked, a note of concern in his voice when he realized the severity of her unease.

"No, no," she replied and gripped his arm a little more tightly. "I will be fine. I trust you."

"Then why are your eyes closed?"

Victoria forced one eye open a sliver and regretted it as soon as she saw the speed with which the scenery passed by—it was a blur of shades of green, blue, and brown. Her eye closed once more of its own volition.

"I cannot help it."

Immediately, the gig began to slow to a comfortable trot, and Victoria began to feel as if she could breathe again.

"Is that better, darling?" Rafe murmured at her side, transferring the reins to one hand and wrapping an arm around her shoulders. She allowed herself to nestle against him as they bounced along at a more reasonable pace.

"Much," she answered with a breath of relief.

"I did not mean to frighten you," he apologized. "We will travel the rest of the way at a more sedate pace." His thumb stroked her upper arm in a comforting pattern.

Already, she was beginning to enjoy the journey much more. With the roofless gig, she could appreciate the sights and sounds of the countryside now that it was not a blur. The air smelled of warm earth and flowers; the scenery was beautiful when she wasn't traveling at a breakneck pace.

"This really is quite lovely when one is not in fear for her life," she commented lightly, tilting her head back to watch a bird swoop over their heads. Then, she realized what she'd said and looked back at her husband. "Not that I believe you would intentionally place either of us in danger."

He chuffed. "Of course."

Several minutes passed, filled by the rhythmic thud of the horse's hooves on the packed earth, the creaking of the gig beneath them, and the sounds of nature. The tower of the town's medieval church gradually began to break the horizon over a hill in the distance. At the pace they were traveling, it would likely be another hour before they arrived at their destination.

"Where did you learn to drive a gig so well?" Victoria finally asked. Was it her imagination, or did he flinch at her question?

No, she hadn't imagined it.

His silence in the wake of her question confirmed that she'd inadvertently struck some tender nerve.

Finally, he answered, his voice low and rough, "Alice's husband."

His sister's husband had taught him how to manage a gig—the same man whose life and that of his wife had been cut tragically short in a carriage accident. Of course, he hadn't been the driver during the incident since no lord steered his own carriage, but her question doubtless unlocked myriad confusing memories, pleasant and tragic, warm and grief-stricken. She reached up and covered his hand with hers in an effort to convey that she hadn't intended to dredge up anything painful, and he surprised her by continuing his explanation.

"I was still fairly young when they married—not yet at University. Alice rescued me from my father's black moods every chance she had, though it was far less often than both of us liked. She did her best to give me all the love and warmth my father's house lacked. Her husband recognized how important our relationship was, and he embraced me as a brother.

"He purchased a new gig one summer, and I was enamored of the thing. It was beautiful—black lacquered with gilt details and his family crest painted on the rear. He had the most beautiful black mare to pull it, too. I was so bloody jealous."

"Jealous?"

He emitted a little derisive snort. "Not only did the man have my sister's love and attention, but he did not have to worry about how empty his family's coffers were. He needn't concern himself with the scrimping and scrounging I was already feeling even at that age. And I was an annoying young buck who longed for the best, though I knew the future of the Blackwood title grew bleaker with every year my father fell more deeply into his grief and apathy.

"Her husband saw this and invited me on a drive one afternoon. I nearly declined out of sheer petulance, but Alice convinced me otherwise, thank God.

"We drove from London and, little prig I was, I did everything in my power to not enjoy myself. As soon as we reached the country roads, however, he gave the horse its head and we *flew*. I was convinced the gig had sprouted wings and we'd begun to soar!"

Victoria smiled at his reminiscing. The tension was slowly draining from his body as he spoke of the memories, old pain gradually giving way to something gentler.

"It was the most exhilarating thing I'd ever experienced," Rafe continued. "When we finally slowed to a stop, he handed me the reins and offered to give me driving lessons." His voice broke slightly on the last word, but he managed to regain his composure. "I felt so fortunate to be a part of his life with Alice. He didn't need to be as kind to me as he was. He was a very good man."

"It sounds like it," Victoria said gently. "And Alice was good as well."

"I didn't deserve them."

"Rafe—"

"I didn't. For all their efforts, I still turned out like this. They could not completely protect me from my father's loathing. I'd tried for years to make him love me, to praise me, to notice me as someone other than the accident that had killed his beloved wife, but nothing worked. So, I think I did the only thing I could do: I began behaving in a way that would earn me his ire. At least that made it feel more justified when he spat his venom and curses."

Victoria pulled her lips between her teeth and bit down. Tears were beginning to burn the backs of her eyes and the last thing she wanted was to break down there in the gig on their way to the village.

"I caused trouble," Rafe continued, shifting his seat. "I chased countless skirts. I did whatever I could to draw attention to myself and have my name listed in as many tabloids as possible."

"So your father would see you…" Victoria guessed sadly.

Rafe's mouth thinned into a fine line; there was a brief pause before he said, "And, now, they're all gone. My father. Alice. Her husband. And I am all that the children have left. They deserve better than me. They should have had their parents rather than me as their guardian."

"Rafe, stop!" Victoria snapped and grabbed his arm. This innocent inquiry had somehow devolved into abusing his character, and she could not listen to it any longer. She could not stand by while he did that to himself. "The children are lucky to have you—do not shake your head! It is a tragedy the way your sister and her husband lost their lives; they will be missed forever. But it is *also* a tragedy that you were raised by a father like the one you had." She watched a muscle tic in his jaw and knew he did not want to listen to her, but she had to make him. "Mourn the loss but also take pride in how you have handled the situation. You never had the example of a home that you should have, yet your instincts when it comes to the children are excellent. You gave them a home, and you have filled it with so much love. Do not speak so negatively about what you have accomplished." She grasped his hand and laced their fingers together tightly. "And look forward to what *we* will accomplish."

He glanced down at their joined hands before returning his attention to the path ahead. "Do you lump our marriage into one of those accomplishments?" he asked in a tone barely loud enough to be heard above the racket of the horse and tack.

She considered his question. A few weeks prior, she might not have. In fact, she'd likely have been insulted to be considered a pawn in a grander plan. Now, knowing her husband as she did, she respected his decision. There was no malice, only a desperate need to provide for his wards. Although he'd never been afforded the warmth of a consistent family, he knew what needed to be done, and he'd done it all at great sacrifice to the lifestyle he'd enjoyed.

"I do," she answered lightly. His fingers squeezed hers; his lips pressed a lingering kiss to her temple.

Chapter Twenty-Two

THOUGH VICTORIA TRIED to guard herself from completely falling for her husband, it was difficult when incidents such as their pleasant trip to town were becoming more commonplace. Not only was he so doting with the children, but he'd also become remarkably thoughtful and intensely passionate when it came to her. He'd made her view him in a new light; he'd revealed facets she hadn't known existed in any man, let alone a former rake such as he.

She also learned that there were distinct advantages to being married to a man with a past like his.

Rafe put his wicked skills to brilliant use at every opportunity, teaching her new heights of pleasure whenever and wherever the opportunity presented itself—against the desk in the smoke-scented study, seated in a chair in the small library late at night, even while standing in an oversized wardrobe in the middle of the day.

On that occasion, she, Rafe, May, and Dominic had been playing a game of hide and seek. Dominic was on the hunt for that round. After helping May hide behind the curtains in the library, Victoria dashed off to find a new hiding place for herself, pausing in the entryway when she spotted the oversized wardrobe. It was an uncommon piece of furniture for the space, and it was also impressively large. It was tall enough so she could stand straight and still reach up until her palms barely pressed to the ceiling, and it was empty except for a cloak she kept there for when she stepped out with the children on breezy mornings. Victoria gathered her skirts, tested the base to ensure it could easily hold her weight, and climbed inside. It took her only a few seconds to settle into the corner and shut herself into darkness. She slowed her breathing and waited in the still silence to be found.

The minutes ticked by until, suddenly, a burst of sunlight filled the space. Her vision had grown used to the darkness, so she shielded her blinded eyes. Victoria laughed, believing she'd been discovered by Dominic, but a large hand closed over her mouth. She was pressed back into her hiding place until her spine collided with the wooden enclosure and the door being pulled shut thrust her into darkness once more. Her vision swam with flashing lights and rainbow fractals, further throwing her off kilter. She might have been frightened had she not been comforted by Rafe's familiar scent, the low sound of his voice as he shushed her.

Then, his hand was replaced by his mouth, and he proceeded to *devour* her. Lips and teeth and tongue tasted and fed and teased, urging her heart into an even more frantic pace. Urgently, Rafe hiked up her skirts, ignoring her half-hearted protests, and pressed the heel of his palm against her mound. That pressure and the rubbing motion he employed left her helpless to resist parting her thighs for him.

"Rafe," she gasped and breathed his name, throwing her arms around his neck. She leaned into his support so she didn't collapse into a molten puddle at his feet.

His middle finger deftly located the slit in her drawers, and he began to stroke her slick folds. As he did so, he alternated between swallowing her tiny gasps and cries and reminding her that they must be very, very quiet.

"You mustn't make a sound," he murmured against her lips. "Even when I do this..." He stroked her faster until she writhed against his hand, rotating her hips to force more pressure on her needy little nub of pleasure. "Or this..." he said, leaving hot, open-mouthed kisses against her throat. "Or this…" Two fingers pressed deep inside her tight channel, stretching her and stroking her while his thumb caressed her swollen pearl. Victoria bit her lower lip so hard she feared it might bleed, but, even then, soft whimpers and moans escaped her throat. She felt the press of his hard length against her thigh, and the evidence that he was as affected by this interlude as she was nearly enough to send her over the edge.

Victoria whimpered, and he shushed her once again and covered her mouth with his palm once more. "If you cannot be quiet, then I shall be forced to do this." He bent his head to her ear and added, "As much as I enjoy hearing you moan and scream, there is a time and place for that. Save it for later." He propped her up as her legs began to give way. His hand between her thighs was stroking and thrusting, curling and caressing a spot that made her gasp against his palm. She clawed at his shoulders in her vain attempt to maintain control and stay as quiet as possible. The squelching of his plunging, rubbing fingers filled the enclosed space; the scent of sweat and arousal was intoxicating.

"Good," Rafe purred as she trembled around him. "Such a good girl. Give yourself over to it. That's it. I'm going to release your mouth…be good and stay quiet now." His hand slid from her face to cup the back of her neck, bringing their foreheads together so their panting breaths mixed in the slight space between them. His skilled touch and erotic words of encouragement made her feel as if she was breaking apart. Her skin sizzled, her nerves sparked, and white light flashed behind her eyes.

And then, all at once, Victoria came apart.

Rafe slammed his mouth against hers, swallowing her cries of pleasure and relief. He continued his relentless onslaught of her body until she was a boneless mass of quaking, overwrought nerves.

When she was finally able to see straight, Victoria focused on the expression of pleasure and pride in Rafe's dilated eyes illuminated by the sliver of light shining in through the seam of the door. His hand slid from between her legs, and his thumb, still slick with her nectar, caressed her bruised lower lip before he replaced it with his mouth for a tender kiss. The flavors of Rafe and her own arousal were a heady combination—one she enjoyed and wouldn't have minded exploring further.

"I don't believe I shall ever have my fill of you, Victoria," he whispered against her lips and began straightening the layers of her clothing. She was still so weak and dazed from the encounter that her sluggish mind struggled to regain its bearings, comprehend what he'd said, and remember why they were hiding in a wardrobe.

She was still using the wall to prop herself up when she finally opened her mouth to speak. Just as she did so, however, the doors flew open wide, and the space was flooded with light.

"I found you!" Dominic crowed triumphantly. "Both of you?" He propped his fists on his hips. "That is rather poorly done. You made it too easy."

She watched Rafe surreptitiously adjust the falls of his breeches before turning to face his nephew. "We shall keep that in mind for future rounds." He stepped down from their hiding place and reached back in to assist Victoria. She was grateful for the strength of his touch, and she leaned into him. His smile told her he knew entirely too well the effect he had upon her.

Instead of embarrassing her, it made her heart flutter even harder.

Even the moments of silence she shared with Rafe were growing more comfortable. Some afternoons, while the girls slept and Dominic was with his tutor, her husband would step away from the study, and he would silently join her as she read or worked on her own correspondence. This quiet companionship was something entirely new to them both, but it was quickly becoming something they both enjoyed tremendously.

One afternoon, Victoria received a heavy envelope as elaborately engraved as any she'd received during her time in London. Slitting it open with her penknife, she unfolded and proceeded to read aloud the invitation to Rafe.

"A birthday celebration?" Rafe commented from where he reclined on the chaise beside her, one leg propped negligently on the back of the furniture.

"It would seem so. Lady Greenleigh did say she would send along an invitation when we saw her at the shops. I'd almost forgotten about it." They'd encountered the woman while shopping in the village the week prior. Rafe had made the introduction and, while there had initially been some jealous curiosity on Victoria's part about the nature of their acquaintance, it had quickly become apparent that Lady Greenleigh was smitten with her own husband. She was planning him quite the lavish birthday celebration the following week, as a matter of fact.

"Yes, you have been rather distracted as of late, haven't you?"

Victoria's head snapped up and she was greeted by Rafe's wicked smile. The cad. She chose to ignore his comment, though she could not fully prevent the blush from creeping up her neck and coloring her cheeks. "How far away is the Greenleigh estate?" she asked instead. He'd spent a fair bit of time in this area of Kent with Mr. Stratford's family, so there was a decent chance he would be familiar with the distance.

Rafe's brow wrinkled in thought for a few moments before he replied. "I would say less than two hours' travel in a carriage."

"Should we send our reply? It might be a pleasant change of scenery, and I have yet to attend a country event. I understand they are less formal than those in Town?"

She looked back at her husband to find him staring at the ceiling, his mouth pulled into a taut line and a muscle flexing in his angular jaw.

"Is everything alright?"

This seemed to snap him out of whatever trance had captured him. "It might not be worth our time," he finally replied. "I've been to these parties many times, and they are never as polished as the ones in London."

"That doesn't matter to me," she said with an airy laugh.

"Now that Faith is improving, we could have some time, just the two of us…socializing with other adults. You cannot tell me that is not appealing, even if the rest of the event is boring!"

The tension eased from his face when he met her eyes.

"Besides, Luke will be there as well," Victoria added. "He indicated in his last letter that he has business with Lord Green-leigh, and it will be so good for me to see my brother again."

Was she imagining his small sigh of resignation?

"We may attend if that is what you wish."

Victoria told herself that she was imagining Rafe's hesitance. He'd seemed quite friendly with Lady Greenleigh in the village; surely, he would tell her if there was a good reason they should not attend?

IT WAS EVERYTHING Rafe could do not to groan at just how horrendous an idea it was for them to attend the Greenleigh party. For one, Victoria's brother had always treated him with poorly veiled dislike (although, admittedly, Rafe would probably hate himself were he in Luke's position). The thought of spending an entire evening with the man was not something he relished.

Then, there was the matter of just how he knew the hosts. Lady Greenleigh happened to be a cousin to his most recent paramour, a young widow who hadn't taken well to Rafe's dissolution of their arrangement. Lady Dallow was no older than Victoria, but she was leaps and bounds more experienced. She'd married young and had been widowed only one year into her marriage. Not a single day had she and her husband been faithful to their vows, and the man's untimely death following a disagreement with his mistress's other lover only set her free. No longer required to mask her indiscretions, Lady Dallow had flitted from one protector to the next. Unfortunately, men did not realize her mercurial nature and unhealthy possessiveness—odd for a woman who did not know the meaning of the word "fidelity"—was often the cause of those arrangements coming to an end. Many a man had been charmed by her ample wares and skills in the bedchamber, only to be run off by one of her tantrums. To say she had been unhappy when Rafe terminated their relationship would be an understatement; however, she had not attempted to contact him since their last meeting. Still, Rafe did not relish seeing her again, and he hoped the chances of an encounter at the party would be slim. She usually stayed in London year-round, and he hoped she would not go through the trouble of traveling to Kent for her cousin's husband's birthday celebration. Perhaps it would work out, and he needn't be so concerned.

He did not relish the possibility of a chance encounter with her. In his experience, those never boded well with a lover who felt jilted.

Even though the women with whom he entered sexual relationships were supposed to have a full understanding that the arrangement was only temporary, things did not always end as cleanly as he hoped. There had been several women who'd optimistically believed they would be the one to change him—to snag one of London's most notorious rakes and set him to heel...to save him...to tame him.

Although he'd expressly told her that their relationship was one of physical fulfillment, Lady Dallow had been one of those women. For all her faults, he'd once thought fondly of her...now he could look back on their time together and see it for the hollow satisfaction that it had been. She'd been a skilled lover and had known exactly what to do to make his body quake with desire, but he knew now—or, at least, he was beginning to— recognize actual companionship.

He was finding it with Victoria.

It was a sobering realization for a man who had thought the notion to be as insubstantial as a fantasy.

Gradually, he was coming to understand that he hadn't known as much about women and relationships as he'd once believed. He knew now that his wife deserved as much of himself as he was capable of giving to her. And, seeing the hope in her eyes and hearing in her voice how excited she was to see her insufferable brother once again made him want to give her everything. If he had to chance seeing Lady Dallow in an uncomfortable situation, then it was a small price to pay to return to Victoria some of the joy she'd brought to his family.

Chapter Twenty-Three

THE DAY OF the party, Rafe took his time bathing and dressing, grateful that he'd brought a formal outfit with them to the country. He certainly hadn't anticipated attending such an event, but it was fortunate that his sense of fashion often won out over practicality.

One never knew when he might be on display, and he had some reputation left to uphold. Whatever would the bucks of London do without his example?

Fitted in his black evening kit, hair tousled and shaped to perfection, he went off in search of his wife.

Victoria had retreated to her own chambers to dress, but he found them empty when he went to retrieve her. After a bit of wandering, he realized she was not downstairs either. He glanced at his pocket timepiece and hoped she had perhaps changed her mind about attending.

Still, there was one more place he had yet to check.

Heading back up to the second floor of the home, he turned at the top of the stairs toward the room occupied by the children.

There, he found Victoria tucking the children in tightly beneath their blankets. Leaning against the doorframe, he watched silently as she kissed each of them atop their heads.

"Wiww I have a dress that pretty one day?" May asked, awe dripping from her every word.

"I'm certain you will," Victoria replied warmly as she brushed the curls from May's face. "I will make sure of it."

Dominic came next, and what the lad did surprised everyone, even Victoria, judging by her little exclamation. He threw his arms around her neck, heedless of her delicate attire, as only a child can be. Victoria held him in return without a moment's hesitation.

"You do look like a princess," the boy murmured just loudly enough that Rafe could hear it from where he stood.

Victoria laughed, but there was a catch to it that Rafe did not miss. "Sweet boy," she replied and stroked his dark hair.

Pushing off the doorframe, Rafe entered the room and said, "I agree. A princess walks among us." Victoria's head whipped around toward him, and Rafe swore his heart stopped. As moving as it had been to watch her with the children, now he was faced with her full beauty. And it was awe-inspiring. He was rendered mute by the dewy glow of her skin and the rosy pinkness of her full lips; he was stunned by how the glitter in her eyes so precisely matched that of her gown—another concoction so expertly made to fit her elegant figure that it should be considered a masterpiece to be studied. He nearly expired when she smiled at him with a mixture of shyness at having been observed unaware and pleasure at seeing him. Several long seconds passed before his body and mind remembered what they were supposed to do, and he crossed the room to bid each of the children goodnight.

"Enjoy yourselves," Nan whispered cheekily on their way from the room. "The children will wish to hear everything about the grand party tomorrow."

"Won't they be disappointed when we tell them a majority of the time was spent talking and eating?" Rafe chuckled.

TRUE ENOUGH, THAT was how much of the evening passed. While the party itself was an elegant affair, it was still just another gathering with many of the same people from London in a new setting. The floral arrangements were lovely—or so Victoria had commented to him upon their arrival—the food and drink were fine. The conversations were all along the lines of what one would expect: The latest gossip, the newest engagements and attachments, a smattering of business.

One unfamiliar factor was the presence of Victoria's brother, Luke. He'd come to know the guest of honor through some of Rockford Shipping's transactions, and the estate had been a natural stopping point for his business on the coast anyway. The timing was certainly fortuitous.

Victoria had all but dragged Rafe across the room when she'd spotted her brother's tall, broad frame. Her steps were too hurried to be proper for their setting, but Rafe allowed her to have her head rather than attempt to restrain her. It pleased him to see her so excited.

There were a few startled gasps and murmurs as the siblings embraced, but neither of them seemed to care in the least that they were starring in a bit of a scene. Their affection toward one another was obvious to even the densest among the guests, and it warmed an unexpected place within Rafe's chest. He liked to think he and Alice would have been that open with their affection toward one another had they not been so stiflingly English. With Victoria in their life, he wondered if Dominic and his sisters would be so unguarded. Warmth suffused him further at the thought.

"How have you been?" Luke finally asked, setting Victoria at arm's length and looking her up and down as if to verify for himself that she was hale and hearty.

No, I have not locked her in a tower and starved her while I fritter away her money... Rafe thought bitterly.

"Quite well! Enjoying the country air. And you? How about Father?"

This sparked a conversation about the elder Mr. Rockford's newfound love of kippers and impending return to America. The siblings were so absorbed in catching up that Rafe might have believed he'd evaporated like a mist had Victoria's hand not sought out his own and wound its fingers with his. The gesture, so small and natural, was enormous in Rafe's estimation. His wife hadn't forgotten about him. She did not wish to be rid of him. She wanted him with her, and this was a show of solidarity. Rafe squeezed her hand back, content to remain silent as she and Luke conversed.

Only after nearly every other topic of discussion had been exhausted did his brother-in-law finally turn to him and offer a perfunctory greeting. "Blackwood." There was a very small pause before Luke held out his hand to Rafe. The whole situation had been about as icy as Rafe had thought it would be, but he took it all in stride. It wasn't anything he wasn't used to. While most of Society adored him, he'd spent much of his life at home, ignored, berated, or sneered at. He could—and would—handle anything Victoria's brother threw at him.

"Rockford." His grin was far broader, and his reply was far warmer than Luke's had been as he clasped the proffered hand. Rafe's other arm slid around Victoria's waist. Not only was it a show of possessiveness, but it was something he desired to do. He enjoyed having Victoria close to him. If it made a muscle in her brother's jaw clench when he saw the gesture, then that was all the better.

Thankfully, they were all rather quickly drawn into conversation with other guests. Rather predictably, guests began peppering Luke with inquiries into his role in his father's shipping company, as well as fishing for any clues as to the business's plans in England. Victoria was pulled aside by their hostess, Lady Greenleigh, and introduced to other Society ladies she hadn't had the opportunity to meet during her time in London. Rafe was, of course, dragged into sharing drinks with man after man. From young bucks who idolized his sense of style, to men closer to his age who wished desperately that some of his reputation with women might rub off on them, all of them demanded a piece of his attention. He was notorious rather than famous, an object of interest rather than a respectable idol. Several conversations turned to the topic of his recent marriage to Victoria; those discussions were some of Rafe's most and least favorite of the evening.

While his bride was a novelty and a delight, Rafe was lauded as a champion for having snagged what was assuredly an obscenely large dowry. Several went so far as to remark how lucky he was to have those funds at his disposal, as well as an entry into what was clearly a lucrative company. For his part, Rafe pasted on a smile, deftly steered conversations away from debasing Victoria to nothing more than a purse, and accepted compliments on his wife's behalf. He knew the truth. He was a lucky man, indeed—not solely because he'd married an heiress, saved his title, and secured his future, but because of the heart and soul Victoria possessed. She'd taught him so much over the duration of their relationship, and he knew he would learn so much more from her in the years to come.

He truly was the lucky one.

"Take care, or some might believe you are in love with your wife," said a familiar smug voice. Rafe turned to find Kempton grinning at him.

"Well, so much for the exclusivity of the evening," Rafe greeted his friend cheekily and held out a hand for Kempton to clasp.

"Greenleigh is a cousin on my mother's side," the marquess answered with a shrug. "I am more surprised to see *you* here." The curious lift of his brow indicated his thoughts were much along the same vein as Rafe's had been. Lady Dallow.

"We encountered Lady Greenleigh in town, and she extended an invitation. Victoria desired an evening out, but I would have been quite happy to remain home for the evening."

"I can see that."

"See what?" Rafe scoffed.

"You can't keep your eyes off of her, mate." Kempton elbowed him in the ribs.

Rafe would have protested, but he knew it was futile. Kempton was one of the men who knew him best in the world, and he also had one of the most stubborn personalities. If Rafe denied it, then that would only spur the man on to continue his ribald observations.

"Is it so bad that a man enjoys the company of his wife?"

Kempton narrowed his eyes, but his wide smile revealed his mirth. "I think it's more."

"More?"

"You've never watched a woman like you are tonight."

"And I did not realize you paid such close attention to my habits. I am flattered."

The marquess chuckled. "I can tell you are a tad sensitive to my observations."

"What I am sensitive to is all these prigs believing I've married a bank account rather than a woman with her own merits."

"You didn't?" Rafe's immediate glare made Kempton wince. "Apologies. That was in poor taste. I may have met her only a handful of times, but you must know I like your wife. She's cheeky and witty; Caro has had nothing but pleasant things to say about her. She's fit in quite well thus far."

"This isn't about her fitting into a role in my life and my world." Rafe was hyperaware that this had been one of Victoria's concerns in the early days of their marriage. She did not want to be viewed as a faceless puppet brought in to fill a vacancy, and he did not see her that way. Not in the slightest. No one could have come in and changed his world as she had. "Of course, I required a wife, but she is more than that."

"She is your partner," Kempton said gently, surprising Rafe. "Your friend."

"Precisely," Rafe answered.

Kempton nodded as if he was familiar with that sort of relationship, and perhaps he was. After all, the man had almost made it down the aisle once before. Something flickered behind his friend's dark eyes—something haunted—but it was quickly chased away and replaced with his usual sparkle. He clapped Rafe on the shoulder, "Well, I'm pleased for the two of you. Truly."

He leaned in and added, "Just don't forget to tell her how much you love her, and tell her often."

"I didn't—" Rafe started to protest, but his friend had already pivoted on his heel and strode over to another guest who had been signaling for his attention...leaving Rafe to wonder at the fluttering in his chest as he caught sight of his wife across the room once more.

SUPPER WAS SERVED late in the evening, as was customary during these events. The estate was much larger and grander than The Cottage, so the impressively long dining table managed to seat every one of the forty-or-so guests—even if they were positioned a bit cheek-to-jowl.

Rafe glanced up from his half-finished bowl of cream soup to glimpse his wife seated across from him. For the most part, spouses had been seated across from one another in an alternating pattern of male and female, which was considered the preferred arrangement for Society dinners of this size. It was supposed to promote interesting conversation and facilitate matchmaking.

Rafe thought it could all go hang.

It was almost startling how much he would much rather have had a quiet night back at The Cottage with Victoria. Hell, he'd have enjoyed another supper with Dominic in attendance if it meant he and his wife could remove their shoes and sip brandy by the fire as they reclined in each other's arms.

Thanks to his wandering mind, he proved to be an unusually poor conversationalist during the meal. Both the countess and baroness seated on either side of him harrumphed when they were forced to repeat themselves time and time again. Eventually, they opted to speak to the men seated on their right and left rather than the abnormally silent viscount sandwiched between them. He couldn't very well blame them when he found it impossible to take his eyes off Victoria. He found himself wishing he were invisible so he might quietly observe her without interruption.

Rafe experienced a sudden and unexpected pang of jealousy when the man seated to her left made her smile and laugh. *He wanted to be the only man who could do that.*

Immediately upon the heels of the thought, he felt the absurdity of it. His wife could interact with other men if that was what she so chose; those men might try to coax her entrancing laughter and beautiful smile from her, but Rafe was the only man who would make her sob in pleasure, to paint a satisfied smile on those lips. His cock throbbed beneath the table, and he knew he had to regain his control lest this turned into a very embarrassing party.

Just then, there was a tickle at the nape of his neck, making him feel like a trapped insect. Rafe's brows twitched in confusion, and he barely managed to stifle a chill of unease as he nonchalantly glanced up and down the table.

It was then that he spotted Lady Dallow.

Her white-blond hair was coiffured to perfection, and her ice-blue eyes stared at him with unabashed intensity. Her ample bosom rose and fell above the daring neckline of her gown, a purple so dark that it appeared almost black in the golden candlelight of the dining room. Onyx and amethysts glittered at her throat and ears; a matching bracelet and ring graced her black-gloved left hand curled around her crystal goblet. The web-like lace of her gown, coupled with the dark color palette she wore, reminded him of a spider.

And she was hunting.

Just as the thought crossed his mind, her cold eyes flicked over to Victoria. Sizing her up. Weighing her.

It had been hours since their arrival, and this was the first time he'd seen his former paramour. Either she'd arrived fashionably late, or she was keeping her distance. Rafe could only hope it was the latter and that she would continue to do so, remaining on the periphery for the rest of the evening. The night had been going well so far, and the last thing he wished was for a confrontation that would sour Victoria's enjoyment of it.

Hardening his jaw, Rafe returned to his food and determined not to spare Lady Dallow another glance. He would not give her the attention she sought. He would not expend the energy when the woman who truly mattered was seated just across from him.

Victoria's eye caught his beyond the rose-and-lily centerpiece. It was funny to him how, with just a slight tilt of her head, he knew she was asking him what had disturbed him. Not only did she know him well enough to recognize that something had transpired, but he could also understand her query without a single word passing her lips. Rafe gave a subtle shake of his head and waited for her to turn back to the man on her right before he resumed eating.

Despite feeling the occasional ripple of unease sent his way from down the table's length, the rest of the meal passed in relative peace. At the culmination, their hostess stood and, raising her glass aloft, invited the party to adjourn outside for a surprise. A display of fireworks had been arranged and would begin in a quarter of an hour.

An excited buzz filled the dining room. Men requested additional glasses of port and whiskey from passing staff to take with them to the terrace. By the time Rafe rounded the endlessly long table and returned to Victoria's side, she, too, was thrumming with the same excitement.

"Have you witnessed a fireworks display before?" she asked him, reminding him a great deal of May when she was unable to contain her joy. He half expected his wife to begin bouncing on her toes until her dark ringlets jumped free of her intricate hairstyle. She wrapped her arms around his in a gesture that was more second nature than a show of possessiveness. He enjoyed it immensely. No matter how the other men had made her smile and laugh during supper, it was obvious that she could not wait to once more return to her husband's side—that it was as natural for her to touch him as it was for her to breathe.

"I have not," Rafe replied, barely suppressing a chuckle at the image she presented. She was so full of unbridled joy, his wife. It was infectious.

"I have only once before, and it was both terrifying and beautiful. I feared for our lives, but Luke calmed me by explaining that the coordinated explosions and colors are created through the use of different chemicals and lengths of wick. It was a glorious dance of chaos!"

"I like that description." He led her along with the flow of the crowd toward the doors and the veranda outside.

The night was comfortably warm, so very few women had taken the time to request their shawls or wraps. The air was scented with night-blooming jasmine and damp earth from that afternoon's drizzle, with a hint of acrid smoke from burning torches. Many guests milled about on the brick veranda, while others had ventured to the manicured gardens and pathways below. The sprawling crushed gravel paths were illuminated by the occasional torch, allowing couples to meander through the curated beds as they waited for the display to begin.

Rafe turned away from the rest of the party and was surprised to notice Victoria was watching him with, what he could imagine was, a similar level of awe and appreciation he'd been showering upon her that evening. The way the flickering orange light and silver moon danced across her face caused her swirling green-and-honey-brown eyes to glitter; her lips glistened invitingly.

"I wish you would kiss me," she whispered intimately, making Rafe's eyes roll back with a sudden bolt of lust.

"Do not tempt me, because that is precisely the sort of thing I would do."

"Then do it." Her voice was husky with need, and it nearly broke him.

"You would not care if we scandalized everyone in attendance?" he murmured, unable to wrench his gaze away when the tip of her tongue darted out to moisten the corner of her mouth.

"Not even a bit." She leaned in closer until they were breathing one another in. Rafe felt the contents of his chest swell with her nearness, making him experience a buoyant sensation unlike any he'd felt before.

"Take care, or some might believe you are in love with your wife."

Kempton's words barely managed to overcome the haze of desire clouding Rafe's mind. They made him pause. What did it matter if people believed he loved his wife? Wasn't that all the better?

What caused his heart to stutter was the realization that it did not frighten him. It did not cause his muscles to tense in preparation for flight or battle. It did not cause alarm to permeate his every thought. Instead, warmth suffused him—similar to the sensation he felt whenever he cradled Faith, played pretend with May, or lightheartedly bickered with Dom. Or when he held his wife in his arms.

That warmth seeped through the very marrow of his bones, welled up through his muscles and sinew, filled his chest and lungs and heart, and threatened to spill over. He knew he must say something, but when he opened his lips, no sound came forth.

Instead, Victoria spoke. "Thank you for accompanying me here tonight; I know you did not wish to. I have enjoyed a lovely time thus far, and it has been so good to see Luke again."

Choked by his unfamiliar emotions, Rafe could only nod his head.

She cast her eyes around them to ensure they were relatively secluded before she added. "There is…something I feel the need to say, and I need you to hear it without interruption or diminishment." Rafe's throat constricted. "You are the most amazing guardian to Dominic, May, and Faith. You are caring and thoughtful and kind. And you make it impossible to stay mad at you for long, no matter how hard I try." She chuckled lightly before continuing. "You've proven time and time again that you are a man of many irresistible and admirable qualities—and don't you dare snigger at me." She patted his chest, right over his thundering heart, and looked up into his face. That heart stopped. "And, despite my best efforts, I am falling in love with you. Now,

I know your feelings on the subject, but I know what is in my heart. I do not say this to pressure you or to cause you discomfort, but to unburden myself. I simply could not watch you being *you* any longer without admitting it." She huffed a cleansing breath. "There. I've said it. There is no taking it back now."

She was falling in love with him.

Once upon a time, those words would have made him laugh in disbelief before running off with as much haste as he was capable.

Now…all he wanted to do was pull Victoria into his arms and forget the rest of the world existed at all.

He was elated. He was overwhelmed by the faith she had in him—to know that she'd been watching his every move and found him worthy of such a thing. He'd long claimed he didn't believe in love, but with Victoria holding the possibility out to him like the gift it was, he recognized that it had actually been a fear of never having the chance to experience what it felt like to give and to receive. She'd deemed him worthy, and that was more important than any other honorific or achievement in his life.

"Victoria, I—"

"You are the American, are you not?" A grizzled voice interrupted the moment. The two of them turned to find an octogenarian with a sparse shock of white hair tottering toward them with his cane.

When Rafe wished the old man would see himself off, Victoria offered him a kind smile despite the gruff greeting. "I am, indeed, sir. Is there something you needed?"

"I've some things to discuss with you," he said brusquely, narrowing his pale, cloudy eyes at her.

"I ASSURE YOU, New York is, indeed, quite the modern city. It might not have the same lengthy history as London, but it is still a bustling hub all the same." Victoria was speaking to Lord Fenton, a doddering old cousin of their host who, apparently, still believed it was 1730. He had more gums in his mouth than teeth, but he seemed harmless enough, especially when the genuine shock and awe lit up his timeworn face as Victoria told him America was becoming a great consumer and producer of goods. His questions about her home country were less insulting than they were curious, so Rafe was happy to sit by and observe. For her part, Victoria was kind and gracious with Fenton—especially when his weary nephew attempted to apologize for his great-uncle's pestering questions and drag him away. She'd simply told him it was no trouble and asked if the hobbling Fenton might join her on a nearby bench because her slippers were beginning to pinch her feet. For all his unsteady faculties, the old man puffed up when presented with an opportunity to be chivalrous.

"Watch out, Blackwell, or he'll be after your bride," chuckled the man's nephew good-naturedly.

Rafe grinned. "I don't doubt it."

Just as Victoria sat, Rafe noticed behind her a woman in a dark lace dress approaching at a steady clip. The torchlight glinted off her pale hair and the collection of jewels she wore.

Every muscle in Rafe's body tensed.

"Excuse me," he murmured and slipped away without waiting for a reply. With any luck, Fenton and his nephew would occupy Victoria long enough that a brief absence would not be noticed.

He managed to intercept Lady Dallow just as she passed near an alcove of hedges on the edge of the veranda. Pulling her into the space with a firm hand on her elbow, Rafe growled, "What do you think you are doing?"

She looked up at him with wide, doe-like eyes, all innocence and spun sugar. "Why, I am enjoying my cousin's party, of course. Aren't you?"

"Do not feign idiocy," he snapped. "What are you doing trying to approach my wife? And do not pretend that you were headed anywhere else but directly to her."

Her expression hardened instantaneously, her eyes freezing

over with such speed that he wouldn't have been surprised to find frost coating the branches around them. "I want to meet the woman who stole you from my bed. I need to see for myself what draw she has."

"She did not steal me." Rafe's voice was a low, dangerous hiss. It was everything he could do not to shake the woman senseless. He hadn't even yet spoken to Victoria when he'd called off his arrangement with the widow; Victoria couldn't possibly have had anything to do with it. Was the woman so jealous, so delusional, that she refused to consider there might be any fault of her own in the termination of their relationship? That she could only lay blame at Victoria's feet? Could she possibly believe that they might still be together had Victoria not come along? "Our relationship terminated before I met my wife. I ended things because we had reached our natural end."

She began shaking her head. "I don't believe that. We *meant* something to each other."

"You were my mistress. We enjoyed bed sport for a time. That time is over." The words were harsh and biting, but Rafe had already tried civility and gentleness with her. That clearly hadn't worked, and he refused to tolerate this woman putting his marriage at risk because she was unwilling to relinquish him.

Bright spots of anger bloomed in her cheeks. "We were so beautiful together, Blackwood. Are you willing to throw all of that away for a plain American woman?

"I knew that it was fate as soon as my cousin told me you would be coming. I haven't seen you in so long, and you never leave London. To hear that you were on holiday in this part of Kent at this precise time? That was divine intervention leading us back to one another." Her tone was increasing, and one glance around told Rafe they were beginning to draw notice. Before Lady Dallow could cause more of a scene, he grabbed her upper arm and all but dragged her down a set of stairs set into the side of the veranda. They were less noticeable than the main ones in the center that led down into the gardens, so guests had not ventured that way yet and he could take advantage of the seclusion to end the confrontation.

"You are embarrassing yourself," he whispered harshly, barely able to make out her features now that they'd ventured further from the flickering torchlight.

"There is no embarrassment in the truth." She flattened her palms against his chest, her fingers slowly curling around the black lapels of his coat. "And the truth is, I miss you. I need you back in my bed," she mewled, pressing herself against him, rubbing her breasts across his chest as if she were a needy cat.

Rafe tried to place some distance between them, to remove her fists from his clothing, but she held him fast. While he was much stronger than she and one good shove would have resolved the situation, he did not wish to hurt her. He'd never physically harmed a woman before, and he refused to allow her to draw him into doing so. They continued to scrabble, but she had latched onto him with impressive fortitude.

"Don't you miss me, too?" she breathed. "I know how to please you—I know what you like. There is no way *she* could ever satisfy you as *I* did."

Rafe opened his mouth to tell her how wrong she was, but Lady Dallow chose that moment to yank his head down to meet hers in a rough, possessive kiss.

Chapter Twenty-Four

"Y OU'RE TOO KIND, Lord Fenton." Victoria patted the elderly man's hand after he complimented her attire for the third time that evening. Despite his age and failing memory, she found him sweet. "You are such a charmer."

"You should have seen me in my youth," he replied, with a wink of a watery blue eye. "I'd have given that husband of yours a challenge for your affections, fair maiden."

"Uncle," his nephew signed and rolled his eyes heavenward. Despite the nearly six decades separating their ages, there was a distinct resemblance in the shade of their eyes, the long, straight noses, and the strong chins. If Lord Fenton had, indeed, resembled his great-nephew in his youth, then he wasn't exaggerating. In Victoria's estimation, he wasn't as handsome as Rafe, but he was remarkably pleasing to the eye.

"It's a shame you met Blackwood before my nephew," Fenton added, glancing between them. "You could have been a marchioness instead of a viscountess; he is first in line to inherit my title when I'm dead, you see."

"Uncle!" exclaimed his nephew in mortification. He scrubbed at his face, clearly wishing he could melt between the bricks beneath their feet.

"What? It is the truth. I'd much rather see you wed to a woman as kind and bright as this than one of those empty-headed ninnies you seem to attract."

His nephew turned to her. "My apologies, Lady Blackwood. My uncle sometimes forgets himself."

"No offense taken, I assure you." She flashed each of the men a warm smile.

The nephew looked grateful. "Come, Uncle. I believe we've monopolized Lady Blackwell long enough."

"Very well," Fenton grumbled and was able to rise to his feet after only two attempts. He leaned heavily on his cane as he bowed over Victoria's hand. "It was a supreme pleasure."

"I agree," she replied, then added, "My family and I are staying at The Cottage just to the north. We would love to have you visit if you find it in your schedule. Otherwise, we will return to London next month."

"My uncle does not travel often anymore, but I have a feeling, for you, he would walk from one end of the country to the other."

The men took their leave and, standing, Victoria began to scan the crowd for her husband. Rafe had disappeared several minutes earlier, but she hadn't seen which direction he'd traveled. As she scanned the gathering, a servant passed by with a tray of champagne; the crystal flutes with their effervescent liquid glittering in the flickering lighting looked so enticing, and she plucked one for herself. She didn't normally enjoy champagne, but this one was quite nice.

She sipped her drink and continued surveying her surroundings when she was approached by a woman in a pale green gown draped in layers of aqua chiffon. The color combination was unique enough that Victoria realized she'd glimpsed her down the length of the table at supper. She had hair the color of burnt caramel and wide-set brown eyes framed by impossibly long lashes. What was odd, however, was her smile. By all accounts, it should have been pleasant and warm...but there was something off about it. It did not reach her eyes.

Victoria had become familiar with such smiles during her time in London Society; they had the potential to be venomous.

Pasting on a forced smile of her own, Victoria waited for the woman to close the remaining gap between them.

"Lady Blackwood," said the woman, making Victoria feel instantly at a disadvantage. This woman knew who she was, but Victoria did not know her.

"My apologies, but have we been introduced?"

Her lips curled into a slightly wider smile. "We have not had the opportunity. I am Mrs. Pfinster."

"A pleasure to meet you."

The other woman's eyes ran up and down Victoria's body as she huffed a small laugh through her nose, telling her Mrs. Pfinster believed it was anything but.

"I have known your husband for quite some time," she finally said, and, just like that, Victoria's stomach plummeted so quickly she experienced instantaneous nausea.

"Oh?" Victoria forced out. Was this woman about to admit that she was one of her husband's paramours? It was one thing to move beyond his past; it was another to have it confront her with animosity oozing from its pores.

"Yes, through my good friend Lady Dallow. You see, I am here because of her. To lend support."

"Support?"

She nodded as if it were obvious, and then she stepped closer. It was all Victoria could do not to recoil. "Blackwood was the wicked rake of the *ton* long before you arrived, you know. He entranced many a lady." She arched a brow. "Has he never mentioned Lady Dallow?"

Victoria shook her head once, experiencing a worsening sense of foreboding.

"No? Well, he was quite attached to the young widow; they had quite the torrid affair."

"I do not judge my husband for his past," Victoria snapped, injecting steel into her spine and standing up straight and strong.

"His past?" She tilted her head sympathetically, and Victoria did not care one bit for the false pity in her dark eyes. "Where do you think he is right now? You did not truly believe marriage could calm a man like that, did you?" Her every word dripped with condescension. "A man like that will never be content with monogamy. Go on; see for yourself." She tilted her chin in the direction of the side of the veranda and the far wing of the house. "The sooner you accept the truth of your situation, the sooner you can move on with reality. Once a rake, always a rake. Once a man has been touched by a passion so great as that of Lady Dallow, he will be forever drawn to it, and what is meant to be, will be."

Victoria's every nerve went ice-cold. Despite her best efforts, her eyes strayed to where the woman had gestured. She was torn between not wanting to give Mrs. Pfinster the satisfaction of watching her attempt to spy on Rafe and, morbidly, wanting desperately to know the truth. Could her husband have been merely tolerating their newfound dynamic these past few weeks, all the while pining for his former lover? Hadn't he always emphasized the power of physical attraction? What if he'd been drawn back to a woman more worldly than she, simply because they were better suited in bed? And here, she'd coerced him into attending this party and effectively tossed him back into Lady Dallow's arms.

Victoria was saved from having to decide before an audience because the woman was pulled into another conversation. This was her chance.

She slipped away, her feet carrying her to the side steps of the veranda of their own volition. Victoria felt strangely as if she were watching another woman creep toward danger as she picked up her skirts in her numb fingers and descended the several steps to the pathway. Her slippers were nearly silent on the crushed gravel as she followed the bend in the path on shaking legs. Manicured hedges were at least seven feet tall on either side of her as she listened for sounds of life.

She stepped around one more corner...and found her husband forcefully wrenching himself free from the grasp of an ethereally beautiful woman. Rafe shoved the blond woman away so hard that she stumbled backward, only barely catching herself on a hedge before she tumbled to the ground.

"What in God's name do you think you are doing?" Rafe demanded through clenched teeth. "You know I am married."

Victoria's spirits soared. The situation was damning, but Rafe's furious reaction to the woman's advance buoyed her. She could not blame her husband for being a victim of Lady Dallow. That was, until the conversation between them continued.

"Since when have marriage vows bothered you?" the woman asked with a pout.

"They were never my own vows."

"Why does that matter?"

"It does."

"I fail to see the significance," the woman scoffed. "You do not love her."

Though she suspected as much, the words were like a blade plunging into Victoria's chest…and Rafe's reply was the weapon piercing her heart.

"Simply because I do not love my wife does not mean I will love you. Nothing about you inspires devotion. You may have been a pleasant diversion, but she offers me vastly more than you ever could."

"Her money?"

"Precisely." His shoulders heaved with his anger. "And I need you to listen and hear me. I will never desire you again. I will never give up what I have gained."

The glass Victoria had forgotten she was carrying slipped from her numb fingers, shattering at her feet and scattering unnoticed crystal shards. The spray of champagne stained the hem of her gown.

Rafe whirled on Victoria, his eyes wide, mouth agape in horror. Surely, his expression was a mirror of her own. Then, his mouth twisted in anger, he turned back toward the other woman who was busy setting herself to rights.

Victoria took that as her opportunity to bolt.

She whirled on her heel, hurriedly gathered her skirts, and ran.

"Victoria!" Rafe shouted behind her, but she wouldn't allow herself to hesitate.

She felt like the most pathetic sort of fool. She'd known how averse her husband was to declarations of love—what little stock he placed in the notion—and she'd gone and done just that. She'd thought she was being so brave, so raw and open with him at the time. And now...? Now she felt as if she were a laughingstock. Oh, how uncomfortable he must have been hearing her admit her feelings. She'd been so blinded by her own growing emotions to step back and realize that a man never changed.

He'd been blatantly honest about it from the beginning, but she'd read too much into his lingering glances, the heat of his kisses, and the care he put into their interactions.

Bile burned the back of her throat as she dashed back up the veranda steps. Her lungs burned from both the physical exertion and the effort of holding back sobs. Heedless of onlookers, she ran back toward the doors leading into the house. She didn't know where she planned to go, only that she needed to be as far away from Rafe as possible. Her heart was bleeding within her breast; her head throbbed with confusion and pain.

She was nearly to the door when a strong hand suddenly closed around her upper arm. The first of the fireworks display began to ignite and ripple the air around them with their colorful explosions, but her tear-blurred vision obscured her sight even more.

"Where are you going in such a hurry?" She would know that voice anywhere. "Has something happened? Is everything alright?" Luke asked her above the din of whistles, pops, and booms when he saw her stricken expression.

All she had to do was shake her head, and her brother swiftly maneuvered them back inside the house, through the ballroom, and into a quiet corridor leading to the foyer and front entryway.

Victoria finally allowed the tears to spill over when her brother pulled her into his arms and wrapped her in a hug every bit as warm and comforting as their father's.

She threw her arms around him and sobbed against his chest. She cried for her broken heart, her shattered illusions about what she'd thought had been blossoming between her and her husband, and the downfall of the family she'd believed they were building. How could she have believed herself in love with a man who could so easily and callously admit that he felt nothing for her?

Because she'd believed him to be different, she had thought Rafe was capable of so much more than he believed he was. She'd felt he hadn't given himself enough credit; now she feared she'd given him too much.

"What has happened?" Luke asked in a tone that was both at once gentle and firm. He was a man who had a depth of sympathy for his sister's pain, but he was also someone who liked to solve problems.

"You were right," Victoria said with a sniff. "I should have listened to you about marrying Blackwood."

"What?" Luke reared back. "You seemed fine earlier. What has he done? I'll kill the bastard, lord or not. I'll—"

Victoria shook her head. "I only wish to go home—to The Cottage. Please."

This did not seem to please her brother in the least. "Why don't you stay here for the evening, and you can accompany me to the coast in the morning? I am certain there is enough room in this veritable castle for one more guest, and we can have some of your things sent for."

"Absolutely not!" Victoria snapped. If Lady Dallow was their hostess's cousin, then the chances were good that she and her malicious friend were staying there as well. The last thing she wished to do was sleep beneath the same roof as the women who would gladly see her marriage crumble. It mattered not that Rafe had rejected the woman; Victoria would not weather her mortification in her vicinity.

No.

She needed to go home.

As much as she did not desire to face her husband, she had nowhere else to go that night. She would sort it out and come up with a plan to enact in the morning. She doubted she'd sleep much that night anyway.

Jaw clenched grimly, Luke nodded in agreement and propped her up as they walked toward the doorway and the drive where the carriages were lined up awaiting their passengers. He exchanged a few words with one of the grooms to have her carriage summoned and her cloak retrieved.

Victoria was numb and cold; her chest and throat burned with the same rage consuming her heart. All these unpleasant sensations vied for her attention as the horses were roused and the carriages in the drive began to shift to make way for hers. Luckily, much of the party was still gathered in the rear of the house for the ongoing fireworks display, so they had no audience. The sky came alight with the pinwheels of light and, several times, horses shied from the unfamiliar assault upon their senses.

"Christ, Almighty…" Luke cursed gruffly, his hands balling into fists.

Out of the corner of her eye, she saw Rafe's familiar figure. His long legs were eating up the hallway between them. Her heart began to pound so hard she no longer heard the fireworks. She was so close to escape. She steadfastly turned back toward the drive, tapping her foot and willing the carriages to move more quickly.

Then, to her horror, Luke left her side and stormed toward Rafe and intercepted him…but not before he called out to her.

"Victoria!" he shouted, and every one of her muscles tensed. She felt a new fissure open up upon her heart. A fresh wave of tears stung her eyes and blurred her vision. No matter how she tried, she could not prevent herself from tilting her head to watch over her shoulder as Luke shoved him, and he staggered back.

She felt as if she were crumbling from the inside-out.

Chapter Twenty-Five

THE SIGHT OF Victoria's tear-streaked face broke Rafe into two. He saw only her, could think of nothing but reaching her and explaining that what she'd seen and heard weren't the truth, so they might begin to repair what had been damaged. He needed to make things right.

Before he could reach her, however, a strong body collided with him, stopping him dead and nearly knocking him to the ground. Before he could fully recover, Rafe was shoved back and around a corner into an unoccupied parlor, and Victoria was shielded from his sight.

Instead, Luke's large frame filled Rafe's vision. His hazel eyes were darkened by fury; his lips were contorted into a snarl. He moved to give Rafe another shove to put him further away from the main entrance, but Rafe smacked his hands away.

"What do you think you're doing?" he demanded of the American. "That is my wife—"

"And that is my sister," Luke snapped back in what was just about the only argument that would have made Rafe pause in his red haze. He, too, had once had a sister whom he would have defended like a hound from hell had she ever been wronged. For all Luke knew, Rafe had truly harmed Victoria. "I have been caring for her a lot longer than you have, and I'll be damned before I stand by and allow you to hurt her. I do not know what you did, and, quite frankly, I do not care. I knew you were unworthy of her from the moment I laid eyes on you—a preening peacock without an ounce of honor or humility." He poked a finger into Rafe's sternum, and Rafe's fists clenched tightly. "Stay away from her tonight—do not so much as breathe her name. I will be by The Cottage first thing in the morning to collect her."

Furious with indignation, Rafe slapped Luke's hand away. "Do not ever touch me again," Rafe growled dangerously. "You may believe you are helping, but you *will not* meddle in this marriage—you have no right."

"You forfeited the right to a private marriage when you wronged her in a public setting," Luke snapped back. "You have done enough damage; now leave it to us who truly love Victoria to pick up the pieces you've left behind."

The sound of a carriage being whipped into motion, the harsh crunch of wheels on gravel, told Rafe he'd lost his wife. He felt as if a curtain had been drawn over his life, blinding him to the light and warmth to which he'd only just grown accustomed.

IT WAS MORE than an hour later when Rafe was finally able to procure a mount to ride back to The Cottage. It was an ill-advised move, but staying at the same estate as Luke and his former lover was not an option. There was no inn between the Greenleigh estate and The Cottage, either. His option was to return home in the dark on horseback or sleep in the stables. Rafe, being who he was, chose the more foolish option.

He'd located Kempton and begged the use of his horse. His friend took in Rafe's harried appearance and immediately agreed without question. It took much longer than it should have with the grooms otherwise indisposed with the guests' horseflesh and the distractions all around, but Rafe was relieved once he was finally in the saddle. Normally, he could have overtaken Victoria's lumbering carriage, but it was unsafe to ride swiftly with only the light of the moon, and he'd also been forced to ride in uncomfortable evening clothes and boots not intended for that purpose. Never had he appreciated the roomier cut of his riding jackets, the thicker material of his usual breeches, and the comfortable cut of his favorite riding boots. Surely, he made quite the sight on horseback. He might have been mortified by the situation had he not been so furious and heartsick over what Victoria must be feeling.

He spent the entire ride back to The Cottage plodding along, holding a lantern aloft until his arm screamed for relief, and replayed Victoria's stricken reaction again and again in his mind's eye.

"Damn it all!" he shouted suddenly, unable to continue bottling up his furious emotions, and the sound was enough to cause his mount to shy and prance to the side. He offered it a silent pat of apology before returning to his torturous reliving of the events of that evening.

Everything had been going so well. Victoria had been enjoying herself. She'd told him she was falling in love with him, for God's sake! He'd been looking forward to holding her against his side as they watched the fireworks display together. Why did he have to so foolishly allow himself to be separated from her? When he'd thought he was preventing a scene, he saw now he'd been playing right into the trap that had been laid. Bloody idiot. He should have seen it. He should have known better. He should never have allowed it to happen.

He berated himself for the first hour of his journey, participated in mental self-flagellation over the possibility that he'd just destroyed what was becoming a beautiful marriage. That he'd quite likely hurt Victoria—the woman he loved—beyond measure. It shouldn't have been possible for him to feel that way about her, but he did. And, whether he chose to accept it or not, that was the only explanation for the depth of feeling he possessed for her, and how it destroyed him like internal decay to even consider that she would no longer be a part of his life, or that of his nieces and nephew. It would destroy them all.

It had been the worst sort of lie when he'd told Lady Dallow that he did not love Victoria. The words never should have crossed his lips, but he'd been desperate for her to leave him alone for good. If he admitted to loving his wife, then the unhinged widow would think there was a possibility of him transferring those feelings to her. No. It was better she believed him entirely incapable of that depth of feeling. He needed to quash any hope her delusional mind had that she might rekindle what had been between them. The words had tasted foul on his tongue and, though he'd said them with good intentions, he felt like a villain for speaking them into existence. Not that it made it much better, but he never intended for Victoria to hear them.

Eyes burning, Rafe pressed a thumb and forefinger into them and allowed the swaying of the horse beneath him to carry him back to the moment everything had fallen apart.

The shattering of Victoria's champagne glass was an apt metaphor for the state of his marriage.

Though he'd called his wife's name, she'd whirled on her heel and taken off in a flutter of skirts that very quickly disappeared around the corner. Teeth bared, he'd spun back to Lady Dallow and thrust his finger at her. "Stay away from me and my family," he snarled.

"What family?" she'd laughed bitterly, sinking a sharp, thin blade between the plates of Rafe's armor. If she had her way, he certainly wouldn't have one come morning—what was his family without Victoria?

Immediate panic and dread set in, and he knew he had to find Victoria; he had to explain what had really happened and what he'd truly meant before she became too upset. Without wasting another breath on his former lover, he dashed off in the direction Victoria had retreated; however, he was blocked by the crowd on the veranda. The milling guests had all paused to stare as the first pinwheel of light flared in the sky. Amidst the entranced oohs and ahhs, he'd dodged between bodies, half-blinded when an explosion happened a bit too low to the ground.

God, what Victoria must have thought of him! Bile had risen in the back of his throat when he'd realized she'd likely never forgive him…and damn him for his past, for it had likely destroyed every chance he'd had had a future worth living.

Were it not for the crowd and getting turned around by heading away from the front door instead of toward it, he might have been able to intercept Victoria before Luke sent her back to The Cottage in the carriage. If only Rafe could have reached her first—if only he'd had the duration of the drive home to speak to her and convince her that he hadn't meant any of what she'd heard and that she, Victoria, was the only woman for him for the rest of his days and that he *loved her*—then he might have had a chance. As the minutes and hours dwindled by, he knew his chances were growing ever slimmer.

By the time he finally arrived at The Cottage, every window was dark and there was not a single sign of life to be seen in or out. He knew it had been a hopeless exercise to seek out the window of the chamber she'd occupied alone, as well as the one they'd taken to sharing, but he couldn't help it. Of course, he was greeted only by more darkness.

Both he and his mount needed to cool off before turning in, so he dismounted and guided the animal to the small carriage house and its adjoining stables. The carriage horses were already bedded down, and they whickered curiously at the disturbance, watching as he carefully hung the low-burning lantern on a peg. Stripping off his ruined coat, he set about wiping down and brushing Kempton's horse, plying it with fresh water and sweet hay for the night. Making sure to douse the lantern, he used the watery silver light of the moon to pick his way across the gardens.

He was unsurprised to realize he reeked of horseflesh and sweat as he made his way to the rear of the house and the entrance to the kitchens. With the way his evening was going, he half expected everything to be barred and locked. Thankfully, he found his way inside with relative ease; even a single low lamp remained lit like a lonely sentinel.

Taking it up, he ascended the stairs like a man on the scaffold—not because he felt as if he had to answer for his sins, but because he dreaded seeing the pain in his wife's eyes all over again. Whether or not he'd put himself in the regrettable situation, the fact remained that Victoria had been wounded, and it fairly gutted him to know he'd been the cause of it.

His feet carried him to Victoria's door, where he stood for several silent minutes listening for any sign that she was awake—that she waited for him. There was nothing. Despite Luke's warnings that Rafe stay away from her, he raised his hand and knocked lightly. He did not want this to fester. He had to reassure her that it was a horrible misunderstanding. He had to tell Victoria he loved her.

"Victoria?" he whispered. "Victoria?" he asked a little more loudly. "Please, darling...please speak to me—allow me to explain."

Nothing.

Not a whisper or a breath could be heard beyond the door.

Jaw set, Rafe wrapped his fingers around the doorknob, but it had been firmly locked. It rattled pathetically, mocking his efforts. He pressed his forehead and palm to the door, sighing heavily. His every muscle cried out to hold Victoria, while his heart ached to be held by her. It was agonizing to be so close to her and yet unable to reach her. Make no mistake, he recognized that she was the victim in these circumstances, but that did not mean he did not feel pain as well. He bloody well loved his wife and, rather than enfolding her in his embrace and making love to her until the sky blushed pink with dawn, he would sleep alone in a cold bed, separated by hallway and a chasm of misery.

The last thing he wished was to wake the children or disturb the rest of the household. If Victoria wanted to bar him from her chamber and have her privacy, then so be it. He would be prepared to see her and plead his case before Luke arrived and she left with him. He was terrified that, if Victoria left, she'd never return to him.

Then, he really would have lost everything.

VICTORIA LAY ON her side in bed, the coverlet pulled up to her ear as she watched the orange light of the lamp retreat from the seam of the door. There was a soft click from down the hall as Rafe went into his own chamber and shut the door behind him.

She swiped furiously at the molten tears stinging her raw cheeks as she admonished herself for the thousandth time for allowing herself to care for such a man—for being naive enough to believe she'd been privy to a special, gentle side of him. Despite knowing better, her heart had not listened to her head and, somewhere along the way, she'd fallen in love with the rake.

How foolish could a woman be?

Chapter Twenty-Six

THE NEXT MORNING, Victoria awoke with a throbbing head. Periods of fitful sleep and tears had plagued her night, and now she felt both hollowed out and as if someone had placed a leaden weight in her chest. What an off-putting juxtaposition.

She was grateful that there was not so much as a raised brow when she requested her maid assist her in donning her navy-blue traveling dress and serviceable brown leather half-boots; nor was there a question when she requested to have her necessities packed away. She'd already decided that she would send for the rest of her things when she sorted out where she would be residing.

How tempting it was for her to consider fleeing back across the ocean and pretending her marriage had never happened.

She knew it would be the option Luke and her father would push for. They would believe only they could provide her with the care and comfort she required during such a trying time; however, Victoria wasn't so certain it was a viable option. According to the law, she was a married woman. She may have married a scoundrel, but there was no denying the validity of their union. And, rather surprisingly, the thought of leaving him created the most confusing maelstrom of emotions to collide and toss themselves around inside her chest. Just when she'd believed her eyes too dry to form any tears, they began to burn anew.

The maid silently procured a cool compress for Victoria's

puffy eyes from the nearby washbasin, which Victoria gladly accepted. Her cheeks were chapped from the salt of her dried tears, and they stung beneath the compress. It was a bracing sensation, and one she was grateful for because the next part of what she needed to do might just be the hardest.

She needed to say goodbye to the children.

Though it would be agonizing, her conscience would not allow her to disappear without facing them.

When she was fully dressed and reasonably sure that her appearance was not as haggard as she felt, she strode down the hallway to the children's room. Nan and the children all greeted her with smiles, but the older woman's wavered when she read the weariness in Victoria's expression. It likely had not escaped her notice that she was dressed for travel. Victoria prayed Nan would not question her, because she did not think she could take it. Instead, she held her arms out for Faith. Nan handed the child over without hesitation and continued her task of brushing through May's tangled mane.

Victoria kissed and cuddled the babbling infant, committing to memory her soft skin and sweet, warm scent. Finally, there was roundness in her cheeks and color to her petal-soft skin. Her eyes were bright and glittering with intelligence, and she clapped her little hands together in joy when Victoria tickled her tummy. How she would miss this.

Next came May. The toddler was not one for prolonged embraces, but Victoria played it off as a game and got nearly as much of a snuggle as she hoped. The child was far more interested in asking Victoria's opinion on which dress her doll should wear that day. After spending several minutes deciding between a peach and a green gown, May was satisfied and skipped off to dress her doll.

Victoria turned to the last child in the room. She'd known Dominic was going to be the most difficult because he, at least, would know what leaving meant. It would do him an injustice if she were to pretend nothing was wrong; it would be worse to lie to him and tell him when she would return when she had no idea when or if she would ever do so. She doubted Rafe would allow her to see the children if he was upset or humiliated by her flight from The Cottage.

Of course, like Nan, the boy had sensed something was amiss the moment Victoria had entered the room. He might not suspect what the cause of it was—she didn't doubt Nan was certain it was marital troubles—but he was a sensitive lad. Even if he tried to hide it behind bluster and bravado, she knew he felt things very deeply, and this was why he'd taken the loss of his parents so hard. Victoria hoped he would fare better after she left, since she'd only been a part of his life a short time. Already, though he watched her with a sullen expression on his face, his arms crossed over his narrow chest.

Heedless of creasing her skirts, Victoria knelt on the floor beside him. Her fingers itched to hold him, but she had to wait until he was ready. If she moved too quickly, he might very well bolt.

"Dominic," she said softly and then waited for him to meet her eyes. "I am leaving for a while, but I could not leave without saying goodbye to you first."

"When will you be back?" he asked warily.

"I am unsure."

"*Why* are you leaving?"

Her heart skipped. "It is…complicated. But you must know that I would not be doing it if I did not feel it was for the best."

"Was Uncle Rafe mean to you? Is that why you are crying?"

Victoria hadn't realized she'd resumed crying until Dominic questioned her about it. She brushed her fingertips across her cheek to see that the grey leather of her glove was stained with dark smudges of tears. She shook her head, unwilling to make Rafe into a villain in his nephew's eyes, no matter how he had shattered her heart. The boy needed a hero. "I am crying because I will miss you terribly," she finally said, her voice watery and thin. "May I embrace you before I leave?"

Three heartbeats of hesitation passed before Dominic walked stiffly into her outstretched arms. His little body buzzed with anger until she wrapped herself around him; he buried his face in her shoulder and twisted his fists tightly in her skirts. He felt so small and fragile, so much more delicate than he pretended to be. Dominic longed to be grown and he emulated everything his uncle did, but the fact of the matter was, he was still a child. He still needed love and security. He still needed guidance and stability. Victoria felt guilty for shaking the foundations of his world all over again, but she had to do what was right for herself. She would be of no use to the children if she was miserable and heartsick.

Victoria held Dominic as long as she could. It pained her to step away, but she knew she needed to. "I hope to see you very soon," she said truthfully. Dominic only glared at her in anger and pain, tears in his eyes, refusing to say anything further.

She said a quick farewell to Nan and escaped the room before she shattered completely. So lost was she in a haze of grief that she hadn't realized she'd traversed the hallway and descended the stairs until she spotted her husband sitting atop her trunk, his head and shoulders propped back against the wardrobe where just days before they'd shared an intimate interlude during that game of hide-and-seek.

Her tears dried almost instantly, evaporated by the heat of her anger. She straightened her spine and swallowed her pain. She was a New Yorker, and she refused to allow Rafe to win.

As she neared him, she couldn't help but notice that he looked far worse than when he'd spent nights awake with the baby. She didn't know how he'd returned to The Cottage, but it had been more than three hours after her own arrival. She wondered if he'd slept at all since then, then reminded herself that she shouldn't care about any of it and would not give it a second thought from then on.

The pomade had been washed from his hair, so he'd bathed, but a shadow of a beard remained on his jaw. She didn't think she'd ever seen him outside of his bedchamber with the dark whiskers on his face. He wore buff breeches and black boots, a clean white linen shirt open at the neck—no cravat, jacket, or waistcoat. There was not a single splash of color on him. It was so unlike Rafe to be so plain and unkempt by his normal standards.

Rafe's bloodshot eyes met hers. "Are you truly leaving?" he asked gently.

"I am," Victoria replied coolly. "My admission last night must have made you quite uncomfortable, but now that I know how you truly feel, I will pressure you no longer to return my affections. I never should have thought I could change what you hoped to receive from this marriage, and that mistake is on my head. I was foolish to believe we'd evolved to a space beyond the early days of our marriage. Your words confirmed to me that I will never be more to you than an income. You have won."

He leaned forward and roughly raked a hand through his hair. "Will you please give me a chance to explain, at least?"

"Why? So you can tell me that I misunderstood what I heard you say to Lady Dallow?" Her voice was bitter and thick, but she did not care. She watched the muscle in his jaw twitch as she continued. "So you can remind me that you *did* tell me you could never promise love, and that what you said was simply the truth?

"I thought I could manage a marriage of convenience—that I could maintain enough detachment from you to guard my heart—but I was wrong, Rafe. I was too stupid and too weak."

Rafe flew to his feet so quickly that she took a step back. "If you gave me half a chance to speak, then you would hear me tell you how wrong those words. I want only you, Victoria!" His chest heaved with his frantic breaths. "My heart wants *you*. I want only you and the way you care for our family—the way you view them as *your* family." Rafe paused briefly, his beautiful eyes dancing across her features as if memorizing them. "I have never before felt a part of a family, and it terrifies me...but I would die before I intentionally did anything to put that in jeopardy.

"I never knew my mother; my father had no idea what to do

with me or how to treat me. I'd only ever known love from Alice, and even that was ripped away from me. I've gone through life searching for love, though I'd never realized it—I recognize it now because of you."

Victoria's knees felt weak. She was torn between desperately needing to search out something to hold onto and not wanting to tear her eyes away from Rafe and his raw admissions.

"Please do not leave," he begged her, his voice barely above a croak and his eyes glittering suspiciously. "If not for me, then for the children. They love you almost as much as I do."

The world seemed to stutter like a guttering candle.

Victoria opened her mouth to speak, but no sound came out.

Rafe's eyes glittered suspiciously.

"I am begging you to hear me. I will fall to my knees if it pleads my case." And he proceeded to do just that. "I love you. I adore you. I am enamored of you. There is no other person in the world who has made me feel whole, like you do. I may not be worthy of it in return, but I am offering my heart up on a platter. Please, allow me to explain why I said what I did. Please."

Behind Rafe, the front door banged open, and the void was instantly filled with Luke's large frame. Hearing the echo of raised voices as he'd stood out in the drive, he'd let himself in.

With emotions as charged as they were in that foyer, it was precisely the worst moment for him to have done so.

Immediately, Rafe shot to his feet and spun on Luke, stalking toward him. "Don't you dare interfere, Rockford." She'd never heard her husband's voice so low and dangerous.

For his part, Luke's anger was just as volatile in his normally cool, calculating gaze. The situation was unbearably tense, to say the least.

Luke stepped further into the house and directed his booming words at Rafe. "There is nothing you can do to stop me from removing my sister if that is what she wishes, Blackwood. It is best now if you step aside and allow it to happen. I am not above striking a lord; despite your sense of entitlement, your blood runs just as red as any other man's."

Undeterred, Rafe stepped toe-to-toe with her brother. "Get out," he snarled.

Victoria, still trying to process all that Rafe had professed before Luke's arrival, was a bit slower to react than she should have been, but she finally came to her senses. She dashed over to the men and tried to shove them apart and insinuate herself between their tall, powerful bodies before the situation came to blows.

She'd never seen her husband so angry. He was usually so playful and light with the children, so continuously thoughtful; however, this was a different side of him she hadn't known existed. Dark eyes, gritted teeth, white-knuckled fists. This was a man who would fight for everything and anything he loved.

Victoria included.

The thought made her heart pound furiously.

Despite her efforts, the men refused to budge. She was no more effective than a gnat attempting to separate two warring stallions.

Annoyed by her interference, Luke made to move Victoria to the side...but Rafe caught his hand quicker than Victoria's eyes could follow.

"Do. Not. Touch. Her." Rafe's warning was deadly and dangerous.

"You have no right—"

"I have every bloody right—*you* are the one who has no right. Victoria is my wife, and I will fight with every breath in my body to see that she is happy. If leaving me is what she wants, then I will not stop her. But I will bloody well not sit by while you barge into our home and demand she go with you. She is intelligent enough to make her own decisions about her life." Rafe released Luke's wrist. His eyes were dark pools of agony when they turned back to Victoria. "Do you wish to leave?" She swore she could hear the shattering of his heart in his voice.

"I—I don't—" she stammered, looking back and forth from

one furious man to the other. Emitting a frustrated growl, Victoria stalked across the entryway and into the library. She shoved the heels of her hands into her eyes and willed the world to make sense once again. She'd been so certain of her choice—of the rightness of leaving her marriage based on money and one-sided love—but could Rafe really be such a brilliant actor as what she'd just witnessed? Was it possible that he'd lied to Lady Dallow and was telling her, Victoria, the truth?

The tap of two pairs of heavy boots entered the library after granting her only two minutes of peace to sort through her spinning mind.

"What is going on, Victoria?" came Luke's baritone.

"Can I not have time to think?" she groaned.

"Why do you need time to think? When I saw you last night, you were—it was upsetting to see you in such a state. Why would you desire to stay in a situation that made you feel like that?"

"If she wishes to have time to think, then allow her to do so," snapped Rafe.

There was a grudging pause before Luke said, "I suppose it will not matter if I take her now or in two hours."

Victoria suspected it took everything Rafe had not to punch her brother square in the nose. Instead, Rafe said to her gently, "You should eat something."

The thought of food made her nauseous, but she nodded and Rafe slipped from the room to find a servant to scrounge up food in the kitchen.

Victoria dropped heavily onto the nearest chair and exhaled heavily.

"Why the hesitation?" Luke inquired cautiously.

"This is my marriage," she croaked, looking up at her brother. "I am not simply walking away from a temporary commitment. We are bound together."

"And arrangements can be dissolved. If you are truly unhappy, come home with me. Come home to Papa. We will care for you."

Victoria's throat began to burn. She thought she'd been wrung dry of tears, but they once more threatened to spill over. "He says I misunderstood what was said," she whispered, her eyes gazing unfocused into the distance.

"What did you misunderstand?" For all his support, Luke still did not know what had transpired the prior evening.

She exhaled a shaky breath. "He says he loves me." A confused silence followed her statement, so she supplied, "I overheard him telling someone he did not love me, could never love me, and had only married me for the money I brought."

"We suspected as much," Luke said through gritted teeth.

"*You* suspected as much." She swiped at the first tear to trail down her cheek.

"And you are far too forgiving."

"Because I've fallen in love with him." This stunned Luke into silence.

The muscles of his jaw worked furiously before he finally asked, "And what will you do today?"

"I do not know," Victoria croaked and dropped her head into her hands.

TWO HOURS LATER, after Victoria had managed to choke down some of the biscuits from the spread the staff had prepared, she felt no closer to a decision. To their credit, the men left her to think, taking up seats on opposite sides of the room and glaring at one another. Each of them wanted so badly to sway her one way or the other, but Victoria refused to speak on it. She desired to keep her own counsel as she considered her choices. Her stomach roiled from the stress, her head pounded from her thoughts, and her heart ached from the torture it was experiencing. As if sensing the pall in the home, a distant rumble of thunder flitted through the grey clouds outside.

Suddenly, there was a frantic pounding of feet as Nan arrived in the doorway of the library, red-faced and panting. "Please," she gasped, "please pardon the interruption. But…we cannot find…" She doubled over, breathing heavily.

Victoria went to her side and held her arm to steady her. "What has happened? What can't you find?" Something must really be wrong to send the normally steady nursemaid so topsy-turvy.

"We cannot find Lord Dominic," Nan said finally. A hint of color returned to her cheeks. "We've been searching the rooms and the gardens. We thought he was simply playing a game and hiding, so the staff didn't want to worry you, but he is nowhere to be found."

Rafe cursed beneath his breath and Victoria's stomach dropped through the floor beneath her feet. It was a testament to how distracted and distraught all of them had been that none of them had realized this was going on in the rest of the house.

"Who is this lord who has gone missing?" Luke asked, clearly confused by the state of panic. "And why are we so concerned?"

"He is our nephew," Victoria explained. "And he is only a boy." More of the staff had collected in the hallway, every one of them with concern in their eyes and anxious stances.

Seeming to deflate, Nan collapsed at their feet and began to sob. "I only went to put the baby down for her morning nap after her feeding with the wet nurse. And he disappeared."

"And we are certain he is nowhere in the house?" Rafe demanded in a tone that was somehow gentle and firm at once.

Another of the maids stepped forward to help Nan, who was too overcome by emotion and guilt to continue. "We found the back door ajar and some food was missing from the larder, including a fresh loaf of bread which had been left to cool on the table in the kitchen," she explained.

Victoria went cold with dread. Dominic had run away—or at least he was trying to. There was no telling the kind of trouble or danger he might encounter. She was sure the expression of horror on her husband's face mirrored her own.

It took two tries, but she was finally able to swallow the lump in her throat. "We will find him," Victoria said to Rafe a little breathlessly. Though she'd meant to be reassuring, the words sounded frantic and uncertain to even her own ears.

Chapter Twenty-Seven

RAFE'S EVERY NERVE screamed with the desire to take Victoria's hand in his; to warm her icy fingers and reciprocate the comfort she was offering him, but he did not.

He could not.

He could not force that upon her.

"What can I do to help?" Luke asked from behind him, making him want to gnash his teeth.

It was on the tip of Rafe's tongue to tell Victoria's brother to go to the devil, but he did not. Instead, he tamped down his pride and looked at the man. This was not about their disagreements; this was about Dominic. They had to find him before he was hopelessly lost or hurt or…God help him. Rafe's heart thudded in his chest.

They had to find him.

Quickly.

"We must form search parties. Nan said the house and immediate grounds have already been searched, so we need to extend the reach. We will fan out from the house in a pinwheel fashion." He looked to the gathered staff. "We must check everywhere; trees, hollows, any carriage houses or other structures we come across. Search gardens and by the pond where he likes to fish."

Much to Rafe's surprise, Victoria told him, "I will go with you." He was so relieved that all he could do was nod. He needed her by his side; he just hadn't known how to put it into words...yet, somehow, Victoria had known. What was more, she'd acted upon it rather than opting to join Luke. It gave him a thread of hope.

Victoria was already fully dressed for travel, but Rafe did not bother to don a coat before they took their leave. With a few more shouted directions, footmen, maids, grooms, Luke, Rafe, and Victoria all set off in different directions.

After some trudging through tall grasses while calling Dominic's name, he and Victoria began following the main path leading from The Cottage toward the nearest village. The search had gradually grown wider until the participants could no longer hear one another shouting for the lad. He had no idea how much time had passed, but he knew every minute felt like an hour.

On the other hand, every minute they were not tracked down by a messenger coming to tell them that Dominic's body had been found drowned in the pond or trampled by livestock in a field was encouraging. It didn't make him want to rip out his own hair any less, but at least it gave him a tendril of optimism, however fragile.

"Dom!" Rafe bellowed through cupped hands, hoping it would carry the sound to his nephew's ears. He prayed that the boy would show up around the next bend or pop out from behind the nearest tree. Though Rafe's heart was racing and the frenetic energy was building within him, he did his best to remain outwardly calm. "Dom!" He tried again but was greeted only by birdsong and sheep bleating in the distance. One side of the rutted dirt road overlooked fields and clusters of trees; the other had a low, mossy stone wall behind which chickens wandered and clucked as they picked through the herbs and vegetables for morsels. The bucolic scene should have been pleasant and relaxing, but every one of Rafe's nerves felt as if a knife were being held to them. "Dominic!" he called again, a little louder and harsher than he had been. He spat a curse beneath his breath when there was still no response.

Rafe raked a rough hand through his hair, scrubbing it back and forth with a growl of frustration. He froze when something caught his other hand and squeezed it.

Looking down, he saw Victoria's gloved hand wrapped around his, holding it as tightly as if they clung together in a storm at sea. That was certainly an accurate description of how turbulent Rafe's insides felt at that moment. Warmth seeped through her hand and into his, instantly providing comfort when he'd believed such a thing impossible so long as Dominic remained missing. His wife offered him a brief flicker of a smile, a small gesture of reassurance he hadn't realized he'd desperately needed. Rafe squeezed her hand in return, and they walked onward together just like that.

"Dominic!" Victoria called, taking her turn. She did not seem to care one bit that it was considered unladylike to traipse through the countryside shouting like a fishmonger's wife, and he loved that about her. He loved that she cared enough for Dom that she'd set aside her anger for him and her plans to leave The Cottage to assist him in locating the boy. He loved her for her priorities, her optimism, and her determination. "Dominic! Dominic, where are you?"

"I meant what I said earlier," Rafe spoke up, and Victoria's head whipped to face him. Though she did not yet try, his fingers tightened around hers so she could not break free. "I realize that this is entirely inappropriate timing, but it simply must be said in case I do not have another chance to speak with you alone. I love you, Victoria. The fact that you are out here with me instead of traveling to the coast with your brother makes me love you all the more."

"You are correct; now is not the time." Her words were harsh, but her tone was not.

"I love you. If I have to say it a thousand times a day, then I will. I will be eternally sorry that you were injured by what you heard last night, and I will gladly spend a lifetime making it up to you. Even if you do not fully love me back—even if what I said has permanently injured your feelings toward me—I know you love the children. I need you. They need you. And I am not too noble a man to use them as a bargaining chip to try to convince you to stay." A sad smile tugged at one side of his mouth for the briefest of moments, but Victoria said nothing. "I needed Lady Dallow to believe that I could love no woman. She is delusional and driven enough that she would do everything in her power to make our lives miserable if she believed there was the slightest bit of hope that I might turn my affections to her once more. If she thought my heart existed, then that gave her a goal. If she thought affection played no role and, instead, I would do everything in my power to keep your money, then that was a battle she could not win.

"I know it is disgusting, and I hated the words when they crossed my lips. I would never have done it if I had thought there was another way. I would gladly stand before the entire country and declare my feelings if I thought it would repair what has been broken, but only you can decide whether my apology is sufficient…whether my words destroyed any chance I might have had of earning your heart."

They'd approached the house whose gardens had been infested with poultry. A woman in homespun brown clothing was busy taking down the washing and dropping it into a basket before the threatening sky followed through on its promise of rain. Victoria hesitated a moment before gently tugging her hand free from his. Her voice was barely above a whisper when she spoke. "You were wrong about one thing." Rafe's breath caught in his throat. "I already fell in love with you." Her eyes were glistening with fresh tears when they met his. "Had I not been in love with you, then I would not have been so destroyed by your adamancy that you would never love me." Rafe was too struck dumb by disbelief to resist when she stepped away. He could only watch as Victoria swiped away her tears and pasted on a smile before approaching the woman working in her front garden.

"Good morning!" Victoria greeted her cheerily, ignoring the

skeptical expression on the woman's weathered face at being approached by a toff in expensive clothing, with a strange accent to boot. "My husband and I, well, our nephew has gone missing. We've been staying at The Cottage just up the road. You haven't seen a lad about yea tall with dark hair and eyes pass this way recently, have you?"

The other woman's eyes softened some at the thought of a missing child. "Just a boy, ye say?"

Victoria nodded. "He just had a birthday a few weeks ago. He is only nine years old, and we are very concerned. He was not located on the grounds and he's not familiar with the area."

The woman turned to the side of the small cottage and shouted, "Ye seen a lad come this way, John?"

"Eh?" came a gruff reply.

"I said, ye seen a lad? One's gone missin'."

A dirt-stained man in a floppy hat that did nothing to protect his sunburned face walked 'round to the front of the house. He still carried the shovel he'd been using. John appeared to be of the right age to be the woman's husband. He took one look at the quality of Victoria and Rafe's clothing, set aside his shovel, and crossed his arms over his barrel-shaped chest.

"I might've seen a lad…but me memory ain't what it used to be—oof!"

"They're missin' a child, and here ye are tryin' to get money from them!" his wife scolded him after delivering a sharp elbow to his gut. "Just tell 'em the truth."

"No," groaned John. "I ain't seen no lad on the road today."

His wife nodded, satisfied with her husband's response. "There ye have it," she said, looking back at Victoria. "I hope ye find 'im. I'll send the boy your way if I do spot 'im."

"Thank you, and thank you for your time," Victoria said earnestly before fishing a coin from the waist pocket of her traveling dress and holding it out to the woman. She looked as if she wanted to decline, but Victoria insisted. The coin quickly disappeared down the woman's bodice with a grateful nod.

Turning, Victoria returned to Rafe's side with a shake of her head. They resumed walking once more.

"I almost feel sorry for John," Rafe muttered once they were out of sight of the cottage.

"Almost," Victoria agreed; "but not quite."

VICTORIA COULD TELL Rafe's patience had just about worn through. His steps were quicker; his breathing was more agitated. Truth be told, Victoria's own anxiety was teetering on the edge of unbearable, but she knew they needed to remain optimistic.

"Why would he have left—what would have possessed him to do such a thing?" Rafe demanded, more to the air than to her.

She had spent a great deal of their walk pondering the same thing. "I did say goodbye to him before I found you in the foyer," she admitted. "But I was careful not to tell him how long I planned to be gone."

"Forever?" her husband asked sardonically.

"Truly? Yes. That is what I planned."

Rafe rubbed a spot in the center of his chest as if she'd stabbed him with a stiletto right there.

"You broke my heart, Rafe. When I heard what you said…when I thought I'd been made a fool for admitting to my feelings—" The words broke along with her voice. She didn't wish to picture the scene again. "I believed you were speaking the truth of your feelings, and that you viewed me as nothing more than an idealistic girl."

"I apologize for that. It was a vile thing to say."

"You told me once that you did not believe in love. You said those words yourself; you cannot deny that you did."

"I was the one who was a fool, Victoria. Not you. Never you. I may not have said them aloud, but I have been falling in love with you more each day. I want nothing more than to be around you. Have these past several weeks meant as much to you as they did to me?"

"They meant *everything* to me, Rafe!"

"I understand now. I understand it all. The thought of you being too far away for me to see, to touch, to speak with, to listen to…that kills me."

"And now you have decided you are capable of love."

"Yes, dammit!"

Victoria was silent for several moments before she said, "It is also clear to me that you love Dominic and the girls a great deal…but have you said as much to them?"

It was as if she'd struck him with a stone; her husband stopped in the middle of the road and pondered what she'd said. "No," he answered, somewhat incredulously. "I do not believe I ever have." He swore and huffed a little derisive laugh. "Despite all my efforts, I did still end up turning into my father—unable to express an emotion that comes so easily to so many."

Victoria shook her head. "It is not an easy emotion, nor is it a simple one. And it is impossible for you to have become your father—not with how much genuine affection you show to the children. You need only improve how you voice it."

He stepped closer to her just as the first few drops of drizzle began to fall, coating his long, kohl-colored eyelashes and dusting his hair. "I am *trying*."

"I know," she whispered.

And she did.

Victoria knew Rafe was doing his best. He'd always been a good man, but that man had stepped aside for so long to allow the selfish rake to take charge. This was an adjustment. A discovery. And he was beginning by professing his love for her.

Like a bolt of lightning, she was struck by the sudden certainty that she did not want to leave him. She believed his explanation about why he said what he had. She believed in his love. For the one incident that had hurt her, there were several hundred other ways he'd proven himself. Wasn't love about trust? That was what her father had always told her and Luke. If now was not the time to place trust in this man who had proven to her a unique level of devotion and determination, then that time would never come.

But they needed to find Dominic first.

"Come along," she murmured and they walked once more in unison, each of them taking turns calling out Dominic's name.

The drizzle became more persistent, further dampening her husband's spirits. His every step was agitated. Though his voice was beginning to grow hoarse from shouting, he refused to give up.

Finally, they came beneath the cover of an enormous oak sprouting between the stones of the ancient stone wall. Weathered rocks had been displaced and tumbled to the earth, while the tree had grown undeterred by the difficulties. The drizzle turned into rain, pattering through the canopy of leaves above their head and quickly soaking Rafe's shirt to transparency.

Fists clenched, Rafe growled, "Fuck!" to no one in particular. Victoria did not flinch and, in fact, could sympathize with the sentiment. Rafe's outburst seemed to deflate him some and, cradling his head in his hands, he leaned back against the low wall. "What if the rain worsens? What if we still haven't found him by nightfall?"

Both of those prospects were unnerving—the chances of Dominic being injured or falling ill were growing.

"I feel like I have failed him," Rafe croaked and lifted his head. He was so lost it made Victoria's heart ache. "I have failed Alice. All I had to do was keep her children safe."

Victoria opened her mouth to reassure him once again, but a bit of movement behind Rafe's shoulder caught her attention.

A gnarled tree stood in the center of the field. Its base was littered with stones too large and inconvenient to remove for tilling, so it had been left to exist alone. The tree, however, was not what had caught her eye.

What looked to be a lumpy pile of dark clothing sat atop one of the rocks against the tree's trunk. From that distance, it was impossible to tell for certain what it was, but her heart already suspected.

When the pile shifted positions, her heart knew.

"Rafe," she squeaked after two tries to make the word come out.

"This is my fault," Rafe continued to fret, not hearing her.

Victoria tried several times to make him take notice, but nothing worked until she finally grasped his cheeks in her hands and turned his head to make him stop speaking and look out into the field.

"There." Victoria pointed.

His eyes squinted and then widened. "Could it be?" he rasped. "Dominic?" he called and then repeated himself more loudly.

The pile sprouted a dark head.

WITHOUT ANOTHER MOMENT of hesitation, Rafe vaulted over the stone wall. His heart was in his throat as he sprinted up the gentle grassy slope leading to the tree Victoria had pointed out, bellowing his nephew's name all the while.

"Dom! Dominic!"

Rafe's boots slipped and skidded along the earth. The skies had opened up, and the ground was running with rivulets of rainwater, but he would not be deterred. He slid on his knees the last few feet and scooped his nephew into his arms and held him so tightly he was probably crushing him. He didn't care. Never in Rafe's life had he been so relieved—not since Faith's health had improved from the brink of disaster.

"How could you run away?" he demanded. "*Why* did you run away? What were you thinking?" The words were a mixture of admonishment and blinding relief. "Tell me now what possessed you to do such a thing," he ordered and held Dominic at arm's length. His eyes scanned him from head to toe. Other than being wet, chilled, and suffering from a snotty nose—which Dominic wiped on his sleeve—he seemed unharmed.

"I—I didn't want Victoria to leave," Dominic responded in between sobs and hiccups. "Why does everyone have to leave?" he wailed.

Rafe did his best to console the lad, brushing his sodden locks from his face and patiently waiting for him to continue.

"I wanted to leave before you left, too," Dominic finally said to him, looking him in the eye.

Rafe was struck dumb.

There was a loud sniff beside them, and Rafe realized Victoria, too, had ascended the hill. He felt guilty about not helping her over the wall and waiting for her, but he knew she understood his need to see for himself that Dominic had been alright.

Rafe kept his eyes on his nephew and said, "I will never leave you. I swear it. You and your sisters are some of the most important things in the world to me. Most days, you make me want to throttle you, but I love you like my own, and I would not have it any other way. You are stuck with me."

At that, all the fight seemed to leave Dominic. The boy collapsed against him and sank into a fresh bout of tears. He buried his face in Rafe's shoulder, hugging him as tightly as his child's arms could. They stayed like that for several minutes, just existing, until Dominic lifted his head and held out a hand to Victoria.

"Are you still going to leave us?" the boy asked in a small voice.

Rafe looked up to see tears streaming down her face, mixing with the tracks of rain cascading down her head and deepening the color of her sodden gown. He found he was anticipating her response as much as Dominic was. The seconds before her response were nearly unbearable.

Finally, she shook her head.

"How can I leave the family I love?"

Rafe shot to his feet, carrying Dominic with him, and pulled Victoria into an embrace, pressing his lips to the top of her head. He was shaking with relief, joy, love, and the overwhelming sensation of finally having everything he'd never dared to dream of, and so much more.

The rain came harder, the heavens splitting open wide. Rafe

tilted his head back and closed his eyes, laughing just as he imagined Alice was doing at that moment.

For the first time in a long while, Rafe looked forward to what his life had in store.

Epilogue

Rafe steadied his littlest niece as she teetered on her unsteady legs. Following their return to London, Faith had continued to grow in size and strength. Her appetite had increased, and it seemed like not a day went by that she wasn't amazing them with some new talent or ability. Dr. McCullom was thrilled with her progress and said more than once that the child was thriving in the environment they provided. This was, of course, a point of pride for both Rafe and Victoria.

"Look! She almost has it!" Rafe beamed as he released Faith's hands and she lurched forward a step-and-a-half before collapsing forward. Rafe caught her before she fell, and she squealed in delight.

"That is wonderful!" Victoria commented with a grin. She'd been helping May retie a bow in her doll's hair and handed the toy back to her for what would be a third inspection. Finally satisfied, the girl skipped off to play. Now that she was free, Victoria sat back on the sofa and watched her husband.

Beneath that gorgeous exterior truly was a man with a heart of gold. He might not have sired these children, but there was no denying that they were *his*. Not once had she doubted that he would give his life for them, and not a day went by that he didn't tell them and show them how he loved them—Victoria included. It seemed that he was making up for lost time.

Victoria and Rafe had discovered companionship most unexpectedly—in their marriage. While Rafe still saw his friends Kempton and Brinley, though he'd drastically cut back on the time he spent with them at their club—not out of anything Victoria did or said, but because, after a few outings, he'd decided he much preferred spending time with her than carousing with his unmarried friends. For their part, the bachelor lords did not seem overly put out by this change.

"Swanleigh and his wife already abandoned us; we figured it was only a matter of time before this one realized he, too, was madly in love with his partner," Kempton had said, gesturing to Rafe and clapping him on the shoulder good-naturedly. He and Brinley seemed content to continue their bad behavior, and not a week went by that Victoria did not see one (or both!) of their names in the gossip rags. Over time, though, she'd come to know them quite well, and she recognized that, like Rafe, they were men with good hearts lurking beneath their charming, irreverent exteriors; they only needed a bit of help to be reminded of it.

Victoria had enjoyed getting to know Odette Stratford and Caroline Bray, Marchioness of Swanleigh. She was gradually finding her niche in London Society. It hadn't been a magical process, but the influence of new connections and vouchers from respected members of the *ton* had been more than a little helpful. Regardless of how Society felt about an American marrying into their fold, she was a viscountess whether they appreciated it or not.

There remained some jealous onlookers and skeptics who occasionally hissed that the Blackwood union would not be a lasting one—that they could not possibly keep up the charade of a happily married couple. Those individuals predicted that Rafe would return to his old, womanizing ways sooner rather than later, and his wife would grow tired of his antics and return to New York. However, none of them knew how grateful Rafe was for his new life, and how he felt as if he'd been given everything and so much more.

While Victoria didn't believe her husband would ever be fully tamed, she didn't wish him to be. She liked his sense of humor, his occasional wild ways; she loved the way he enjoyed life. There were still some nights when he would go out; he was still the heartbeat of any gathering they attended, but she never worried he wouldn't come home to her. Without fail, he'd return to their bed, crawling naked beneath the coverlet with her, holding her close and waking her with tender kisses upon her bare skin. His appetites remained voracious, but Victoria was only too happy to indulge in that vice.

In addition, Rafe and Luke seemed to have come to a sort of an accord after Victoria had told her brother that she did not wish to leave with him—that a reconciliation had taken place and she was determined to never be parted from her husband and their wards. After Luke returned to The Cottage, filthy and drenched from searching for Dominic, the evidence of his efforts in looking for the boy seemed to have endeared him to her husband. Victoria's adamant support of her husband helped do the same for her brother. Regardless, there was no love lost between the men; they did not care for one another (it seemed, solely on principle), but they'd gradually come to a silent agreement. As long as Rafe kept Victoria happy, then Luke wouldn't have to kill him; as long as Luke stayed out of their marriage, then Rafe would return the favor.

Victoria's first sign that things were truly taking a turn for the better between the men came the week following their return to London. Rafe had come home and admitted to something quite shocking.

"I met with your brother today," he'd said, his tone entirely flippant and unbothered, as if he hadn't just told her his life had been in jeopardy.

"You did? Whatever for?" Her eyes had skimmed him, but found no injury. Even his knuckles were unscathed, and she would have expected at least a little scuff if he'd struck Luke.

"I've decided to invest some of the money I received from your dowry back into Rockford Shipping, among a few other diverse industries." Victoria's concern quickly gave way to pride as he began discussing his plans with her. It was clear he did not take investing lightly and had given it a great deal of thought. "My solicitors and I have seen the figures, proper inquiries were made, and I am confident that, with the expansion plans in place, this could prove to be a lucrative endeavor. Luke and I agree that the profits, alone, from the investment should keep us quite comfortable and promise to allow us to explore other interesting and blossoming industries. Production and industry are the way of the future. I refuse to commit the sins of my forefathers and fall back on tradition. I will do whatever it takes to keep my family safe, comfortable, and well-provided for." He'd paused and taken her hands in his. "I want to give you and the children all the security I never had."

Smiling through her tears of pride, Victoria had cupped his cheek and whispered, "And, for that, I love you all the more."

What she had, in the early days of their marriage, seen as selfishness and duplicitousness were only the beginnings of Rafe exploring his protective drive. She'd watched him come into his own as a lord, as a husband, and as a surrogate father. Watching him interact with the children was something that brought her endless joy. What a remarkable man he was, and she would fight tooth and nail to prove how sorely and gravely mistaken anyone was who believed otherwise. He could be a little bit rugged, a little bit brash and impulsive, but she vowed to continue to work to make him feel worthy of the love and happiness he now possessed.

Victoria began to gnaw on her lower lip in coy excitement. She'd been planning her words for a long time at that point, so she had to struggle to make them seem natural rather than rehearsed.

"It is a good thing Faith is beginning to walk. Two babes in the nursery would make for too much work for just Nan on her own."

Rafe, preoccupied with steadying his niece on her feet once

more, only half heard her. "Pardon?" he said with a frown of concentration.

"I said, it would be a busy nursery with two babes for Nan to tote around all the time. She would not have hands for the other children."

The dense man made a thoughtful sound, clearly still not having processed what she'd said. Victoria huffed a frustrated sigh.

Unable to bear it any longer, Dominic piped up from the corner where he'd set up his soldiers in yet another bloody battle. "She is going to have a baby, Uncle Rafe," the lad said without bothering to look up from his toys. This finally made Rafe's head snap up. "She told me two weeks ago," Dominic added with all the exasperation of a child who has held onto a secret for far too long.

Rafe's eyes jumped from the boy and back to Victoria. She watched as comprehension dawned slowly and then all at once. He leapt to his feet, careful to dodge the toys and the children crawling across the rug, and caught her hands in his. It was simultaneously the clumsiest and most elegant feat she'd ever witnessed.

"Is it true?" he asked, his voice thick as treacle.

Victoria nodded; the blatant joy in her husband's eyes made her tear up.

Rafe scooped her up and into his arms with a laugh, swinging her around as she clung to his neck. The world was a whirl of colors and possibilities around them.

"Why did Dom know before I did?" he asked with a chuckle. He'd stopped spinning, but he showed no signs of setting her on her feet.

Dominic supplied the answer once again. "She vomited during morning lessons."

"Dominic!" she scolded him, mortified.

"It went everywhere!" The lad made a broad sweeping gesture with his arms.

"It did not," Victoria said indignantly, and then grumbled, "I mostly made it to the chamber pot." Her cheeks burned furiously, but Rafe's chuckle helped her mortification dissipate.

"I hope you are feeling better now. I wish you had told me you were unwell."

"It comes and goes." She smiled up at his beaming face. "I take it you are surprised? Dominic did a good job of keeping the secret?"

Rafe leaned his head in and murmured into her ear, "Darling, for a man who has spent his entire life hoping to avoid hearing those words—" She swatted at him playfully. "Yes, it is a glorious surprise," he finished with a chuckle.

Victoria tightened her arms around his neck, bringing his head down to hers to meet in a passionate kiss.

"Must you do that?" Dominic complained and crinkled his nose.

"Absolutely," Rafe replied matter-of-factly and then turned to his nephew. "You will understand one day when you realize you've reached the point where you don't believe you could possibly be any happier."

Love reading about reformed rakes?

Find out what happens when the Marquess of Kempton encounters the one woman who shatters his heart. <u>The Rake's Revenge</u> is coming later this year!

Acknowledgments

To everyone who has continued to follow me on my journey as an author: THANK YOU! This would not be possible without you. This book launches my second series with Dragonblade Publishing, and I am so grateful for the opportunity to continue sharing my world and my spicy stories with you. I am constantly overwhelmed by the love you show for my works, and I hope you continue to get as much enjoyment from reading them as I do from writing them.

This book would not have been possible without my amazing editor, Brenda. She has helped me transform this story into something I adore. She constantly pushes me, making me a stronger writer and storyteller. The edits for this book presented a unique challenge in that we decided to add chunks of plot, but it all took place during a difficult time for my family. To Brenda: Thank you for your patience and support as I worked through all of this.

Thank you to my friends and family. I am overwhelmed by their constant well of support and love. I would not be able to do what I do without them.

To my husband and son: I love you to the moon and back.

About the Author

Kelsey is an Illinois native, author, wife, mother, animal lover, and owner of an obscenely large To-Be-Read book stash. She fostered her love of reading and writing after a heart condition sidelined her childhood. Early one, she learned the joy of living a thousand lives, experiencing hundreds of new worlds, and, eventually, the true pleasure of providing that same escape to others with her writing. Her passions continued to develop long after surgery restored her health and, to this day, it's difficult to find her without a book in her hands. She dove headfirst into the romance genre (perhaps) a bit earlier than the recommended minimum age and became rather adept at disguising her reading material. Once exposed to the glittering world of historical romance, she was forever changed. Her love of writing and all things British translated into her future collegiate studies in both English (with an emphasis on British Literature) and History (mainly British and European). She would go on to earn Bachelor's Degrees in both English and History, as well as a Master's Degree in English. She finished penning her first story fresh out of high school and has never looked back. Her debut novel, *The Baron's Folly*, was published in 2023.

When she's not reading or writing, she's usually watching reruns of her favorite shows, streaming just about any true crime show or podcast; obsessively collecting architectural designs, crafts, and recipes on Pinterest; or sketching, crocheting, cooking, and spending time with her family making the amazing memories she's always dreamt of. She is a diehard supporter of the Oxford Comma and is glued to the TV whenever le Tour de France is on. She is on a never-ending mission to convince her husband that they need pygmy goats, highland coos, and silkie chickens to make their lives complete.

authorkelseyswanson.my.canva.site